ANGEL OF DEATH

"Doctor Leonard McCoy, arise!"

McCoy sat up in bed suddenly, staring wildly about him. Then he saw the figure and froze.

"I am Death, and your time has come. You must go with me. You see, Dr. McCoy, you stand between me and my goal. There must be peace in the Universe, there must be a détente between the Romulans and the Federation. We have had enough bloodshed. I am tired of bloodshed. I grieve at the bleeding bodies I must deal with day after day. I am the Angel of Death, and as long as there is no peace in the Universe, I must go on plying my trade. . . .

"Come, Leonard. Come with me."

Don't miss any of these exciting classic *Star Trek* titles from Bantam Books!

DEATH'S ANGEL

A STAR TREK® NOVEL

Kathleen Sky

BANTAM BOOKS
NEW YORK • TORONTO • LONDON • SYDNEY • AUCKLAND

DEATH'S ANGEL
A Bantam Spectra Book

PUBLISHING HISTORY
Bantam edition / April 1981
Bantam reissue edition / June 1995

This book is published by Bantam Books under the license from Paramount Pictures Corporation. Star Trek *is a Trademark of Paramount Pictures Corporation. Registered in the United States Patent and Trademark Office.*

Mark Lenard's image portraying Sarek appears on the cover of this book with the permission of Mark Lenard.

SPECTRA and the portrayal of a boxed "s" are trademarks of Bantam Books, a division of Bantam Doubleday Dell Publishing Group, Inc.

ISBN 0-553-24983-5

Published simultaneously in the United States and Canada

Bantam Books are published by Bantam Books, a division of Bantam Doubleday Dell Publishing Group, Inc. Its trademark, consisting of the words "Bantam Books" and the portrayal of a rooster, is Registered in U.S. Patent and Trademark Office and in other countries. Marca Registrada. Bantam Books, 1540 Broadway, New York, New York 10036.

PRINTED IN THE UNITED STATES OF AMERICA

RAD 0 9 8 7 6

To Ruth Rigel, Fuzzybutt, and all the creatures great and small we know and love in veterinary medicine

ACKNOWLEDGMENT

I wish to thank Bjo Trimble for her help and the creation of the *Star Trek Concordance,* a book of great value in my work on both *Vulcan!* and *Death's Angel.*

1

Medical Log, Stardate 6914.6, Dr. Leonard McCoy reporting:

It's been ten days since the return of the survey party from Delta Gamma Four, and as yet the survivors have not regained consciousness. Included among the survivors were both the Captain and the First Officer. Three members of the survey party—Security Officer Jamison, Security Officer Matthews, and Medical Technician 2nd Miriam Raymond—have all died of massive cerebral breakdown due to spore infestation. I've been able to rid the remaining survey team members of the spores, and there is no evidence of brain damage in any of them, yet there remains this strange coma, for which I have no explanation. . . .

Dr. McCoy had told James Kirk on more than one occasion that his presence was totally unnecessary in a survey team on an unfamiliar planet. But Jim would laugh, complain of itchy spacelegs, and cheerfully beam himself off into the unknown. On the occasion of the Delta Gamma exploration, Dr. McCoy had been only too correct in voicing his objections.

One of the great difficulties of planetary exploration is that it is only possible to visit a small fraction of a planet in a given timespan; it sometimes requires several expeditions before the nature of the planet can be adequately assessed. This particular planet had been visited only briefly by one scouting expedition, in the dead of winter, in the southern hemisphere. The *Enterprise* party landed in the northern hemisphere in high summer. The area that the *Enterprise* picked seemed perfect; there was adequate water supply, plants, lower life forms—a truly marvelous place for a potential colony.

The planet was located in that band of space between the Federation and the Klingon Empire, and the Organian Treaty made it to the Federation's advantage to discover and colonize as many planets as possible, to keep them out of Klingon hands. When the Federation found that the *Enterprise* was passing close to the Delta Gamma system on its usual rounds, orders were given that an exploratory party be sent down to the fourth planet, which seemed the most suitable for a Federation colony.

Captain Kirk and Mr. Spock had reported from the planet's surface that everything seemed in order. Kirk had even waxed poetic over the beauty of the quadrant they were exploring, and had raved for several minutes about the distant fields of blue poppies that stretched to the horizon. He had, in a burst of whimsy, nicknamed them "Oz poppies." They were not truly flowers, as Mr. Spock was quick to point out, they were something not quite animal and not quite plant—mindless, yet possessed of a fascinating beauty. They had an undulating motion which caused the fields of flowers to look almost like ocean waves, and Kirk had not been able to resist ordering the survey party to explore that expanse of beautiful yet deadly creatures.

The survey party had wandered freely through the fields of blossoms, and reports from the surface never made it clear whether it was the action of the people crushing the plant-beings underfoot, or simply some normal part of their life cycle, which caused the massive clouds of spores to rise suddenly and begin choking the crew; but the end result was a sudden cessation of conversation from the survey party, and Captain

Kirk's feeble, half-delirious cry for help before his voice ceased altogether.

A rescue party had been sent down clad in protective clothing, and the nine-member survey team was brought back to the *Enterprise*. They were all in a state of coma, and nothing McCoy did could change that fact. He had watched with horror the convulsive, painful deaths of three crewmembers, and had been utterly helpless to stop them.

The deaths had occurred within the first twenty-four hours of the survey party's return to the *Enterprise*. Autopsies had revealed the presence of spores from the poppies packed tightly into every vein and capillary of their brains. McCoy had quickly prepared antibodies for the survivors and soon was able to report the complete absence of spores in any of them. He could find no abnormal toxins in their systems, but there was *something* very, very wrong with the Delta Gamma Four landing party. In the subsequent nine days, there had been no change in the conditions of his patients.

McCoy wandered aimlessly from bed to bed, reading the life-support panels. Captain Kirk, Mr. Spock, Dr. M'Benga, Dr. Carter, Security Officer Robinson, and Biologist Temple remained exactly the same. The life-support systems read perfectly normal; pulse, respiration, and blood pressure normal; blood chemistries normal. There was nothing whatsoever wrong with them, except they did not wake up. McCoy had tried every possible stimulant known, and there had been no visible success. He had even, out of desperation, attempted the use of a depressant; that too had done nothing. He had run blood-chemistry readings looking for hallucinogenics; again, nothing.

McCoy could do nothing but pace and curse James Kirk's insistence on going along with the survey party. The ship could technically spare either Captain Kirk or Mr. Spock, but to have both of them incapacitated was a calamity. Scotty, of course, was in command of the ship and was doing an excellent job. Fortunately, there had been no Klingon attempt to contest their exploration of Delta Gamma Four, and McCoy had a nagging suspicion that the Klingons might have known a great deal more about the planet than the Federation—and that James Kirk's "Oz poppies" might be the reason the Klingons had been in no hurry to claim Delta Gamma Four as their own.

The door to the medical ward slid open and Nurse Christine Chapel entered, carrying a tray with the equipment for taking more blood samples. Her face had for ten days worn an expression of anxiety, and McCoy, noticing that she went to Spock's bed first, knew the reason for that anxiety. The Vulcan might at any moment die of the same massive hemorrhage that had killed the other crewmembers, and there was nothing McCoy or Chapel could do to stop it.

McCoy watched the nurse take the blood samples one by one; and then, when she asked, "Is there anything we haven't tested for?" he was only able to shake his head and sigh. He had no answer.

He walked over to the side of Jim Kirk's bed and reached out to touch his captain's face. Kirk twitched slightly at the stimulus but did not awaken.

"What *is* it? What could it *be*?" McCoy said, knowing that even voicing his frustration was useless. If the Captain and the rest of the party came out of the coma, it would be in their own time, and not from anything he could do. He turned and watched Chapel leave the room, knowing that her next few hours of work would be utterly futile. But he was also aware that she found relief in doing *something*. He was past the point of finding any satisfaction in make-work; there was nothing to do but pace and wait.

The communicator panel on the wall whistled for his attention; when he flicked it on, he heard the reassuring voice of Lt. Cdr. Scott. "McCoy, would you come up to the Captain's cabin for a moment or two? I'd like to have a talk with you—that is, if you're not in the middle of doing something important for the Captain." Scotty's voice held an edge of hope. His faith in Dr. McCoy's ability to come up with cures was sincere and also very touching.

"No, the situation's the same, Scotty. But unless it's

very important, I'd prefer you come down here. I hate to be away—you know, just in case. . . ."

"Aye, if I were in your place, I'd feel the same. I'll be down in a moment. Scott out."

McCoy thumbed the communicator panel off and walked out of the ward into his office. He preferred to have his conversation with Scotty away from those six quiet, accusing bodies. While waiting for the engineer, he absentmindedly shuffled some papers and signed two medical requisition forms. Even this minutiae of his normal routine seemed utterly pointless.

Scotty came into the office wearing the burden of command heavily on his shoulders. Scott was an engineer, not a starship captain.

"I was wanting to know, Doctor, when you were planning to leave this accursed planet and get the captain and the others to a proper medical lab. I'm getting more than a little itchy, hanging about here and waiting for the Klingons to show up. I don't feel up to a fight with those laddies, with the Captain lying cold and still—and I'm sure you feel the same."

"I know, but we've been over this before. I keep thinking the answer to our problem lies down there on Delta Gamma Four, and if we leave here, we lessen our chances of finding out what's wrong with the Captain."

"But man, you've sent out a survey team every day!" Scotty exploded. "I canna be risking it anymore! I know they've got protective clothing; I know they're shielded; but they've found nothing. They've done every test possible to those stinking plants, they've done everything but bring them aboard the ship, and I willna have that—I willna have the entire crew sleeping like Captain Kirk." Scotty was working himself into a rage, and McCoy knew it was entirely justified.

"I still have some hope of finding out what those spores were up to," McCoy said. "Dr. Rigel was on that last search team, and she feels the connection is something in the makeup of those rodents she found. She says they're telepathic or pretty damn close to it. But the only thing they seem to respond to is the spores. Ruth wants to run a few more tests down there.

Maybe she's got something . . . it's more than I have. . . ."

"I canna see how telepathic mice will help us none. If we canna communicate with the wee beasties, it's a bloody waste of time, Doctor. I dinna care about mice! My only concern is for the Captain and the rest of them puir souls a lyin' so still in there."

"But the rodents might be an answer! Ruth says there's some sort of symbiotic relationship between the poppies and the animals, and if she can just figure out what it is. . . ."

"All right, all right. I gave you and your vet a few more days, but you had no results for me worth the mention. I'm takin' the *Enterprise* out of orbit, and that's my final word on the subject."

The Doctor had insisted they remain in orbit around Delta Gamma Four, and he had a right to insist on that precaution; but after ten days and no success, it was beginning to seem futile. Scotty was probably right. Dr. Ruth Rigel had found nothing of any help in the rodents' behavior, and McCoy was able to say with certainty that there were no spores left in the bodies of the Delta Gamma party. They should get the Captain and the others to a proper medical facility.

McCoy buried his head in his hands and murmured, "I know you're right, but I keep thinking that in one more day we might find something. That's Jim in there! I'm so afraid of risking his life. . . ."

"And are you not risking it by staying here?"

"His condition is stable; it's exactly the same as when he came on board. Oh, I don't know, I just don't *know*!" McCoy slammed his fist suddenly onto his desk. "You don't understand how helpless I feel, Scotty. I'm a doctor, I'm supposed to heal, I'm supposed to cure people, and I can't do anything! I'm helpless as a five-year-old with Down's syndrome. There's nothing I can do, and the agony of it is more than I can stand."

Scotty looked alarmed and hastened to the other side of the desk to put one hand reassuringly across the doctor's shoulders. "There, there. We know you're doing all you can. And I know it's a terrible burden. But we canna hang here doing nothing. Do you think it's easy on me? Why, I can't even tell my top from my bottom anymore. I'm supposed to be an engineer and a captain both at the same time; the puir engines are suffering at the hands of my second-in-command—who's a good lad, but he's not me! And there I am, sitting up there in Jim Kirk's place, knowing I haven't the guts or the gall to be a proper captain—and I'm so muddled about that I can't even remember when I've signed the fuel consumption sheet or not! There I was, fashing my poor yeoman over it, until she pointed out I had signed the thing. . . . Why, I canna even finish a cup of tea without someone needing me for something. Sulu and Chekov are as hangdog as a couple of common criminals, and Uhura does nothing but sit at her console and sniffle. The whole lot of them's gone to Hell in a handbasket, and it's up to you to do something about it, or to get the Captain and Mr. Spock and the rest of them to someone who *can* do something!"

"Doctor, Doctor! Come quickly!" Nurse Chapel burst into the office, her face alive once more. "They're waking up! They're waking up!" She grabbed McCoy by the front of his uniform, shaking him. "Hurry! Mr. Spock and Captain Kirk are waking up!"

McCoy reacted so swiftly in leaping from his recliner that his shirt was torn. It didn't matter. Captain Kirk was waking up. He ran into the hospital ward with Scotty and Chapel at his heels.

The six people in the ward were showing various signs of awakening. Jeff Carter was stretching, catlike; and Spock had turned over and curled up in a childlike pose. Captain Kirk was sitting up on one elbow, staring at the wall across from his bed, a strange expression of mingled horror and surprise on his face.

McCoy skidded to a stop at the side of Jim's bed. "Jim! Jim, are you all right?"

James Kirk turned slowly to stare at his medical officer. He blinked once or twice and ran an exploratory tip-of-tongue around his lips. "Am I awake, Bones?" he asked weakly. "Am I really awake?"

2

Dr. McCoy swiftly ordered neurological tests for the survivors of the landing party. Dr. M'Benga had had the most difficulty in coming fully awake and seemed too dazed to even understand where he was. Spock had simply sat up on the edge of his medical bed and pronounced himself fit. The person who worried McCoy the most was Captain Kirk.

James Kirk seemed to be suffering from a difficulty in recognizing the reality of his waking state. The neurological tests revealed nothing whatsoever wrong with him; a complete Sigmund showed only that he had developed a mild terror of sleeping at night and some irregularity in his REM pattern. There was nothing to indicate that he was unfit to resume his duties as captain of the *Enterprise* and, with great reluctance, McCoy released him from Sick Bay. The other survivors of the party he insisted on keeping in check and observing.

Mr. Spock was annoyed—if such a word could be used to describe an attitude in a Vulcan—by McCoy's excessive solicitousness, and more than once complained that he knew he was back to normal and perfectly capable of resuming his duties. Bobby Robinson, the security officer, was returned to light duty; his superior, Lt. Cdr. Greg Collier, put the man to work handling some of the paperwork of the security department. It was as though the entire *Enterprise* was collectively holding its breath while watching for any sign of peculiarity or loss of ability on the part of the survey crew.

Captain Kirk in particular felt pained by the crew's lack of confidence. He was aware that there was something wrong, and that he, Spock, M'Benga, Jeff Carter, Grace Temple, and Bobby Robinson had not been the same since their adventures on Delta Gamma Four.

There was nothing Jim Kirk could point to and say, "This is how I am not the man I was before I went down to the planet"; there was no piece of his mind missing, no lack of awareness of his abilities or his position. But there was a problem of occasionally finding himself dozing in his command chair. When he would yank himself back to attention, he would realize to his dismay that no one on the Bridge had even noticed he'd been nodding. Indeed, when he questioned Sulu or Chekov about the brief catnaps, both men denied that the Captain had in any way appeared asleep.

Kirk took his problem to Dr. McCoy, and a twenty-four-hour EEG reading was tried. There were several occurrences of those strange catnaplike sensations, but the EEG readings indicated James Kirk had been wide awake. He admitted that he could be mistaken, but there was still a strange feeling that he could not control falling asleep at odd moments.

Leonard McCoy pointed out one other slight discrepancy in the EEG readings: when Captain Kirk was indeed asleep, his REM, or Rapid Eye Movement, readings—indicative of the dream state—were much more intense than those from earlier tests taken a year before during Kirk's regular physical. McCoy ran similar tests on the other members of the survey party and found the same pattern. They all showed evidence of much more intense dreaming. Yet when questioned about their dreams, they could not remember them, not even the simple ramblings of the subconscious mind attempting to resolve the problems of the conscious mind while in the dream state.

Kirk, getting no satisfaction from McCoy, talked to

Spock about the problem and found that the First Officer was also troubled by the problem of dreams.

"Captain," Spock had said, "I have a theory that there was something the spores were trying to make us do for them—some form of pollination, I suspect—but we are now free of them and only an echo of their command lingers. I am sure it will disperse in time."

"Yes, Dr. Rigel said something about that to me. She said the spores traveled to new meadows using the telepathic rodents. It seems we've just been mistaken for rats, or something like them. Not an amusing thought, eh, Spock?"

"No, Captain, it is not amusing. Three crewmen died because of those spores, and the rodents . . . the rodents did not travel, they only dreamed. Dr. Rigel's tests proved that to my satisfaction. The rodents spread the spores but did not move from the area. Also the rodents were telepathic and spent most of their lives dreaming. I wonder what a creature of so low an intelligence factor dreams of. Most curious."

"I wish I didn't dream," Kirk said. "I seem to be the only one out of the whole survey party who does dream. McCoy can't figure that out at all. At least I think I dream. I can't tell half the time if I'm even asleep or not. Tell me, Spock, do you dream too?"

The Vulcan looked away for a moment, and Kirk was not sure he would answer. "Yes, Captain, I dream. But I wish I did not have such a talent. Dreams are not for Vulcans. I wish for no more dreams for either of us. Dreaming is illogical."

After several weeks, McCoy was forced to admit that the incident was over. He had no conclusions; whatever had happened on Delta Gamma Four would simply be filed under unknown phenomena. A report would be forwarded to Star Fleet Headquarters that Delta Gamma Four was definitely unsuitable as a colony planet.

It had been a month and a half since the abortive exploration of Delta Gamma Four, and the ship had returned to normal. The crew, to all intents and purposes, had returned to its usual well-functioning unity.

There were no major difficulties. Grace Temple reported a weight gain; Bobby Robinson demanded a return to active duty; and Jeff Carter picked a fight over a chess game with Spock, but McCoy filed these data as trivial. McCoy, Kirk, and Spock had all congratulated one another that the episode was now conveniently behind them, and the *Enterprise* resumed its quiet patrolling of its assigned quadrant of space.

Captain Kirk sat in his command chair, Dr. McCoy standing at his side, Spock at his science console, and everything on the Bridge was completely normal. There was a bleeping sound from Lt. Uhura's communicator panel as it lit up to indicate a top-priority message coming in from Star Fleet. Lt. Uhura adjusted her earphone and listened intently, her head tilted to one side. She murmured a few words of confirmation and then turned to face her captain.

"Sir, we've been rerouted to Star Base Seven. It seems that we're going to get some guests, important guests." Uhura smiled slightly, a bitter edge to her voice. "They're going to saddle us with more ambassadors, sir."

Kirk swiveled in his seat to face the Communications Officer. "What is it now? A blather session on Babel? If I have to put up with another group of ambassadors running amok on my ship, I swear I'll resign my command and take up captaining a garbage scow. It's both quieter and a lot less smelly."

There were sounds of stifled laughter from a number of the officers on the Bridge. Only Mr. Spock looked disapproving. "May I remind you, sir," he said, "that on that particular journey to Babel, one of the ambassadors on board this ship *was* my own father . . . and while I admit that his medical condition did lead to some difficulty, I fail to see why you would feel the necessity of resigning your command rather than deal with such a situation again. We are, after all, a Federation starship, and we are expected to handle whatever the Federation assigns us. That *is* only logical, sir. . . ."

Kirk chuckled. "I was being facetious, Spock, and as usual forgot to take into consideration your intensely literal mind. No, I've no intention of resigning my command . . . but I do wish it wasn't a group of ambassadors, nor that we were going to Babel."

"But sir," Lt. Uhura said, "it's not Babel we're assigned to. We've been given the job of taking a delegation of Federation ambassadors to a special meeting place which has been established in the Romulan Neutral Zone. This meeting is for the purposes of a possible détente with the Romulans."

There was a silence on the Bridge as each person considered the implications of such a détente.

3

Captain's Log, Stardate 6968.4:

Announcement of a potential detente with the Romulans has caused considerable friction among my crew. I realize, of course, from my own feelings, that such a peace with our erstwhile enemies would not be an easy thing to accept quickly. I have noticed indications that members of my crew have been quarreling, and there's even a possibility that such quarrels have led to physical violence. This morning, Dr. Jeffrey Carter of the ship's medical department was sporting a spectacular black eye, which he insisted he got by walking into a door. I was not able to get any other explanation from anyone in the medical department.

My concern at the moment is that we will be adding to the volatile situation on the *Enterprise* an as yet unknown number of Federation ambassadors. Potential for violence is already present. The ambassadors may serve as additional fuel. I remember too well other occasions when the *Enterprise* carried Federation representatives and the chaos such visitors can cause. My only hope is that my senior officers can behave with the dignity expected of them, and will preserve tranquillity as best they can. As for the ambassadors, I will have very little control over them—but I must admit to a feeling of confidence and relief when I was informed that

their senior representative was Ambassador Sarek of Vulcan.

Star Base Seven resembled a cross between an Oriental bazaar and a zoo run amok. Captain Kirk and Mr. Spock wandered the corridors of the Federation Embassy on their way to a meeting with Ambassador Sarek. Kirk was finding it very difficult not to gawk at some of the strange and exotic creatures parading the hallways. There was one being, a bright yellow lobster, who he swore had to be at least three meters long; Kirk watched nervously as it slithered down the corridor on its tiny legs. The creature's gigantic claws, clicking in rhythm with its speech pattern, were less than reassuring. However, when Kirk got a closer look at its companion, even the lobster didn't worry him very much. The other ambassador was a gigantic gray cat, with enormous fangs and yellow, narrow-slit eyes with a gleam of fanaticism. Something in the creature's body language made Kirk feel very nervous and very, very frightened.

"Spock, what do you make of those two we just passed?"

Spock stopped, turned slightly to gaze after the now-receding figures, and said, "What do you wish to know, Captain? Their names? Characteristics? I am capable of telling you about both beings. The large crustacean is Ambassador Telson of the planet Manteiga; he's quite a pleasant gentleman, my father approves of him immensely. His work in the Federation Council has been known to be both moderate and intelligent. So if you are having a typical Terran reaction to something outlandish in appearance, you may relax; there's nothing to worry about. It is my hope, indeed, that Ambassador Telson is assigned to the *Enterprise*. He is a being of great intelligence, and he and I will have many things to discuss. He is also a Grandmaster chess player."

"How very reassuring," Kirk said with a half-sigh. "But I notice you said nothing about his companion. Any reason for that, Spock?"

Spock frowned and appeared to be considering just

what to say. It was as though his natural Vulcan reluctance to commit himself to an unpleasant statement was struggling with his Vulcan respect for the truth. Finally, it seemed the truth won out. "Ambassador Neko, from Gyuunyuu, is not considered to be reasonable. He is . . . *difficult* to deal with, my father says."

Spock had ceased speaking, and Kirk, anxious for more information, grabbed his elbow and said, "Out with it, Spock. You know more than you're saying. There's something about that ambassador that's fishy. I want to know about it. Given the tensions we have on the *Enterprise*, I don't want a repeat of finding a dead ambassador on my ship."

"Captain, I cannot swear to the statements I am about to make—and I have an aversion to gossip. But I will say that the ambassador has very sharp claws, which he has been known to trim on his fellow ambassadors—and I do not mean that figuratively, sir."

Spock had retreated into his most rigid Vulcan mode, and Kirk knew he would get nothing further out of the Vulcan concerning Ambassador Neko. But James Kirk knew that if he had any choice, that particular ambassador would not be on board the *Enterprise*.

James Kirk found out very quickly that the choice of which ambassadors would be assigned to the *Enterprise* was not his to make.

The office that had been temporarily assigned to Ambassador Sarek was quite comfortable. It was decorated in soft shades of blue and green, and there was an ocean motif to the upholstery on the furniture. The wall facing the door had been decorated with a beautiful mural of dolphins and mermaids and other sea creatures, and the massive driftwood desk was topped with a sandstone slab and a beautiful piece of blue coral, sculpted into the shape of a water nymph.

Kirk found himself wondering how the Vulcan ambassador, used to a dry, arid world, was reacting to all this emphasis on ocean around him—and then realized that to Sarek the decor probably meant very little. The ambassador was seated at the desk, busily shuffling a large stack of papers. He looked up as Spock and Kirk approached and then stood to acknowledge their presence. He shook hands with the Captain and reached out to grip his son's elbow. Spock, moved by the gesture, took steps to control his features as best he could and returned the grip, murmuring a Vulcan greeting.

"Now, gentlemen," Sarek said, "if you will be seated, I will continue reviewing this manifest for the *Enterprise*. It's a listing of the ambassadors who will be traveling aboard your vessel, and I was reviewing their opinions regarding the Romulan détente." The ambassador seated himself again, and Spock pulled two large seashell-shaped chairs into position in front of the desk. He indicated the one on the left for the Captain, and then seated himself.

"We met two of the ambassadors in the hallway," Kirk said. "Spock informed me that they were Ambassadors Neko and Telson."

"I beg to differ with the Captain," Spock said. "We did not meet either ambassador—we merely passed them in the hall. There is a difference."

Kirk grinned slightly, realizing that Spock was being especially Vulcan for his father's benefit. "I stand corrected—as my First Officer has stated, we did merely pass the ambassadors in the hall. Spock seemed quite impressed by Ambassador Telson, and I hope he'll be included in that group of ambassadors assigned to the *Enterprise*."

"Oh yes," Sarek replied, "Telson is a very old and dear friend, and I insisted on his presence on the *Enterprise*. He is, like myself, a moderate, and his voice will be very important in the upcoming meeting. But you did not mention the other ambassador. Has my son told you anything about Neko?"

Kirk glanced quickly at his First Officer. Spock, his fingers steepled, seemed to be studying intently the blue coral carving on his father's desk. It was obvious he was not going to reply to the question. "I was given the impression, sir," Kirk said, trying to be very precise and careful about what he said, "that Ambassador Neko can be—I believe the word was 'difficult.' I would appreciate your opinion of him; and if he is, shall we say, difficult, is it possible to keep him out of the group assigned to my ship and let some other captain deal with the *difficulty*?"

Sarek had steepled his fingertips in a gesture so like Spock's that the Captain realized where his First Officer had gotten that affectation. If it had been possible, Ambassador Sarek would have smiled. Instead, he merely lifted one eyebrow in an expression that was the Vulcan equivalent of amusement. "My son has the makings of an excellent diplomat. I would not have used the word 'difficult' in regard to Neko; I would have used the words 'utterly impossible.' I quite agree with you, Captain—I do not wish Neko aboard the *Enterprise*. But unfortunately . . ."

Sarek shuffled the manifest sheets again until one rested on the top. Even upside down and from where Kirk sat, he could see that it had Neko's name on it. "Ambassador Neko is a fanatic, and he dislikes Romulans," Sarek continued. "I might also add that he extends that dislike to Vulcans. There is something about our pointed ears—I think he finds them offensive."

Kirk glanced swiftly at the ambassador's face in hopes the man was making some kind of joke, but it was obvious that Sarek did not and would not make any sort of joke about this subject, or any other.

"Then there's no way we can keep him off the *Enterprise*? I thought, sir, since you were officially in charge of the party, you would have some voice . . ."

"Indeed, but I have included Neko for one very good reason. There are two ambassadors included in the group traveling on your vessel that are able to control him. One is Ambassador Telson, whom you have already encountered, and the other is Ambassador Karhu. I am not sure you have met him, Captain, or even passed him in the hallway. He is from the planet Hunaja and can be quite a fearsome creature in his own way. He is also a moderate. Karhu and Telson are the only two beings that I have ever found capable of making Neko listen to reason. Of course they have a very simple method—if he will not listen to reason, they utilize force. And both of them are capable of dealing with Neko's rather unpleasant method of debate."

Kirk remembered Spock's comment about Ambassador Neko's use of his claws. He sighed, spread his hands in a gesture of resignation. "Well then, it appears that we have Ambassador Neko."

"Yes, and twelve others, including myself. That makes thirteen." Sarek paused, eyeing Kirk. "I do hope, Captain, you do not suffer from the Terran flaw of superstition. It would be so inconvenient. I have handpicked the group of ambassadors traveling on the *Enterprise,* in hopes that they will be a balance, each to the other. And that also the time spent in travel might be well utilized in discussion of this situation. I assure you on my honor as a Vulcan that there will be no unpleasantness to mar this journey. I too remember very well the last time a group of ambassadors traveled on board your ship, and it is very much to my dishonor that that trip was not pleasant. I shall attempt to rectify the situation."

"I hope you're right, Mr. Ambassador. My crew is already in a state of ferment over this proposed détente. Tempers are running high, and it wouldn't take much to cause a major disturbance. I'm not happy about the situation." Kirk paused, trying to think of the best way of admitting his problem. "I know it appears that I should have better control of my own crew, but as your son can explain to you at a later time, the *Enterprise* underwent a traumatic incident several weeks ago in our exploration of the planet Delta Gamma Four, and while there are no residual ill effects, there is still a question of normalizing my crew's morale. It was almost perfect until the announcement of the Romulan détente. I do not want a situation on board my ship that could lead to anarchy or mutiny—and I am counting on you, sir, to make sure the ambassadors you've chosen assist me in maintaining calm aboard my ship."

Sarek nodded and again shuffled the stack of papers; he then neatly aligned them and handed them to the Captain. "You'd best read these; they will give you some idea of what you will be encountering, and it will familiarize you with the general characteristics of your passengers. There is to be a reception this evening for the group chosen to be aboard the *Enterprise,* and you'll have a chance to meet them all. I would like you to read the psychological surveys of each ambassador, Captain; I would like to avoid any unpleasantness, or potential faux pas, on your part. You see, this group of ambassadors is . . . quite alien, as you will see."

It was obvious that the interview was over. Kirk rose, as did his First Officer. "Spock, if you would care to stay here, or," Kirk swiftly amended, "if your father wishes to discuss anything with you, I would be perfectly amenable to your being away from the *Enterprise* until later this evening."

Spock glanced at his father, noted the ambassador's brief nod of acceptance, and said, "I would appreciate such a leave, Captain. I will see you at the reception later."

4

Captain Kirk had asked Dr. McCoy, Mr. Scott, and Lt. Uhura to join him for the reception at the embassy, and he was very pleased to see that his officers had made their best effort to look as smart as possible for the delegates. Scotty was in full family kilt, red velvet jacket, sporran and all; Dr. McCoy was particularly distinguished in his full dress uniform. But it was Lt. Uhura who quite stole the show. The woman was wearing a cinnamon silk-chiffon sari, shot with gold, that displayed a great deal of her not inconsiderable charms. Kirk was quite pleased with the turnout and positive that his group would outdo the representatives of any of the other eight starships waiting to carry ambassadors to the rendezvous point in the Romulan Neutral Zone.

The ballroom of the Federation Embassy was gigantic, and for a moment, Captain Kirk felt as though he had walked into the middle of a giant caucus race straight out of *Alice In Wonderland*. The room was packed with hundreds of aliens of every size, shape, and conceivable physical description. For a moment he wondered just how he'd recognize his own group of travelers. He began scanning the room for some sign of Ambassador Sarek—and then he realized how cleverly the ballroom had been designed. What appeared to be a large open space was actually divided into sections by crystal banners that hung from the ceiling to the floor, marking out the gathering point for each ship. The room had an openness that would allow the various ambassadors to move from section to section and would avoid any sense of claustrophobia. Yet the sections had also been clearly marked with a design, woven into the floor covering, of the insignia of each of the selected Federation vessels. Kirk gathered his group together and started moving toward the part of the room where he could see the design that denoted the *Enterprise*.

Spock materialized at his elbow, as if from the crystal banners themselves. "My father sent me to make sure that you did not get lost, Captain. This affair does appear to be quite crowded." Spock wrinkled his nose slightly. "They have allowed a number of the staff members of the embassies to be present to meet the local celebrities. It's not often that the whole Federation diplomatic corps is gathered in one place at one time."

"Aye," Scotty said, "and it seems to me a dangerous thing. When you consider that they're all going to be together on one little station in the middle of the Romulan Neutral Zone, all it would take for those laddies would be to drop a wee clutch of photon bombs and, poof, there goes the Federation and its diplomats."

"I'm afraid you are in error, Mr. Scott," Spock replied. "You must understand that there is a considerable difference between the diplomatic corps and the Federation Council itself. The corps merely advises; the Council legislates. While some ambassadors are also on the Council, such as Sarek and Telson, that is not universally the case. If we were to lose every creature in this room, including ourselves, the Federation would still continue."

"Are you saying, Mr. Spock, that diplomats are unnecessary?" McCoy was being deliberately provocative; he waited for the Vulcan's answer, enjoying himself immensely.

Spock frowned and considered the comment. "Not useless, Doctor, but certainly expendable. However, should the Romulans attempt to destroy the Federation's ambassadors, they would harm only themselves.

The result of such an aggressive action would only be automatic war—something the Romulans obviously do not wish. The very fact that they have agreed to a détente meeting proves that."

"I quite agree," Kirk said. "The Romulans, whatever we feel about them, are no fools. A Klingon *might* decide to destroy the whole diplomatic corps simply because he was a Klingon—but not the Romulans. I feel that this détente meeting really is something they want. In all my dealings with them, I've found them to be at least honorable—stubborn, bullheaded, but honorable."

Thanks to Spock's judicious steering of the group through the mob, they easily reached the area marked out for the *Enterprise*. Kirk swiftly spotted Ambassador Sarek, and with him an extremely beautiful woman. She was a pale shimmery sky blue, her slender naked body iridescent with fish scales; her eyes were enormous, clear, and beautiful as faceted aquamarines, and her hair, hip-length, the same color as her eyes. The ambassador swiftly made introductions.

"Captain Kirk, I would like you to meet Sirenia, ambassador of the planet Cetacea. I think you will find her quite charming company, and well able to introduce you to the rest of our group. I fear I must be excused; I am to receive some last-minute instructions from the head of the diplomatic corps. If you will excuse me," Sarek executed a perfect bow, "I shall join you on the *Enterprise* later this evening."

With that, the tall Vulcan took his leave, moving gracefully through the crystal panels toward a throne-like platform at one end of the room. Captain Kirk recognized the being seated on the throne as Marmeluke of Antares, the chief of the diplomatic corps.

Kirk turned to the lovely ambassador at his side and realized on closer inspection that the woman was not, as he had first thought, nude; she was wearing body jewelry of pearls and aquamarines which blended almost perfectly with the slightly scaled quality of her skin.

"I am so pleased, Captain Kirk, that Ambassador Sarek has entrusted me to this position. I shall do my best to please." Her voice was as gentle and soft as seafoam, and Kirk realized his interest in meeting any other ambassadors was fast fading.

"If you would be so kind," he said, "I would like to meet the rest of your colleagues—because," he smiled, "if I don't meet them soon, I'm not sure I'll want to. None of them is likely to be as fascinating as you are."

She nodded and accepted the compliment with a calm gaze and a particularly sweet smile. "Very well, let me begin by introducing you to one of the ambassadors who will be the most difficult for the *Enterprise* to deal with. Not," she added, "because of his position on the issues, but simply from the complications of his situation." She led Kirk to a large rectangular tank, its base heavily studded with dials and controls. The upper part of the tank was a clear lucite material, open at the top, and filled with slightly murky fluid. It was not easy to see the creature inside but, to Kirk, it appeared to be something slimy and snakelike. He found that the old cliché about something making one's flesh crawl was accurate; this thing in the tank gave him an itch that was less than pleasant.

"Captain, I would like you to meet Agnatha, ambassador of Jezero," Sirenia said, placing one hand gently on the fluid at the top of the tank. There was a swirl of motion in the fluid, and suddenly a head, large and scaly with bulging eyes, appeared, its mouth an open maw of busily waving tentacles. The creature paused at the surface only long enough to envelop Sirenia's hand in its tentacles, and then vanish again into the viscid liquid that was its home.

"He wishes to convey his greetings, Captain, and requests that we adjust the translator so he may speak to you personally." Sirenia pushed a series of buttons at the base of the clear tank, and a strangely metallic voice issued from the machine.

"I greet you, Captain James Kirk." The voice was precise, as though it were forming each word separately and not quite sure how to put them together. "I must tell you I am unhappy about this meeting with the Romulans. I do not approve. I have little choice—I am a diplomat. But the Romulans are evil." The creature splashed vigorously in its tank. It was clearly agitated. Sirenia again placed her hand in the fluid, and her very presence seemed to have a calming effect on Agnatha. The surface was again still, and the creature silent.

"You will have three other ambassadors on board your vessel who feel very much the way Agnatha does," Sirenia explained. "The others are Ambassadors Neko, Rovar, and Naja. It is my hope, and Sarek's, that we may convince them to take a more openminded view before we reach the meeting." The woman smiled sweetly. "I think it can be done. This détente is too important to allow ill feelings to stand in the way of peace."

Captain Kirk nodded his agreement and glanced again at the thing only dimly seen in the tank. He had noticed the gentle touch Sirenia had given it and found himself almost envying the strange lampreylike creature. It was obvious there was a certain rapport, if not actual affection, between the two ambassadors.

"And now I will introduce you to some of the other ambassadors." But before Sirenia could continue, it was obvious that a quarrel was breaking out at one end of the refreshment table that had been set up in the *Enterprise* sector. There were four beings standing at the end of the table; two of them were vigorously engaged in a quarrel. One of them was Neko; beside him on the floor was Ambassador Telson, his claws clicking like castanets. Across from them stood a humanoid, tall, slender, and black-haired, his eyes as red as burning coals. He was dressed entirely in black, and there was something about his pale face and glittering eyes that reminded Kirk of strange nursery tales and things undead.

The fourth ambassador was in and of himself enormously reassuring. Dressed from shoulders to ankles in a white fur ceremonial cape, he was the largest, most cuddly koala bear Kirk had ever seen in his life. The very sight of him instilled warmth, comfort, and a feeling that nothing could go wrong in his presence.

It was the handsome humanoid and Neko who were doing the loudest arguing. Telson seemed to be attempting to run interference, and the teddy bear, as Kirk had mentally nicknamed him, was merely standing by the table, his eyes half-closed, meditatively chewing a fistful of slender green leaves.

Neko, obviously incensed by something the humanoid had said, made as if to strike the ambassador; and then with surprising swiftness the bear lost his sleepy quality. He reached out one surprisingly long arm and grasped the gray, catlike ambassador by the scruff of his neck, lifting him effortlessly into the air until his legs dangled off the floor.

"Neko." The bear's voice was sweet and soft and gentle. "I don't like fights at parties. I don't approve of fights at parties, and I will get *very* upset with you if you continue it." The bear appeared to be in total control of his temper, and even a little bored by the situation, but it was obvious from the look of fear on Neko's face that it had not been an idle threat, and that Ambassador Neko knew only too well that this large, sleepy, cuddly koala could *do* something about his dislike of fights at parties.

"All right, all right, Karhu!" The cat was trying very hard to present a pleasant expression on his fanged face. "If you'll be so kind as to put me down, I assure you I will not disturb you again."

The bear slowly lowered Neko to the ground and with one hand (which, Kirk noticed, was as amply clawed as Neko's) he gently smoothed the fur of the Gyuunyuu ambassador. "You have to be understanding about these things, Neko," the bear said. "Disturbances of this nature are so tiring. Now drink some of that lovely punch and be the diplomat you claim to be."

The cat glared at the humanoid and then stalked away to the other end of the refreshment table, where with enormously expressive gestures he helped himself to a cup of punch. It was clear he was doing it only under protest and because he had been ordered to by a teddy bear.

Kirk was almost tempted to laugh at the scene but realized it was far more serious than it had seemed and that laughter would not be appropriate. Sirenia led him up to the handsome humanoid and proceeded to make introductions.

"Captain James Kirk, I would like you to meet His Excellency Damu, ambassador of Chiroptera. He's a gentleman of much wisdom, but is inclined to speak his mind a little too freely." She smiled at the tall humanoid to take the sting out of what she'd said, and he smiled back, revealing a mouth filled with perfect, even white teeth.

Kirk felt a sudden shock in recognizing the source of the nursery tales. Damu was the perfect image of a vampire.

"And now," Sirenia continued, "I would like you to meet two more of your ambassadors: Ambassador Telson of Manteiga," she indicated the lobster-creature, who gravely lifted his tail to the Captain, "and of course, our own dear Ambassador Karhu of Hunaja." Karhu nodded to the captain; it was obvious that he had retreated into his sleepy, relaxed pose of a few minutes before. He had again busied himself in masticating a large wad of the aromatic green leaves, which seemed to interest him far more than meeting a starship captain.

Sirenia laughed and patted the large furry marsupial on one arm. "Captain, you must pardon Karhu; he takes such trouble with his affectation of being sweet and adorable. We really mustn't destroy the illusion by commenting on his little disturbance with Neko." She laughed up at the bear, watching his eyes crinkle as he grinned slightly in admiration at her ability to catch him out.

"Well, you have to admit this is more enjoyable than going around being gruff and fierce and mean," Karhu said. "I am not ursine, even though I am frequently mistaken for a bear. And growling and showing my claws are both so fatiguing." He reached for another leaf and nibbled it, closing his eyes and affecting an air of great weariness.

Sirenia took Kirk by the arm and led him away from Karhu. "Don't let that foppish, cuddly quality fool you, Captain. Karhu, when pushed, is an extraordinarily dirty fighter. He just appears harmless. He's not."

"Yes, I got that impression, but he is going to have difficulties on board the *Enterprise*. He's so—*cute*—my crewwomen are going to find him absolutely adorable."

"Oh dear," Sirenia said, "that's the one thing he can't stand—being called cute. Please warn your ladies of that. It is the one word that will cause him to lose all his affectation and sulk quite vocally."

Kirk laughed and said, "I'll make sure everyone is informed. Now for the rest of the ambassadors."

The next few minutes were a blur of strange and marvelous creatures. With the exception of Sirenia and Damu, none of them were humanoid. Kirk had vague recollections of a crocodile, a snake, a large insect, and a tall slender thing with bat wings, an enormous chest, and rather sharp-looking mandibles who was introduced as Ambassador Spiracles. There was also a tanklike creature, close to the ground, which vaguely resembled a giant armadillo. Kirk was positive the *Enterprise* had never seen so strange an assortment of creatures in its entire history; but he was in for one or two more surprises in the way of ambassadors.

Lt. Uhura had joined Captain Kirk and Sirenia, her eyes wide with amazement as she took in the details of the various creatures that would be inhabiting the *Enterprise* for the next few weeks. She picked up a punch cup from the buffet and remarked to the Captain, "Look at the piece of sculpture in the center of the table, it's a perfect pyramid. I wonder what it's made of. Do you think it's edible?"

"No, madame, I am not edible!" The indignant small gray pyramid suddenly had eyes, ears, and a large mouth. "I'm Hotep, ambassador from the planet Djoser. I'm not a table decoration, either. Karhu lifted me up here so I could reach the food. Now if you will excuse me, I must rest. I had entirely too much punch for my system to deal with effectively." The creature gave a loud burp and subsided into his former faceless form.

"Good heavens, Captain, I've never seen such a strange array of ambassadors in my life. But I must say that Ambassador Damu is incredibly charming. I'm really rather fond of him."

"Ahh, lovely one," a strange, lisping voice had added itself to the conversation. "But you have not yet had a chance to meet me. I assure you I will make you forget Damu swiftly."

Lt. Uhura turned to see behind her a giant blue crocodile, his head towering above her own. He wore a flowing red velvet cape lined in sapphire satin, and on his head a small red velvet skullcap with a magnificent sapphire-blue ostrich plume. His jaw was long and narrow, and when he smiled—or it seemed to be a smile—it was apparent he had two rows of incredibly sharp teeth. He sketched a magnificent bow, the point of his snout almost touching her small brocade slipper.

"Queen of my heart," he said as he rose from the bow, "I am Si-s-s-s(click), ambassador of the magnificent and marvelous planet Gavialian. And I might only add that it is to my great s-sorrow that you have met the other ambassadors before observing myself—for I fear you may have lost your heart to another, when I would claim it." He again bowed deeply.

Uhura was stunned by the sight of so exotic a creature. It was clear from her face that she was not at all sure how to take the excessive romanticism of his language. She swiftly curtsied to him and smiled.

"Lt. Uhura, Communications Officer, USS *Enterprise,* at your service, sir."

"Oh how niccce; someone who knows how to curtsey. May I kiss your hand, madame?" He reached out for her hand and Uhura, taking a second look at that incredible jawline, retreated a step.

The large crocodilian's eyes filled with tears. "Alas, alas, like most Terran ladies you do not trust me. It is a pity. Of course," he eyed her slowly from the crown of her head to her toes, "I must admit you *are* beautiful enough to eat." He laughed, leaving the exact meaning of his comment open to interpretation. "Perhaps another time, when you get to know me better. I wish s-so much to know more about your Terran customs of romanticism—they are s-so beautiful, s-so lovely, s-so filled with panache. I am a great admirer of your writers Dumas and Shakespeare, and your romantic poets Shelley and Byron and Keats. Oh, it is such a beautiful thing, and I shall strive to live up to them and prove to you I am a romantic lover beyond your wildest dreams." Si-s-s-s(click) bowed again and backed out of Uhura's presence as if she were an empress.

"Good heavens, Captain," was all Uhura could say.

"Don't mind Si-s-s-s(click)," Sirenia said. "He's given to fads, you see. He reads a great deal and admires every culture but his own. It's a common failing with ambassadors; and his own culture, I'm afraid, is terribly dull. You should consider yourself fortunate you didn't meet him six months ago; he was quite enthralled with a warrior culture from Rigel 6, and he went around in full armor challenging everyone to a duel. I believe he killed six beings before he was restrained from further bloodshed. I personally find the romantic mood quite restful—but," she laughed and then smiled at the beautiful Terran, "I would advise you to be careful. He is a carnivore, and when he says you look beautiful enough to eat, he just might mean it."

5

Captain Kirk had been looking forward to getting Ambassador Sirenia alone, perhaps for an intimate little dinner in his cabin with conversation and whatever else might develop. But unfortunately, protocol did require that he attend to the comforts of his other guests. Ambassador Agnatha, of course, required that his tank be properly installed in his cabin; Scotty and some of his engineers spent a great deal of time adjusting all the gauges and dials to assure the ambassador the environment that was most suitable for him. A similar problem arose over the comforts of Ambassador Telson. He was somewhat aquatic and needed a much larger shower and bath ensemble in his bathroom. Spiracles suffered from too much oxygen, requiring air regulators on his door and nose plugs for his visits to the rest of the ship.

In the ensuing few hours, Kirk found himself being run ragged by his Alice-in-Wonderland collection of ambassadors, and learned three new Scottish oaths from his chief engineer.

"Captain," Scotty complained after having to make his third change in the quarters of Ambassador Rovar of Hemiptera, "I canna tolerate any more complaints of that great ugly bedbug. Would you believe it's not his comfort he's concerned about, it's bloody aesthetics? He says the walls are the wrong shade of green, and he doesna care for the softness of the mattress of his bed. For two credits I'd take that large stripy bandersnatch and throw him into me own engines, save that he's so nasty-tempered I'd never get the beauties working again. I tell you, Captain, I will not put up with one more complaint from that great bug of a beastie."

Captain Kirk was inclined to agree. Rovar had proved to be a pest. He had an unfortunately strong resemblance to a bug; his six arms and three eyes were disturbing, particularly since the eyes, on rather large stalks, had a tendency to look in several directions at once, and his rather flat, shiny-striped body reminded Kirk forcibly of some sort of flea or tick. His temper, unfortunately, matched. Rovar had complained bitterly over everything about the *Enterprise* the moment he stepped on board, and Kirk made a mental note to speak to Sarek about the possibility of shortcircuiting some of these complaints. An ambassador such as Rovar was only a short-term aspect of the *Enterprise;* a chief engineer like Mr. Scott was vital.

The various ambassadors did have individual requirements which Kirk and his crew had tried to anticipate as far as possible. But it was still extremely difficult. Kirk had, in a burst of goodwill, ordered appropriate food and beverages delivered to the quarters of the various representatives; he asked Sirenia whether she drank wine and was pleased to hear that she did, but he was drawn up short when Damu said in his silken voice, "I thank you, Captain, for your kind thoughts, but I never drink . . . wine." He bowed to the Captain and then, taking Sirenia's arm, escorted her to his cabin.

Kirk was torn between jealousy and a nagging suspicion that Damu's comment about wine had a great deal more meaning to it than appeared on the surface. His fear was borne out a short time later when Dr. McCoy, as part of his duties of making the ambassadors comfortable, commented that Damu had brought on board large quantities of the blood of some mammalian creature from his own planet and had asked McCoy to store it in his medical facilities.

"Dammit," Kirk exclaimed, "I *knew* the man was a

vampire! I won't have it, not on my ship! I won't have some fanged bat running around sinking his teeth into heaven knows who or what! I don't care if he is an ambassador, I want him off this ship."

"There, there, Jim, you're getting a little too upset," McCoy said, placing a reassuring hand on Kirk's arm. "Damu doesn't have fangs, nor is he capable of biting anyone. His principal source of nourishment *is* blood, but I gather from what he's told me that his methods are entirely humane—it's similar to the customs of the Masai tribesmen on Earth. They raise these animals on Chiroptera and drain their blood periodically as a food source. The animals aren't killed, they're simply tended and fed, and the blood regenerates within twenty-four hours. It's actually much more humane than what we do to a cow to obtain steaks. As for Ambassador Damu being a vampire, don't let his appearance or all that pure elegance fool you. He's no more immortal than you or I—and down in my Sick Bay he reflected perfectly well in the mirrors. I've heard all those nursery tales too, and I can assure you we have nothing to worry about from Ambassador Damu. He's one of the gentlest of all the ambassadors, next to Sarek, of course. I rather like him. The one that bothers me is Si-s-s-s(click). He had several crates of long-eared critters brought on board, and he says he always eats alone in his room with a live animal as food. May the gods pity anyone on this ship who believes in the Easter Bunny." McCoy shuddered.

Somehow Kirk did not find this entirely reassuring. Eating rabbit, alive or dead, was understandable, but he had too vivid a memory of having been read Bram Stoker's classic *Dracula* at a young age by his father; and black-haired beings that seemed likely to turn into bats weren't at all to his taste.

Ambassador Spiracles proved to be a bit of a problem for the doctor. His oxygen needs were far less than the average Terran, and he had begun to show all the signs of heavy oxygen intoxication. McCoy had to put him in a low-oxygen chamber for two hours to detoxify him and then insisted that the ambassador remember to use his nasal plugs when he left his quarters. Karhu caused no difficulties whatsoever, much to everyone's relief; the Hunaja ambassador simply looked over his room, nodded acceptance, curled up, and went to sleep. Ambassador Edentata from the planet Tandenborstel was equally easy to deal with. This was the ambassador whom Kirk had likened to an armadillo—and indeed, the slow, relaxed attitude of the heavily armored creature was reminiscent of that gentle Terran beast. His only request involved substituting a shallow box of sand in place of the standard starship bed.

Bit by bit, the job was accomplished. Thirteen ambassadors had all been accommodated, their tastes catered to and their complaints handled to the best of the *Enterprise*'s ability. Captain Kirk found himself the victim of massive weariness, and he began to suspect that he had not fully recovered from his adventures on Delta Gamma Four. He was suffering from a headache, tension in the deltoid and occipital regions of his back and neck, and an overwhelming wish to find someplace warm and comfortable to curl up and fall asleep.

However, even though Kirk was exhausted, the thought of the beautiful Ambassador Sirenia itched at his mind. After all, what would it hurt to invite her to his cabin for an apertif and a little conversation? It would even serve to banish some of the weariness from his mind and body. He went in search of the woman but found her cabin empty.

He had almost decided to give up the half-realized notion of getting to know Sirenia better when he noticed Sarek approaching Sirenia's cabin, obviously also in search of her. Kirk leaned against the doorframe of her room and waited for the tall Vulcan to reach him.

"I see Madam Sirenia has not yet returned from Sick Bay," Sarek said. "I did feel it unnecessary for her to take all the medical tapes to Dr. McCoy personally; she might have delegated the job to an aide. But then, she's always been a woman who enjoyed doing things on her own. She finds it almost impossible to delegate authority—a definite drawback in an ambassador."

Kirk nodded, unsure of what reply Sarek expected. He personally had no interest whatsoever in her ability to delegate authority; how she handled her job was her business. But he realized that, out of politeness, he ought to say something to the Vulcan.

"I'm very glad, sir, of your assistance in getting everyone settled in. If Sirenia has taken it upon herself to be equally helpful, I'm afraid I haven't much cause for complaint. You did say she was down in Sick Bay?"

Sarek's eyebrows lifted slightly. "Yes, and she should still be there. But Captain, I would advise . . . no, you probably have no need of my advice, so I shall refrain from giving it. Unneeded or unwanted advice is illogical." With that rather cryptic statement, Sarek bowed gravely to the Captain and continued down the corridor.

As soon as the Vulcan was out of sight, Kirk sprinted for the nearest turbolift and set it for the Sick Bay station.

He saw Sirenia as soon as the doors opened. She was just leaving Sick Bay, and he called to her to wait. She turned, startled by the sound of his voice; she looked pensive—and it was apparent from the droop of her shoulders that she was more than a little tired herself.

"Uh, Madam Sirenia—I've been told by Ambassador Sarek how much help you've been in getting the records to Dr. McCoy. I appreciate that, and all you've done in establishing your fellow ambassadors aboard ship. I was wondering if you'd care to come up to my cabin for a drink before retiring for the evening. But I can see that you look as tired as I feel, so if you want to put it off until another time, I do understand," he said with a mild tone of regret in his voice.

Sirenia studied the handsome captain for a moment or two before replying, and then said, "Did you honestly have in mind simple liquid refreshment, Captain? Or were you wishing to indulge in an act of reproduction?"

The bluntness of her reaction rattled Kirk. He blushed slightly, then decided honesty was probably the best policy with this woman. He grinned and shrugged. "Well . . . I did have something of that sort in mind; but I must admit that I'm pretty tired from the day's activities, and I suppose you are too—so if you just want to make it a drink, let's leave it at that."

"Yes, Captain, I wouldn't mind something of that sort—I would find it relaxing. But I think we should discuss the question of biological reproduction right now, because I have a feeling that you also have that in mind—if not tonight, then on some future occasion. I find it necessary to explain that there are certain basic difficulties involved in such an act between a being like yourself and a woman of my world. Have you studied biology, Captain?"

"I don't see what that has to do with the subject at hand," Kirk said, "and besides, I wasn't really thinking in terms of reproduction. I'd been considering it more—well, as recreation."

"Yes, but you see, on my world it *is* done only for reproduction." Sirenia smiled and reached out to touch his sleeve with one blue-tinged hand. "If you have studied biology, Captain, you know something about the mating habits of fish, or frogs, on your own planet. I think you've failed to take into consideration that I am from Cetacea and, as such, an amphibian."

Kirk stared at her for a moment, an expression of shock on his face as what she said penetrated his mind. He knew very well from his biology classes the reproductive habits of fish and frogs—and primarily that there was no physical contact between the male and the female. The female laid eggs and the male swam by and fertilized them. He found himself wondering whether Sirenia knew there was a swimming pool on the *Enterprise,* and then blurted, "But that doesn't sound like much fun!"

Sirenia smiled again, patted his arm in almost reassuring fashion and said, "Captain, I have made a thorough study of the biological habits of your race, and frankly I find your sexual customs to be . . . excessively sweaty and a great deal of labor for very small results. I must admit—" She tried to look apologetic, but it was apparent that she really wanted to giggle and was suppressing it. "—I find your method of reproduction to be somewhat disgusting! I mean, all that *clutching*! I'm afraid it won't do, Captain. I am very flattered, but I'm afraid it just won't do." She turned away and signaled the turbolift.

Kirk leaned against the wall near the door of the Sick Bay wondering what he should do next. The conversation with Sirenia had been a bit of a shock and deflating to his ego. He reassured himself that she hadn't turned him down personally—it was simply a matter of their species' incompatibility. But still it was frustrating to have so beautiful a woman aboard the *Enterprise* who wasn't exactly a woman. He had finally decided that bed—alone—was the best answer when he noticed Dr. Rigel, the blonde veterinarian, approaching Sick Bay.

"Captain, Dr. McCoy has been looking for you. He wants a consultation with the two of us," she said, her round face lighting with a smile. Dr. Rigel smiled frequently. She was a cheerful woman and almost totally unflappable—which was necessary considering she spent most of her working hours dealing with a collection of very odd animals in her veterinary lab located near Sick Bay.

Captain Kirk noticed that Dr. Rigel was not accompanied by her pet mongcat, a fact which made him profoundly grateful. He sometimes found Fuzzybutt too demanding of Dr. Rigel's attention, and every time he saw the petite doctor cuddling the creature, he wondered again why he had not prohibited pets aboard the *Enterprise*.

"A conference? Did he say what it was about?"

Before Kirk could say anything further, the door to the Sick Bay opened, and McCoy stuck his head out into the hall. "I thought I heard your voice, Jim. You and Ruth get yourselves in here, I've got a problem."

Kirk nodded assent and followed the veterinarian into Sick Bay. He hoped whatever McCoy wanted to discuss wouldn't take too much time; the tension in his occipital region had become a definite pain, and there was a throbbing sensation at the back of his head warning him he'd probably have a splitting headache if he didn't get to sleep soon. "All right, what is it, Bones?"

McCoy signaled the two officers to take a seat wherever they were comfortable. Kirk chose the recliner behind McCoy's desk, while Rigel perched on one corner of the desk.

"Look, Jim, these ambassadors . . . they're too much for me. I mean, they are some of the *weirdest* beings I've ever encountered in my life. It's like being in the middle of a bloody zoo! Now I'm just a plain old country doctor. I can handle the problems of the *Enterprise*; I can even handle Spock—and heaven knows he's put together strangely—but *these* creatures! I'm going to have to have help. That's where the problem comes in. The only one really capable of assisting me in analyzing their medical reports is Dr. Rigel, but she's a veterinarian!"

"I don't see the problem," Kirk said. "If you need Ruth's assistance, use her. Now if you don't mind, I want to get to bed." He started to rise from the seat, but McCoy indicated that he hadn't finished explaining the difficulty. Kirk settled back and waited.

"You don't understand, Jim. It's the fact that she's a *veterinarian.* Can you imagine me telling Ambassador Neko that I'm going to have a *cat doctor* look after him? And what would he do to *her*? Have you seen the claws on that creature? Now what I need from you is a general order to the entire crew that no one, but no one, is to mention to any of the ambassadors that Ruth is a vet. What we'll do is put her in an office here in Sick Bay, give her a fancy title like Extraterrestrialist, and we'll tell everybody she's a doctor. That way if we have any problems, we won't have a diplomatic crisis on our hands."

"There is one possible trouble spot with our zoo," Ruth said, "and I don't mean Neko. Did you know that Ambassador Naja is a hundred and fifty-seven of our years old? That's pretty advanced, even for his people. If that snake up and dies on us, we're in a sticky spot because, while I'm a vet, I'm no herpetologist."

"But we still need you, Ruth," McCoy said. "Naja wouldn't be on this trip if he wasn't fit. I won't let you use one feathered snake as an excuse to wriggle out of a promotion to physician. Besides, think of the joys of working with Rovar. I sure can't handle him!"

Kirk nodded. McCoy and Ruth had made a valid point; two or three of the ambassadors, Neko and Rovar in particular, would not be pleased to be told they were being treated by a vet rather than a physician. "Handle it any way you want, Bones. You write up the order and I'll see that it's implemented. Now is that all you needed?"

"That's it. You can take your weary body off to bed. And as your doctor, Jim, I'd prescribe that. You're tired and I don't think any more work tonight is recommended. You've done more than your share to get the ambassadors settled in and enough is enough, even for a starship captain."

"Don't worry, Bones. Bed it is. But I do feel that this fatigue of mine is a bit more than it should be. I wonder if I'm really over Delta Gamma Four. There are times when I feel almost too tired to get out of bed in the morning. You think I'm okay?"

McCoy nodded. "Jim, I've checked you out every way possible. You are 99.9 percent recovered from Delta Gamma Four. Sure, there's a little fatigue expected—you went through a lot there. But if I felt you weren't up to your usual ability, I'd have said so before I ever allowed you back on duty. So get to bed, and I'll see you in the morning."

Kirk found his doctor's advice relatively easy to follow. As soon as he got to his cabin he stripped down, leaving the clothes where they fell, and dropped into the bed. He was asleep almost as soon as his head hit the pillow, but his mind was not at rest.

The dream began swiftly. It was extraordinarily vivid. Kirk found himself moving along the corridor toward Sirenia's quarters. There was a feeling of hunger in him, a desire for something. But her cabin was empty.

He drifted slowly down the corridors of the guest accommodation area, and as he turned a corner he noticed, at the end of the hall, Sirenia entering the room reserved for Agnatha, the lamprey-being from Jezero.

He stopped and watched the woman slip into the ambassador's quarters. He realized with pain that Agnatha was probably closer, both physically and emotionally, to the beautiful humanoid than he was. He found himself struggling with feelings of jealousy, lust, and an overwhelming sense of loneliness. He leaned against the wall and wanted to weep. She didn't want him, but she wanted that slimy thing. She wanted that slimy thing. She wanted Agnatha. She wanted. . . .

He lurched down the corridor, barking his shins against a piece of sculpture, and started to swear through his tears. . . .

Kirk came awake suddenly with a groan. He felt strange, disoriented, and then realized that he was in his own bed. The dream had been very vivid, and more than a little painful. He felt around on his bedside table until he found the packet of sleeping pills Dr. McCoy had given him when he had first suffered from nightmares after Delta Gamma Four. He took two of the pills and curled up under his bedcovers in a semifetal position. He fell asleep, his mind still trying to deal with the feelings of loneliness his dreams had given him.

6

Captain's Log, Stardate 6970.7:

By common consent, the main Officer's Lounge on Deck 4 has been selected as a meeting room for discussions of the Romulan detente. These discussions were suggested by Ambassador Sarek, much to my own surprise. I have found him rather reticent about engaging in free-form discussion in the past, but he obviously has his own reasons for allowing it on this trip. Unfortunately, he has not considered it necessary to inform me of these reasons. Sarek has also made these meetings open to any members of my crew who wish to attend, and he has also requested that they speak out and give their opinions on the detente. I find the suggestion brazen. There are many members of my crew who have violent opinions on one side or another of the question, and I am concerned that these detente discussions will turn into verbal free-for-alls, or, far worse, a brawl. Sarek has assured me, however, that he will maintain order. I hope he can manage it. . . .

The meeting room on Deck 4 was convenient to the guest quarters of most of the ambassadors, and it had been enlarged by taking down the barrier between Officer's Lounge A and B, creating a strange half-moon shape, since the room was located at the central core of the deck. The room had been stripped of tables and recreational equipment and was empty save for a scattering of benches and one long table, which Sarek had appropriated as a podium. There was a constant flux in the number of persons in the room, and not all thirteen of the ambassadors were present at all times.

Captain Kirk, after only two visits to the meeting room, was able to establish the political opinions of the assorted ambassadors. Sarek, Si-s-s-s(click), Telson, Karhu, and Sirenia were all in favor of the détente, while Agnatha, Rovar, Naja, and Neko were equally opposed. Ambassadors Damu, Edentata, Spiracles, and Hotep were, as nearly as Kirk could tell, neutral on the subject.

The meeting took the form of one polarity or another discussing the subject while anyone else in the room listened. The crew found the debates fascinating, particularly when they realized that they, too, could contribute to them. The one ambassador who seemed to attend all the meetings was Karhu. It was not that the large ursine creature was that fond of politics—it was more that his lulling presence served to curtail most attempts at violence.

Captain Kirk had come off duty and after dinner had decided to see what was going on in the meeting room. He found a noisy discussion in progress. Sarek, Si-s-s-s(click), and Karhu were present, and speaking in favor of the détente. Neko and Rovar were seated in the audience, as was Damu. Kirk looked around the room and spotted his First Officer and several members of the engineering department. Dr. McCoy and Dr. M'Benga were also there, and there was an empty seat beside McCoy. Kirk realized that the Doctor had saved it for him, and acknowledged his gratitude as he settled in to listen to the debate.

Sarek had the floor, and seemed to be discussing some involved economic point. Economics were not Kirk's strongest field, and most of what the ambassador said might as well have been in Vulcan for all Kirk could make of it. He glanced around the room and saw that many of his crewmembers were equally in the dark. But Sarek was drawing to a conclusion of some sort and after two or three more statements concerning trade ratios, gave up his place to Si-s-s-s(click).

The large, bulky reptile had a flamboyant speaking style in keeping with his equally flamboyant appearance. "O gentlebeings of the Federation, we must understand the necessity of placing our hand gently in that of the Romulans and giving them the friendly clasp of welcome. We must not let them wander aimlessly in s-s-space, unaware of our willingness to meet with them. Gentleness, s-s-simplicity, and kindness must be our manner in dealing with our Romulan brothers, for we are all brothers. The Federation is made up of many races, but yet we have managed to band together in a network of cooperation. We can add the Romulans to that network without difficulty or strain if we are willing to do so. I ask of you, fellow members of the Federation, favor this détente; welcome the Romulans into the light of our democracy, that they may be one with us-s-s." There was a scattering of applause as Si-s-s-s(click) took off his feathered cap and bowed to the audience. He then took his seat with a flourish of his cape, and Sarek stood again.

"I now throw this discussion open to comment. Is there anyone in the audience who would care to comment on the question of détente?" Sarek scanned the room and then acknowledged Spock.

"We Vulcans," Spock said, "have a particular interest in seeing the Romulans joined in a treaty with the Federation. There are a number of Federation planets which are concerned over this fact; they fear that we may be attempting a coup d'etat, but this is not so. What we are actually hoping for is that we, through the teachings of Surak, will help persuade the Romulans to a view of logic similar to our own, so that they too will in a few hundred years manage to throw off their violent, overemotional characteristics."

As soon as Spock could finish speaking, one of the ensigns from engineering got to his feet. "That's all very well, sir, but do you remember what it was like fighting the Romulans? You were up on the Bridge, you at least had a chance to see what was going on—

but down in engineering we didn't know why we could have been killed in the next minute. The only thing we could be sure of was that the barrage of fire that would have killed us was Romulan. I don't know how you can forget that, sir. I don't think I ever will."

Dr. M'Benga signaled that he wished to comment, and when acknowledged, he too stood. "Tell me, ensign, did it feel any different when it was Klingon fire we were under? Could you tell whether you were about to die in a Klingon battle or a Romulan one? Death is death, and it's something we must end. We need peace in the Galaxy; we need the opportunity to explore, to fulfill our destiny—and as long as there's war, killing, and the threat of it, we must constantly be on guard. The *Enterprise* is a battleship rather than a flagship of scientific exploration. The Klingons are a danger to us, the Romulans are a danger to us, and together they can destroy the Federation. We must not let them join forces against us. I feel that war of any sort is wrong, and I'm in the same position you are: when I'm in Sick Bay or my quarters and there's a red alert, I won't know who's shelling us or why. I just know that I'll be needed shortly to patch up some crewman. The fact of knowing or not knowing what's happening has nothing to do with the problem at hand—what matters is knowing that it will never happen again." There was a scattering of applause for M'Benga's comments, and the large dark-skinned doctor ducked his head somewhat in embarrassment.

"I don't usually make speeches, Captain," he said across McCoy to Kirk. "I guess I just got a little carried away. But it's something that's so important to all of us."

Kirk nodded, and then got to his feet to speak. "I have to admit I'm in a position that can best be described as neutral," he said. "I'm not at all in favor of war, I don't enjoy it. But gentlebeings, it's what I've been trained for. If there is no war, I'd prefer that—but if there is battle, be it with Romulans, Klingons, or anyone else who menaces the Federation, I'm going to do battle. If we can remove one enemy, if we can make that enemy our friend, we've benefited—and that's something to consider. At the same time we must never let the Romulans think we're bargaining from a position of fear or weakness. The Federation isn't crawling on its belly, screaming for peace. We are the equals of the Romulans, if not even their superiors. We must never let them think they have the upper hand. That's my only concern about this détente—will they take advantage of it, and of us?"

"That's something I worry about, Captain," Neko's silky voice answered. "I don't trust the Romulans. While we're all out gathering flowers and leaves for peace garlands, they will be arming themselves to destroy the Federation. I can never allow that—nor can I allow the increase of any more . . . pointed-eared beings in the Federation. There are too many of them as it is." Neko's remarks were intentionally provocative; unfortunately, he was provoking in the wrong direction. Sarek merely shrugged and did not consider the comment even worth answering.

It was Karhu who lumbered to his feet to address his fellow ambassador. He rumbled something in his own tongue that was not intelligible to Kirk but was quite obviously a well-executed curse, for Neko quailed visibly.

"I tell you, we need this détente," Karhu said softly, switching to Federationese. "It's necessary to all of us." He blinked his eyes for a moment, almost as though he had lost his train of thought. "You see, we can't continue having something like the Romulan Neutral Zone as one of our borders. It isn't wise; there are too many messy things that happen within the Neutral Zone. I'm sure Captain Kirk knows what I'm talking about; he's had his share of problems patrolling that sector of space, and he knows as well as any of our other gallant ship captains that to stray into that Neutral Zone is to invite retaliation and possible intragalactic warfare. We don't need that; we don't need a so-called Neutral Zone."

"Would you prefer no barrier at all, my furry friend?" Neko said. "Would you like the Romulans to go rampaging through Federation space any time they chose to? I wouldn't—but then my mind is so much more agile. And so is my body." Neko flexed one arm, claws extended in demonstration. "I can see the danger involved even if you can't, my furry friend."

Karhu turned to Sarek and in a rather loud stage whisper commented, "If he calls me 'furry friend' one more time, I will take his tail off at the root. I think that would be amusing, don't you, Sarek?"

The Vulcan ambassador chose to ignore the remark, just as he had ignored Neko's earlier attack on the Vulcans. He asked whether there were any further comments, and since there appeared to be none, dismissed the meeting for the evening. The discussion broke up into small clumps, and Kirk found himself bored by the whole situation. He wondered whether anything was really being accomplished by these meetings. The neutral-minded members of his own crew seemed to be in a minority, and there had been only the one neutral ambassador present; it was hard to say what Damu's opinion had been, as he'd said nothing. Kirk left the room wondering if this was only a foretaste of what the détente discussion would be. But there would be Romulans at that meeting.

There was a gradual change in the meetings. Nerves went taut, and the arguments grew louder. Captain Kirk was forced to put Dr. Carter on report for conduct unbecoming an officer when the doctor attempted to assault Ambassador Neko. Carter would have come out much the worse for wear if Karhu and M'Benga hadn't stopped the fight in time.

The closer they approached the Neutral Zone, the more charged the air became. The situation polarized into three camps: those who were for were more violently for; those who were against were more loudly against; and those who were neutral seemed intent on building citadels around their neutrality. Captain Kirk was counting the days until they reached the station designated for the détente meeting. He knew, once he got rid of his ambassadors, he would finally breathe easier.

But other than a great deal of shouting, arm waving, and carrying on, he wasn't expecting any particular problem—that was, until Ambassador Agnatha was found dead in his quarters, his water tank a shattered mass, revealing for the first time the full length of his dead, slimy body.

7

It was Sirenia who discovered Agnatha's body. She had an appointment with the ambassador for breakfast, and when she'd gotten no response to her signal at his door, she became concerned and asked Captain Kirk's assistance in forcing the door.

Kirk and Scotty made short work of unlocking the door. Barely had the metal panel begun to move when a stream of water flooded out into the corridor. Sirenia gasped and forced her way through the widening doorway. Kirk and Scotty followed as soon as the opening was wide enough.

The sight in the room was apalling. The large tank which had held Agnatha was on its side, its plastiseal panels smashed, the floor awash with the murky fluid the ambassador had lived in. At first Kirk didn't recognize the body as being that of Agnatha; he had only seen the ambassador's head and circular tentacled mouth. It was difficult to relate that to the flat, eel-like body with its furled fins that was lying in the midst of the debris.

Sirenia bent over her fellow ambassador, attempting, so it seemed, to apply some sort of artificial respiration; but it was obviously too late. She looked up, her face tracked with tears.

"He's been dead for several hours, gentlemen. And I would recommend that you have your ship's physician perform an autopsy. I am not sure this was an accident."

"But . . . but ma'am," Scotty said, "it would have been very easy for the ambassador's tank to have fallen. It wasn't the most stable of environments, and I wasna happy with the way it was arranged. It may well have been an accident."

"It was no accident," Sirenia answered. "Look at the bolts on the floor." She pointed at the large metal bolts that had held the tank firmly to the deck. They had been wrenched and twisted out of their place. "This tank was pulled back and forth violently by someone or something. I suspect Agnatha was murdered. And if he was," her voice grew very cold and hard, "I want to know who did it. That being and I will have a great deal to settle between us."

"I know you and Agnatha were very close," Kirk said, going to Sirenia's side and slipping an arm gently, comfortingly around her shoulders, "although you did disagree on the détente situation. But you're reacting emotionally. There may possibly have been something wrong with Agnatha himself. This tank wasn't the most efficient environment for a being like him. I hadn't realized how big he was—the murkiness of the fluid, you have to understand—but he may have done this himself. It may have been something he ate. He may have been ill. He could have thrashed back and forth in the tank and tipped it over himself. I'll talk to Dr. McCoy and I will very definitely ask for an autopsy. But try to keep an open mind. Don't yell murder until we can be sure it really was. I don't want the rest of the ambassadors, or my crew, upset—and until we know precisely what happened to Agnatha, anything you have to say could damage the cause you're involved in. Consider your responsibilities as an ambassador—and think. I beg you, don't say anything yet."

Sirenia nodded acceptance. Gently removing herself from Kirk's encircling arm, she knelt again beside her friend's body and began a keening wail that was obviously a song of mourning. Kirk did not know whether the song came from her culture or Agnatha's; he was only aware of how terribly sad and lonely it sounded.

8

Captain's Log, Stardate 6976.5:

Dr. Rigel, in her position as temporary physician, has performed the autopsy on the body of Ambassador Agnatha. She was assisted by Drs. McCoy and M'Benga. I find the results of the autopsy disturbing. There was no indication whatsoever of foul play; to all intents and purposes the ambassador died of completely natural causes. The only oddity was a high percentage of ongrene present in his blood, a chemical which is a close equivalent of the Terran compound adrenaline. Whatever Agnatha died of, he was extremely agitated at the time of his death. This fact disturbs me, and unfortunately it has caused Ambassador Sirenia to again demand some sort of investigation into the death of her friend. I have called for an official meeting of the ambassadors, the medical staff, and the Chief Engineer. I hope something useful can come of this meeting. We are less than four days away from Detente Station One; I only hope there will be no other occurrences on board my ship to mar the detente meeting. But I have my doubts that we will reach the rendezvous point without some further trouble.

The meeting was held in the Officers Lounge with all the ambassadors present. McCoy and Rigel had given a concise rundown of the medical findings; their opinion that Agatha's death had been from natural causes was only partially accepted by most of the ambassadors. Kirk could tell from the tension in the room that his engineer had better come up with some kind of explanation, no matter how farfetched, for the destruction of Agnatha's tank.

Kirk, as moderator for the inquest, called his chief engineer to the witness seat and watched as the computer identified him and adjured him to speak the truth.

Scotty hunched forward in the seat, his hands placed firmly over the truth discs. His face was tense, and it was obvious he was attempting to be as accurate as possible in an area that seemed to allow for very little in the way of absolute truth. "Well, gentlebeings, I began my investigation of the damage to the ambassador's habitat by studying the plates in the floor. To the best of my knowledge, they were pulled loose by stress incurred from a violent side-to-side motion. This indicates to me that the tank was rocked back and forth with a great deal of savagery."

There was a buzz of speculation from the ambassadors, and Scotty held up his hand for silence. "Na, na, that's not to say that anyone or anything was rockin' that tank. In fact, from a careful examination of the plastiseal walls of the tank, the only rocking was bein' done inside by the ambassador himself."

This again produced a loud burst of comment and questions from the ambassadors. Captain Kirk was forced to ring the ship's bell in front of him several times to silence the group.

When the bell's echoes faded from the room, Scotty again spoke. "You must understand how a piece of plastiseal breaks. If it's pushed from the outside, the shards show it; they will implode inward. There'll be marks that you can look at under the microscope, and you can see the pressure points. Well now, I gave it every test I knew, and the results are always the same. The pressure on that plastiseal was from the inside. In my opinion Ambassador Agnatha destroyed the tank himself. He was a big laddie; and if upset enough, he was quite capable of smashin' that environment tank to smithereens. Which is precisely what he done. There canna be no other explanation. His room was locked, we had to break into it, there was no other way in or out. Whatever happened to his tank, the ambassador did it himself. And if anyone in this room can prove otherwise, I will be glad to hear of it." Scotty leaned back in the chair and waited.

No one in the room seemed prepared to contradict his testimony. But one fact was quite apparent: in all the testimony there had been no discussion whatever of why Agnatha had felt such hysteria that he would have lashed out to destroy his own habitation and, in effect, his own life.

The ambassadors left the room silently, leaving Kirk, McCoy, Rigel, M'Benga, and Scotty alone. Kirk bowed his head over his interlaced fingers and sighed. The inquest had not been a total success. It had proved nothing, but at least it had fulfilled Sirenia's request for an investigation.

"Ruth," the captain said, "is there any chance you could have missed something? I'm not questioning your competence," he added hastily, "but I know your field is primarily nonsentient animals. Could there have been anything in the brain, some kind of damage, some indication of hallucinogens, anything . . . ?"

The veterinarian shook her head slowly, and then looked to McCoy for confirmation. "Remember, Jim," McCoy said, "I assisted. And while I have to admit that what I know about beings like Agnatha wouldn't coat the bottom of a test tube, I do know a great deal about the brain. There was no indication of damage whatsoever. As near as I can tell he was as well as you or I, and as sane. The only problem is, he's dead. I have no way of knowing precisely what his mental state was at the time of death, but it's my best guess that he was absolutely terrified."

"If I had all of his responsibilities on my shoulders, I'd be terrified too," M'Benga said. "The ambassador was preparing to go into battle in a very, very touchy situation, and he was working from a position of opposing détente—it couldn't have been easy for him. Perhaps in the loneliness of the night, considering what he might be doing to damage peace in the Federation, it all got to be too much for him."

Captain Kirk considered the doctor's viewpoint for a moment. "Mem, are you insinuating that Agnatha committed suicide? I find that a little hard to believe, and I'm sure it's an opinion Sirenia wouldn't accept."

"I'm a little inclined to agree with M'Benga," said McCoy. "I can't think of a better explanation, and he was to all intents and purposes the leader of the opposition party. That is a lot of responsibility. Right now I'm afraid we're going to have to leave the whole case filed under 'cause of death: unknown.' Perhaps when his body is returned to his world they'll be able to establish a little more about the cause of death than we could. After all, they'd be a lot more familiar with his anatomy and psychological makeup."

"I'm sorry we couldn't give you more," Dr. Rigel said softly. "I know you wanted a simple answer, Captain, but sometimes in medicine there aren't any. It had nothing to do with my being a vet, or Dr. McCoy or Dr. M'Benga being unfamiliar with Agnatha's mental makeup—it's just one of those things we have to live with. There are too many unknowns in our field, more than a lot of us like to accept. We're not omnipotent—we simply try to do the job that was given to us, and we did it to the best of our ability. There are times, sir, when it's impossible to establish that black is black and white is white. There are simply too many shades of gray."

Captain Kirk rose wearily from his seat. He patted Ruth on the shoulder and smiled; he knew that under very difficult circumstances the woman had done her best. It was a considerable strain on the ship's vet, masquerading as a doctor; but she had risen to the occasion with all the skill and tact at her command. He couldn't find fault with her, and he admitted to himself that she was right—he *did* like nice simple answers, black or white. Shades of gray were something he preferred not to acknowledge.

"You all did your best, and I'm proud of you. Now let's get this ship to the rendezvous point and try to keep the ambassadors content. I know that isn't going to be easy, but I'm counting on all of you to help. Thank you very much." With that he turned and left the room, but Dr. Rigel could see by the way his shoulders were sagging that he was not happy with the whole situation.

9

The ship seemed very quiet after Agnatha's death. The arguments in the Officers' Lounge were subdued, and only Ambassador Neko seemed compelled to take up Agnatha's mantle as spokesperson for the anti-Romulan party. He could be heard at almost any hour loudly declaring that any form of détente with the Romulans was unthinkable. He argued viciously with Sarek and Spock, to the point that the First Officer refused to involve himself in any further discussions; he absented himself from the Officers' Lounge and could be found either in his quarters or on the Bridge. Kirk couldn't find it in his heart to blame Mr. Spock; Neko's disposition was difficult, and the large cat seemed to go out of his way to antagonize everyone in sight. It was almost as though he were attempting some sort of vengeance on the entire ship for the death of his party's leader. The only two people on board the *Enterprise* who seemed at all interested in discussing the situation with Neko were Sirenia and Dr. M'Benga.

M'Benga had seemed quite fascinated by Neko's views, and had questioned him at great length on his reasons for disliking the Romulan détente. Unfortunately, as Sarek and Spock had found, Neko's arguments contained very little logic, only aggressive rhetoric. Neko seemed opposed to the détente simply for the sake of opposition. Captain Kirk was convinced that given half a chance, Neko would take either side of an argument, as long as he could continue to argue at great length at any time, on any subject. Captain Kirk found himself growing very short tempered, and were it not for the necessities of protocol, he too would have absented himself from the Officers' Lounge.

The *Enterprise* was within two days' journey of Détente Station One, which had been built at the edge of the Neutral Zone. It was the first watch of the day, and when Captain Kirk strayed into the Officers' Lounge he was surprised that Ambassador Neko was not in attendance. He found Rovar and Naja waiting for their confederate. The feathered serpent had rolled himself into a large ball on the floor of the lounge, with only his flat head showing above his coils. His breathing was agitated, stirring the luxuriant wings which framed his fanged jaw.

Rovar paced back and forth in the room, his long striped tail lashing back and forth in a very good impersonation of Neko. "Where *is* he?" Rovar snapped in the strange metallic high-pitched voice of his people. "He promised to meet us here twenty minutes ago. It's not like Neko to be late. I find it very disquieting. In fact, I suspect a plot. Captain, the security on board this ship has been extraordinarily lax. I would have suspected that after the death of the unfortunate Agnatha, you would have placed guards around the ambassadors' quarters. I fear there has been some foul play. Neko is known to be in opposition to the détente, and since Agnatha's death I suspect that someone on this ship would not like to see us succeed. There are entirely too many pointy-eared beings present." Rovar was consciously using Neko's phrase in reference to Sarek and Spock.

Kirk found the Hemipteran's attitude annoying. "There was, as you well know, no accusation of foul play in the death of Ambassador Agnatha. I resent your implication that something has happened to Neko simply because he may have overslept or indulged in a large breakfast. If you're so concerned for his welfare, why don't you go down to his quarters and ask *him* why he isn't here instead of pacing around in that totally useless manner?"

"We tried that," Naja answered. "He didn't open the door. We also contacted him over the intercom; there was no answer, Captain. If he slept, it was a very deep sleep indeed. I would advise that we find out a little more about that sleep."

Kirk nodded assent and quickly requested a security team to report to the door of Neko's quarters.

It was with a strong sense of déjà vu that Captain Kirk watched Scotty and his fellow crewmen cut through the door of the ambassador's quarters. But the scene inside was entirely different than that which had met their eyes when they opened Agnatha's door.

Neko's room was in perfect order; there was no sign of any struggle or anything untoward. Everything was in place. The large ambassador lay curled up in his bed in a strangely ludicrous position. His body was arched in a catlike pose; his legs and arms tucked up against his body, his long tail wrapped around his nose. His eyes were closed, and his body seemed absolutely relaxed and calm.

It was also stone cold. Neko had been dead for quite some time.

Pandemonium reigned in the corridors of the ambassadors' section for the next hour. Dr. Rigel and Dr. McCoy had the body removed. The various ambassadors had taken turns viewing the scene in question, and their agitation was obvious to the Captain. It was entirely possible that Agnatha's death had been accidental, but a second ambassador's death on a mission so serious stretched coincidence too far. Even Kirk himself was worried about the outcome of the autopsy. He was not in the slightest reassured when Ambassador Naja requested a private audience in his quarters.

Captain Kirk entered Naja's room fully prepared for some sort of diatribe on the lack of security provided. He found the ambassador again coiled up in his snakelike pose, his head resting calmly on his coils.

"I wanted to speak to you alone, Captain," the ambassador said, "because what I have to say I do not want to repeat at large. It will either cause panic or concern for the loss of my sanity. You see, Captain, last night in my quarters I was visited by the Angel of Death, and he is, by his own word, the being responsible for Agnatha's and Neko's departure. I would suggest that you get help of some sort, and I recommend a Special Security Division officer. The Angel might fear an SSD investigator—I know that I fear them, and my conscience is clear. The SSD is the only group I know which fears nothing at all. . . ."

10

A special security division had been established very early in the development of Star Fleet. The black-clad group of elite security investigators was sometimes jokingly referred to as the Federation's equivalent of the Texas Rangers. But there was also an undertone of fear and dislike in Star Fleet's relationship with the SSD. There had been accusations of Gestapo-like techniques, and a general feeling that the end justified the means; also, the strange esprit de corps that existed among the members of the Special Security Division was frightening to many of the Federation's other ranking officers. The Special Security Division felt no loyalty to anything but the Federation and the SSD. They gave no quarter in their investigations, and should a high-ranking Federation official be implicated in a crime or misdeed, there was no bargaining with the Special Security Division. *Justice* was their motto, and let the chips fall where they might. They respected no one, and their loyalty to their code of ethics was unbreakable. They were a necessary force but a feared one.

Colonel Elizabeth Schaeffer had been an official member of the SSD for twenty of her thirty-five years. She had been born in an SSD creche, chosen as a cadet at the age of fifteen, and had devoted her entire life to the Special Security Division. She knew she wasn't always loved on the assignments she was handed; she even accepted the fact that it was necessary to *force* people to like her. Love was a concept that very little concerned Schaeffer. That was one of the major complaints in her relationship with her husband, Col. Alexis Schaeffer, also of the SSD.

Elizabeth had tried to explain her point of view in their last meeting nearly three months before. "Love," she'd said, "is not something that jumps out of a cuckoo clock every hour on the hour. It changes, it varies in degree. Sometimes, Alex, I love you more than I can ever put into words. And there are times I simply love you because you exist, like the Sun, the air I breathe, the food I eat—and then, too, there are times when I'm not sure I love you at all. But it all evens out, so I can't understand why you insist on some uniform degree of involvement on my part. It's unreasonable."

"But I need the reassurance that you love me all the time. I need it to be there. I need your love as part of my existence, Elizabeth. I can't have this on-again, off-again attitude of yours. Make up your mind."

Elizabeth knew that it was simply one more futile argument in a series of arguments that had become all too frequent. Part of the problem was their marriage itself. With both of them being active officers in the SSD, their ten-year marriage had been frequently interrupted; and once, in a moment of introspection, Elizabeth had calculated how much time they had spent with one another in ten years. It added up to less than nine months of scattered meetings, brief weekends snatched between assignments and passionate encounters on out-of-the-way planets. At first there had been a certain excitement to this pattern of separation and reconciliation; it had made for an intensity akin to repeated honeymoons. But recently the quarrels had outnumbered the interludes of warmth and desire.

In two months it would be time to renew their marriage contract. Both Elizabeth and Alex would receive renewal papers, and if either party decided not to sign those papers, the marriage was null and void. She found herself wondering what she would do. It would be so easy to end the farce, to let Alex go his own way and stop the silly quarrels, the demands for unending love which she could not give. She found herself incapable of lying to him about her feelings. It was, he had insisted, her chief flaw. She would praise his body, his intelligence, his skill in bed; she would flatter him; she would soothe and comfort him; but she would not say "I love you" unless she felt it.

But Alex demanded verbal reassurance over and over and over again. It didn't matter to him what the feeling was behind it, as long as he heard those three magic words that meant so much to him.

Elizabeth was beginning to find the situation, and those three words, exceedingly tedious.

Their marriage had at one time been an almost perfect relationship; they were both in the Department, they understood the necessities of their respective jobs, they even realized at that first ceremony so long ago their need for separation. It had seemed ideal. It had been a marriage of two people in the same profession who were totally aware of the pressures of that occupation. But unfortunately time had eroded that bright and beautiful concept, and Elizabeth had come to Détente Station One at the edge of the Romulan Neutral Zone for one purpose only: to see Alexis again, and find out if something could be settled between them, some compromise in their marriage before the renewal papers arrived.

According to her orders from the Department, she was in charge of security for the various ambassadors, Romulan and Federation, and to make sure in her own way that the détente discussions went as smoothly as possible. She was one of only three SSD officers who would be present, but they were the senior officers in charge of the détente, with a crew of regular Star Fleet security personnel to back them up.

It was a heavy responsibility. She realized with guilt that she was not putting her full energies into coordinating the upcoming meeting; she moved like a sleepwalker through the assorted preparations, checking and double-checking the security watches and safety facilities that had been built into the various ambassadorial quarters. It was a job that any competent redshirt could have handled, but she found a certain serenity in making these familiar rounds. It gave her time to think, and while she mechanically checked alarm systems and pressure-sensitive wallplates, her mind circled round and around the same track: her marriage, Alex, her feelings.

Alexis had suggested that they both sign up for the détente station security force. It had been, in his opinion, an excellent opportunity to get together and give their marriage one more chance. Elizabeth wished he wasn't so eager to continue what was rapidly becoming a farce. The whole idea of a weekend snatched here and there over a period of years did not constitute a marriage—and for him to cling so desperately to something as thin as the molecules of deep space seemed ludicrous.

She was beginning to find his attitude almost pitiful, and the last thing she wanted of her marriage was for it to end on a note of pity. Elizabeth was not sure that agreeing to the meeting had been a good idea. But she was here on the station, and the *Excalibur* would not be arriving for six hours and thirty minutes. On board the *Excalibur,* Alexis would be waiting for his meeting with her.

11

The communications room of Détente Station One received the emergency message from the U.S.S. *Enterprise* with shocked silence. Two ambassadors were dead, and there was a possibility that the deaths were not accidental. Lt. Col. Derek Gleason of the SSD stared over the shoulder of the communications officer at the visual screen as he listened to Captain Kirk explain the details of the deaths. As soon as the transmission had ended, he swiveled in his seat and beckoned to a waiting Star Fleet security officer.

"Find Col. Schaeffer for me, Lieutenant. I think she's in Quadrant Four; she was checking the insulation on the temporary guest quarters. Tell her to meet me at Security Control Central on the double—I think we've got an emergency."

The lieutenant saluted and moved out of the room at a swift trot. He too had been listening to the transmission. Two dead ambassadors was no way to start a détente meeting. There was going to be hell to pay, and Col. Schaeffer had been handed the job of making the payment.

He found the black-clad colonel in Quadrant Four, along with two engineering experts, examining the mechanism of a security door leading to one of the temporary meeting rooms. He waited politely until she'd finished her conversation with the two engineers, then requested a private consultation.

Elizabeth looked up from her study of the door mechanism with some surprise. What could have gone wrong aboard the station that two engineers should not be privileged to hear? But she had spent most of her life in Security and understood the fondness for cloak-and-dagger maneuvers, particularly among some of the lower-grade officers. She moved away from the engineers and joined the young lieutenant in an alcove at the end of the corridor.

"All right, Lieutenant, what's the problem? Food supplies? A Romulan ship showing up too early? I do hope it's something crucial."

"Yes, ma'am, it is." The young lieutenant straightened his shoulders and tried for as formal an attitude as possible. "We have received a transmission from the U.S.S. *Enterprise.* Two ambassadors to the détente meeting are dead. It is presumed that they met their death at the hands of another. It has been requested that a member of the SSD be sent to the *Enterprise* for investigation. Col. Gleason has requested your presence in Conference Room 3A, level four." He paused for breath, waiting to see whether the colonel had noticed the dignity of his recitation. He had only been on board the station for three days but had managed to convince himself that he was in love with the beautiful Col. Schaeffer.

She had noticed and suspected that the lieutenant had ambitions of eventually becoming someone whose love she could return. It was very unlikely, but he wasn't the first young man to mistake love for simple lust. She wanted to laugh but knew the situation was beyond levity. A young boy in love and two dead ambassadors could not under any circumstances be considered amusing. "Was there any report of who the ambassadors were, and what their position was on the Romulan détente?"

"Yes, ma'am. It was Ambassador Agnatha of Jezero and Ambassador Neko from Gyuunyuu. Both were opposed to the détente meeting."

"Well, that puts the Romulans right in the middle of

the briar patch. I suppose the captain of the *Enterprise* suspects sabotage. Of course, in his position so would I—but then I'm not in his position, and I don't intend to make any snap judgments. Come on, Lieutenant, let's have a look in on Col. Gleason and see what's to be done about the problem."

The lieutenant was obviously flattered by his inclusion in the discussion and followed the colonel down the hallways, giving her as much of a verbatim description of the transmission as he could remember. His memory was good.

"Captain Kirk stated that he had at first felt Ambassador Agnatha's death was accidental. They did an autopsy and a coroner's investigation; it appeared that the ambassador may have had some sort of fit and killed himself. But when Ambassador Neko died, it looked a little more suspicious. And then too, from what Captain Kirk said, when Ambassadors Naja of Dalzell and Sirenia of Cetacea began demanding another official investigation, the autopsy on Ambassador Neko revealed nothing in the way of foul play either. But Captain Kirk had decided to give in to the pressure not only of Naja and Sirenia, but of their fellow ambassadors as well. Also, there's some sort of scuttlebutt about an 'Angel of Death' on board the *Enterprise*. I get the feeling, ma'am, that they're running kind of scared out there, seeing ghosts and all." The lieutenant had added that last as his own interpretation. "Anyway, Ambassador Sirenia wants to call out a whole detachment of Star Fleet security, but Naja talked her into making it an SSD investigation, and he figured one SSD investigator was sufficient."

"Sort of a one-riot, one-investigator theory, Lieutenant? Or should it go two-murders, two-SSD investigators? It sounds a little like someone's panicked. Oh well, we have to take on jobs like this, whether it's a result of panic or not."

They had reached the conference room, and Elizabeth found Gleason, two minor Star Fleet officials, and an assortment of security people waiting for her.

"Well, Gleason, the lieutenant's been filling me in on

most of the details. I gather that you think I should go out there."

"Colonel, you're the highest-ranking SSD officer present, and for public relations' sake, it's advisable that we send someone of equal rank to the captain of the *Enterprise*. According to the computer, the only two Security people of sufficient rank assigned to the détente station are yourself and Col. Alexis Schaeffer. He won't arrive for several hours—so I'm afraid, ma'am, the assignment falls to you."

"Have you consulted SSD Central on this, Derek?" She used his first name as a verbal clue that she would like to speak to him alone. Derek was an old friend, and he instantly picked up on her request.

"I was about to contact them for further orders, ma'am. If you wish, we can handle the transmission together. It ought to be encoded, in which case top-secret methods do apply." He looked around the room at the rest of the personnel. "If you'll excuse us, ladies and gentlemen, that will be all." The young lieutenant's face fell. He gave Elizabeth one mournful glance and then left the room with the others.

Gleason waited till the room emptied, then turned to Elizabeth. "What's the matter, Beth? Don't you want the assignment? Or do you think Kirk's just got a tribble in his trousers?"

"I think it's a bit of both. You see, Alexis and I haven't seen each other in three months. He set up this assignment so we'd have a chance to be together. Our marriage contract is up for renewal." She was using a verbal shorthand; she and Derek had worked together before and had been close—very close. She knew that there was no need for long involved explanations.

"Is the meeting more important to you or Alexis? I suspect he wants it more than you do. It is an important job, Beth. SSD Central is very worried. If those two ambassadors did die as a result of Romulan sabotage, consider the consequences. Within the next three days we'll have two hundred and fifty ambassadors lodged on Détente Station One. If the Romulans intend to kill the Federation delegates, it's not going to look good on our record."

"You know, Derek, that's one thing I love about you PR types. The fact of that many lives doesn't interest you in the slightest—it's just how it will reflect on the SSD. Of course ambassadors are, as a class, expendable; I'd be more inclined to get myself in a twitch if it were actual Council members we were discussing. Ambassadors are as useful as legs on a snake; even the Federation Council knows that. Why else would they be sending them here instead of coming themselves? I almost think they do suspect the Romulans are going to kill off their precious delegation. But doing it one by one is silly—all the Romulans would have to do would be wait until everyone was here on the station and blow it to kingdom come. I'll take the assignment, Derek, even though I suspect that Kirk, Naja, and Sirenia are all overreacting. But there's one thing you're going to have to do for me in return. *You* are going to have to tell Alexis why I'm not here, and I don't envy you the job."

"Coward." There was a note of affection in Derek's voice. "You just haven't got the nerve to tell him yourself, and I can't say I blame you. If I were in his position and coming halfway across the Galaxy for an interlude with a woman as beautiful as you are, even if you were my wife, I'd be in quite a temper if I found you'd gone off on some half-baked assignment. But we don't really have the time to wait until Alexis gets here so we can play pick-up-sticks and decide who goes out to the *Enterprise*. Central has put out the word; they want a bigwig on this job and, frankly, right now you have the biggest wig around. I've got a speedcraft waiting down on the hangar deck. Good luck with the *Enterprise*." He smiled and patted her gently on the shoulder. "I'll talk to Alexis. Although I assure you, my dear, my charming presence will be no substitute for yours.

"Oh, and speaking of charming presences—watch out for Captain Kirk; he's quite a ladies' man. I'm sure Alexis is as much aware of Kirk's reputation as I am."

Elizabeth laughed. "He's going to have to be pretty special to take my mind off a murder investigation—if that's what it is. And then of course, if I'm not worrying about the investigation I've got Alexis to worry about, I've got a détente meeting to worry about, and I've got the fact that until Alexis arrives, you're in command, to worry about. All of the above is guaranteed to keep me from any romantic interest in this Captain Kirk. So you can reassure Alexis that I'm only doing my duty for the greater glory of the Special Security Division. God rest our souls."

12

Captain's Log, Stardate 6980.6:

Due to the demands of the ambassadors aboard my ship, I have requested the services of the Special Security Division, and I have been informed by Detente Station One that they are sending Col. Elizabeth Schaeffer to investigate the situation. The question of calling in the SSD displeases me very much; it reflects badly both on my ship and on the capabilities of my own security officer, Lt. Cdr. Greg Collier. The ambassadors, however, feel they need a top investigator, and the SSD does qualify as the cream of the crop. I hope Col. Schaeffer can complete her investigation swiftly, and that her results will match those of my own officers. I am still of the opinion that the deaths of Ambassadors Agnatha and Neko were accidental, and I have the fact that all medical examinations indicate no sign whatsoever of foul play to back me up. The only thing that persuaded me to call in outside assistance was the strange report of Ambassador Naja that he had seen the Angel of Death. Even I am unable to come up with a rational explanation for what he observed in his cabin.

Naja's announcement of having seen the Angel of Death had very definitely caused a problem on board the *Enterprise*. The story was all over the ship within hours. The ambassador claimed to have been awakened from a sound sleep by a brilliant light in his cabin; and there, floating above his head, was an enormous winged serpent. It was the image of the being the people on Dalzell, Naja's home planet, knew to be the forerunner of death. The being had called Naja by his egg-name, and had spoken to him softly. The death angel stated that he had not yet come for the ambassador; the time was not right. But because of the great love he bore for the son of his people, he was there to issue warning: Naja must not vote against the Romulan détente. The détente was a good and valuable thing, necessary to peace in the Universe. The death angel had admitted that such a peace would in the long run give him much less business, but he felt almost a sense of relief at that, for even the Angel of Death must rest—and Naja, by favoring the détente, would give the angel some slight relief on his rounds. But should the ambassador persist in opposing the détente and be stubborn and stiff-necked, the Angel of Death would have no choice but to visit him again, and this time would take Naja with him into the great western lands, as he had taken Agnatha and Neko. With a final burst of colorful pyrotechnics, the angel had vanished, leaving the room in utter darkness.

Naja had assumed he'd merely dreamed the encounter, but it was a dream of such vividness that it left him with a sense of strong uneasiness—and then, when he was informed of Neko's death, he realized it had not been a dream. The Angel of Death *had* visited him, and it was also very likely that whatever death angel Neko believed in had come to the large cat—but had not issued warning. The very fact that Neko had been found curled kittenlike, in a position of gentle resignation, indicated there had been no struggle, that Neko had gone calmly to his death. Such was the custom of the people of Gyuunyuu. Death was not feared; it came merely as the gentle messenger of a new life. Only the Angel of Death could have entered Neko's cabin and received no argument from the ambassador.

Kirk was inclined to consider this blather about the Angel of Death in much the same way he would view a statement by Dr. McCoy that he had seen Santa Claus in the Sick Bay—yet he was well aware, from his anthropology training, that most cultures did have a tradition of some harbinger of death. He didn't believe that what Naja had seen was really the Angel of Death, but he strongly suspected that someone on board the *Enterprise* was getting very cute. There were a number of possibilities—hallucinogenics, holograms, posthypnotic suggestion, or simply an excess of the baked clams that Naja was so fond of, and had eaten to excess at dinner that night. If the ambassadors felt that only the Special Security Division could cope with Death's Angel, so be it. Let one of those black-clad minions of Justice run around chasing a ghost. He, Captain Kirk, had better things to do with his time—such as getting the *Enterprise* safely to Détente Station One, which was less than a day and a half away.

In the meantime, he felt he'd better rustle together some sort of official delegation to greet Col. Schaeffer. He supposed he could shuffle the responsibility off on Spock or McCoy, but at the same time, since the colonel was his rank equivalent, he felt he should at least put in a formal appearance on the landing dock when her speedcraft arrived. He hoped she wouldn't be too much of a bore; SSD officers were not known for witty repartee, nor were they inclined to have any sense of humor. There was something about the black uniform and the gold-embroidered Scales of Justice prominently displayed on the right side of the tunic top that tended to dampen a nonofficial relationship with someone from the SSD.

Captain Kirk had chosen the welcoming delegation for Col. Schaeffer: his First Officer and his Chief Security Officer. As the three men stood outside the airlock, waiting for the atmosphere in the landing bay to come up to normal tolerances, Kirk watched Lt. Cdr. Greg Collier fidget from foot to foot. The tall, handsome black looked magnificent in his red velour tunic; his muscles caused the fabric to ripple across his back as he shifted weight. He, more than anyone on the ship, would be affected by the presence of an SSD officer. The very fact that the ambassadors had demanded the presence of Special Security showed their lack of confidence in Collier.

The indicator light blinked "safe" and the wide door slid open, exposing the massive landing bay. The tiny needleshaped high-speed ship seemed lost in the wide expanse of the docking platform. It was a small silver sliver, hardly visible on the geometric patterning of the field. Kirk, Spock, and Collier walked slowly toward the vessel. It was obviously designed to hold only one person and was probably, Kirk speculated, one of the latest developments in the SSD arsenal. He had a strong suspicion that, fragile as the craft looked, it was probably capable of doing as much damage to a planet as the entire *Enterprise*. The SSD had a reputation for thoroughness, justice, and the ability to be judge, jury, and executioner in one being.

An exit hatch opened in the top of the craft, and the pilot began to slither smoothly out of the machine. It was obvious that the colonel had barely enough space inside the craft for her body; there was no waste. It had been designed for maximum efficiency.

The three men reached the edge of the landing disc Col. Schaeffer had chosen, just as she slid down the side of the craft and removed her helmet. She turned to face the three officers, and Kirk felt a sudden wave of panic strike him. It was as though her very appearance were a physical blow.

Elizabeth Schaeffer was easily the most beautiful woman James Kirk had ever seen in his life. She stood as tall as he was, her body slender and delicately made. Her complexion was the delicate pink of angelskin coral, and even the heavy piloting helmet had not managed to crush the candycotton swirls of her silver-white hair. There was a shimmer to her, a glow like the inside of a pearl. The tilt of her eyes, the faint point to her ears, and the configuration of her skull and facial bones indicated that she was quite definitely of mixed blood. Kirk was convinced that whatever that mixture was, it ought to be mixed more often.

Her eyes were a deep turquoise, exactly matching the mandarin collar and wide satin stripe that ran down the side of her black tunic—the collar and stripe that indicated her rank as full colonel in the SSD. The long-sleeved black tunic fitted her slender body to perfection, and the ankle-length black trousers revealed a figure as slender as that of a wood nymph. She appeared to be a creature of mythology, a being deserving of gossamer dragonfly wings. She barely appeared to touch the ground with her black boots; she flowed more than walked, and Kirk knew in an instant that everything he had felt about the SSD was rapidly undergoing a change.

"Captain Kirk?" Her voice was as gentle and delicate as the rest of her. "I'm Col. Elizabeth Schaeffer. I believe you have a problem."

Kirk shook himself quickly to clear his mind of thoughts of Titania or Venus rising from the sea. He had to remind himself that this *was* an officer of the Federation, and fully his equal. "I hope, Colonel, you've not simply been sent out on a wild goose chase. Some of our ambassadors have panicked a little. I admit we've had two rather mysterious deaths, but I don't think it was necessary to get your department involved in it." He smiled, realizing that what he said might have sounded a bit insulting. "I'd like you to meet Lt. Cdr. Greg Collier, my Security Chief. I hope the two of you will manage to work together on this problem." Kirk gently prodded Collier forward. It was obvious to the Captain that his Security Chief was just as stunned as he was.

"It's a pleasure to meet you, ma'am," Collier said, extending his hand. "I know there's always been a feeling of rivalry between our two units, but I do hope, as the Captain said, that we can work together."

Col. Schaeffer took Collier's hand between her own and held it gently before releasing it. She smiled, and Collier found himself trembling.

"I quite agree with you, Mr. Collier. There has been a great deal of rivalry between our two branches, but the détente meeting between the Federation and the Romulans far outweighs any petty feelings you or I may have. I promise you," she chuckled and looked rather pointedly at his tunic, "that I will not refer to you as a redshirt if you in return refrain from calling me a blackjak. And by the way, my name is Elizabeth. I would much prefer it if you'd use it. 'Colonel Schaeffer' is rather intimidating, and it doesn't always help with my investigation. Try to think of me as a person, not as a uniform."

There had been a visible lightening of the atmosphere. Kirk wasn't sure whether it was due to a change in his own feelings about Elizabeth Schaeffer or some sort of magic that Schaeffer herself had. It was quite clear that she and Collier were rapidly forming a mutual admiration society, and Captain Kirk decided that he had best reinforce the fact that *he* was captain of the *Enterprise*. "Elizabeth, I'd be very pleased if you would join me for dinner, and then afterwards I can give you a tour of the *Enterprise*."

"Captain," Spock said, immediately bringing it to his captain's attention that he had not been introduced to Col. Schaeffer, "I would tend to suspect that the Colonel would be most interested in seeing what we have done so far concerning the deaths of the two ambassadors, and she will probably be very interested in going over the records of the medical examinations with Drs. McCoy and Rigel. A tour of the *Enterprise* at this time strikes me as being both superfluous and illogical."

"Uh—Spock, I only wanted to familiarize her with the terrain where certain events took place," Kirk added hastily, trying to cover what had been an obvious bit of inefficiency on his part. "By the way, Elizabeth, this is Mr. Spock, my First Officer. If you have any problems with logic, he's the one to see."

Elizabeth assumed a semiformal stance and lifted one hand in the proper Vulcan salute, and then, in exquisite Vulcan without the slightest trace of accent, greeted the First Officer. A look of surprise crossed Spock's face; then recovering swiftly, he raised his own hand in salute and returned the greeting.

"Colonel," he asked as soon as the formalities were completed, "where did you learn to speak Vulcan? *Are* you Vulcan? I'm very interested in your lack of accent; it's amazing. You must have been trained from childhood." Spock was, for Spock, babbling.

"Thank you very much, Mr. Spock," Elizabeth said. "You flatter me on my Vulcan; I do have some Vulcan blood, but I can only manage a few phrases beyond formal greetings. I have been doing a great deal of study of the language, and would appreciate any help you can give me with my grammar. As for my speaking it since childhood, to a certain extent I'd have to say yes—I was raised in an SSD creche, and we're given training in most Federation languages. But you must understand it's only a familiarity. I can greet various Federation delegates in their own tongue, ask for basic necessities, and perhaps make a flattering statement or two about their own home world, but beyond that I'm totally at a loss."

The First Officer had visibly thawed, and Kirk saw to his horror that Spock, too, had joined the Schaeffer Appreciation Society. He was going to have to fight off every male member of his crew the minute they caught sight of Elizabeth Schaeffer. He found himself with an odd sense of wishing he could confess to the murders if it would serve to get her undivided attention. He realized that this was probably the secret of her ability as a security officer. There was nothing terrifying about Elizabeth Schaeffer; she was obviously quite skilled at charming her opponents to death.

13

"Captain," Elizabeth said in a calm, reasoning tone, "would you please contact your Bridge and order the engines turned off?"

Kirk stared at her openmouthed. Her request coming so soon after her arrival on the ship seemed bizarre, to say the least; she'd not even left the landing bay and already she was giving him orders concerning *his* ship. "Col. Schaeffer," he found himself sliding swiftly into the formal mode, "would you mind telling me what reason you have for that rather extraordinary request? I do have eleven ambassadors on board who are in a considerable hurry to get to Détente Station One; I don't think they'd appreciate being told that the ship was coming to a complete halt in space. And come to think of it, I don't like the idea very much myself."

"Well, you see, Captain." Elizabeth moved closer to Kirk and reached out to touch the sleeve of his uniform lightly. "I'm putting your ship in quarantine. You must understand, Captain, I'm only doing my job."

"And what happens if I choose to contact Star Fleet," Kirk said, "and have your request countermanded? We are on a top-priority mission."

"Captain," Mr. Spock said, joining the conversation, "you are failing to take into consideration the fact that the orders or requests of an SSD agent supersede any orders from Star Fleet. I would suggest that if Col.

Schaeffer has suggested shutting down the engines, we should proceed exactly as she has suggested and remain here in space while she continues her investigation."

"And if I decide you're wrong?" Kirk asked Col. Schaeffer. "What if I ignore you and continue on my way to Détente Station One? You see, I'm inclined to believe that the orders of Star Fleet supersede anything you have to say. Particularly, *Colonel,* since you've made this rather arbitrary request before seeing any of the medical records on the deaths of the two ambassadors or doing the slightest bit of investigating."

Elizabeth Schaeffer nodded quietly and rolled back the sleeve of her black tunic, revealing a thin, translucent band around her wrist. "I understand your position, Captain, but you see, before I left Détente Station One I ascertained that there had been no other deaths on any of the other ships carrying ambassadors to the station. This automatically makes the situation suspicious—and we are so close to the station that I can't risk endangering the lives of other Federation ambassadors.

"So I am—if you'll pardon me—placing the *Enterprise* in quarantine by fiat. It's a matter of my orders against yours. I know you don't like that very much—it is, after all, your ship—but I don't have a lot of choice in this. I've been trained to function a certain way and follow a certain set of rules. I'm sure you can understand that; our mindsets are very similar. You, too, have rules and regulations to follow—but in this circumstance mine *do* supersede yours. I'd like to keep this in the nature of a request. If I have to make it an order—well, it's not nearly as pleasant, and it can damage the relationship between us." She looked up at him, and the pressure of her hand on his arm increased ever so slightly. It was a way to let Kirk know she could tighten her hand, hawklike, and smash his wristbones.

"You see," she continued, "this little bracelet I'm wearing—it's a triggering device. My ship, an XK Needle currently sitting there on your landing pad, is a bomb. All I have to do is pull off this bracelet, putting pressure on the right spot, and the *Enterprise* is reduced to atoms. It's something I'd rather not do, and I assure you it's not an action I'd take with undue haste—but I will do it when I have to. When dealing with disease, the next step after quarantine is generally destruction of the potential host. The death of one ambassador might be considered coincidental; the death of two makes me suspicious—and the references in your report to a being known as the Angel of Death make me downright paranoid. It wouldn't take much to convince me that the destruction of the *Enterprise* would be for the greater benefit of the Federation; and I'm sure, Captain, that neither of us wants a confrontation that could lead to any rash actions on my part."

Kirk looked down at the slender plastic band, hardly wider than a hospital identification tag, and then looked up into the woman's face. Col. Schaeffer was completely calm, almost unconcerned; but he could see in her azure eyes a quiet conviction that she would do precisely what she'd threatened. "But it means your death too, Elizabeth." He deliberately used her first name, trying for some degree of intimacy.

"My life is relatively unimportant in the general scheme of the Universe." Her voice was as calm as though she were discussing the state of the weather. "You see, I am trained to die as an SSD agent as much as I am trained to live; and I do assure you that if I considered it necessary to destroy the *Enterprise,* nothing whatsoever—especially any thought for my own safety—would stop me."

"Captain," Spock said, "I would tend to believe that Col. Schaeffer has, at the moment, the upper hand. And from the standpoint of the overall view of the Federation, her premise is a logical one. Until the question of the deaths of the two ambassadors is answered to her satisfaction, perhaps it *is* best to let the *Enterprise* remain where it is."

Kirk glanced at his First Officer. He felt a strong temptation to say, *"Et tu, Brute?"* but decided it would simply be an unnecessary display of a classical education. He bowed in the direction of Elizabeth Schaeffer, and said, "Well, it appears you win this time. The *En-*

terprise will not continue any further toward Détente Station One. But I'll leave it to you, Colonel, to explain to the ambassadors on board this ship *why* they're stuck here. And as for you, Spock"—he turned to his First Officer—"*you* give the order to the Bridge. The idea of shutting down my ship doesn't appeal to me very much. It's too much like pulling the plug on a lifesupport system of someone I love very much."

Spock nodded, walked over to the communications screen on the wall of the landing bay, and relayed the Captain's orders to the Bridge. Within seconds there was a quiver that ran through the ship, something Kirk could identify almost as the death throes of his vessel; and then there was silence. The constant hum of the engines was so much a part of the background noise that he was hardly aware of it until it was gone; and even though he could hear the hiss of the atmospheric systems, it was as though something was missing from his ship.

"Well, Colonel, we are now officially in quarantine," he said. "I'll issue orders that no one is to leave the ship by transporter or shuttlecraft, and we'll sit and wait while you do your investigating. Are there any other little surprises you have up your sleeve?"

"Oh no," she said cheerfully. "I assure you, I don't enjoy doing this, Captain; it's simply a matter of necessity. I'd suggest also that you not try removing my ship from the landing bay. It's a very delicate piece of machinery, and should there be any attempt to use a tractor beam to remove it to deep space, it would explode before it even cleared the landing pad doors. And the effect on the *Enterprise* would be just as messy as my using the bracelet-trigger. You see," she smiled up at him, "I'm here to stay and so's my ship, so we'd best get on with the investigation. I think we should start with your medical department. Would you be so kind as to escort me to your Sick Bay? Or have you seen enough of me and my SSD uniform for a while?"

Kirk smiled at the way she was maneuvering him, and accepted the necessity of it. "Madam, I would be only too honored to escort you to Sick Bay. It will give me great pleasure watching you make life difficult for Dr. McCoy rather than myself. Shall we go?"

The door to the landing bay hissed open as Kirk led the slender black-clad woman out into the corridors of his stilled ship.

Dr. McCoy was waiting in Sick Bay for the SSD colonel. A very nervous Dr. Rigel stood beside him, wringing her hands. "Dr. McCoy, she's going to know within minutes that I'm not a regular doctor," the vet said, a certain amount of panic creeping into her voice. "Then there'll be hell to pay. It's against regulations, and you know how the SSD is about regulations! We could both be broken in rank for this! I hope she's the understanding type—from what I've heard about the SSD, they don't understand much of anything beyond the rulebooks."

"Don't worry, Ruth." Dr. M'Benga had joined them, his hands still damp from the work he'd been doing in the pathology laboratory. "The SSD are sticklers for rules, but they're also fair; and much like the Vulcans, they're inclined to be logical. I'm sure she'll understand the necessity for what we did. So relax. I don't think we have much to worry about." M'Benga had hardly finished speaking when the door of the Sick Bay slid open and there was Captain Kirk with Col. Schaeffer.

McCoy's reaction to the elegant woman was similar to the Captain's. If she had not been his superior in rank, he would have been tempted to give a low whistle of sheer admiration. No matter what rules and regulations this woman might be involved with, at the very least she *was* decorative.

"Col. Schaeffer," Kirk said, "I would like you to meet the chief members of my medical staff who have been involved with the ambassadors. This is Dr. Leonard McCoy, chief medical officer; Dr. Ruth Rigel, specialist in exobiology; and Dr. M'Benga, our specialist in alien races, particularly Vulcans."

Col. Schaeffer acknowledged the introductions, shook hands with each of the team members, and glanced around the room. "I don't see a chief nurse present. You do have one, don't you, Dr. McCoy?"

"Yes, but Nurse Chapel is currently giving a bit of first aid to one of the ambassadors. It seems that Ambassador Si-s-s-s(click) of Gavialian attempted to do a flamenco with a rose between his teeth, and he didn't remove the thorns beforehand. He has some superficial lacerations of the upper palate, and he requested Nurse Chapel's assistance for the first aid. He's in a romantic mode, you see, and is very fond of having the ladies wait on him."

Elizabeth laughed. "Oh dear, a Gavialian! I'm familiar with his people. What is he being this time, a Spanish gypsy? Or something more exotic? You'd think if he'd done any reading in the area, he'd realize that roses do have thorns . . . Oh well, it's safer than some possibilities. I once had to deal with a Gavialian who fancied himself as a Rigellian space-pirate; he almost removed my left ear with his cutlass before I could get it away from him. It sounds like thorn-scratches are a very minor price to pay."

McCoy grinned and said, "I'm glad *someone* is familiar with Gavialians. Si-s-s-s(click) has been a holy terror to the whole ship. Not that he means any harm, he's really quite charming; but he's asked every female crewmember we have if he could kiss her hand, and he hasn't found a single volunteer. It's probably made him a little irritable, and it may explain the flamenco dancing and the rose. But speaking of things medical, I assume, Colonel, that you're here for your standard physical and sigmunding. I'll be set up in a couple of minutes when Miss Chapel is finished with the ambassador."

"I'm sorry, Doctor, but a physical—and particularly a Sigmund—on an SSD officer on duty is specifically prohibited to a Star Fleet medical officer. It's not my idea, you see." She smiled meltingly at the doctor. "I'd like nothing better than to have someone as handsome as you are doing a physical—but there have been too many adaptations made to my body. Some of them are top-secret; you do understand, I hope, that it just isn't possible.

"And a Sigmund would be utterly out of the question. I cannot allow anyone but an SSD physician to have access to my mind. I do assure you, though, that if I should become ill, or if any problem develops, I would of course place myself in your hands. At the moment I'm in perfect health, and you shouldn't have any difficulty coping with emergencies. My racial background is primarily Terran with Arcturian bloodlines, a small percentage of Vulcan blood, and some other minor racial blends. Nothing too difficult for a doctor of your skill to handle, I'm quite sure."

McCoy was somewhat at a loss for what to say. Elizabeth had flattered him shamelessly, and yet it was quite clear that in a battle of wills over a physical or a Sigmund, she was going to win. And as intrigued as he was to learn what curious adjustments and augmentations had been done to her body, he had a strong feeling that it might not be safe to try finding out too much.

"Now that we've got that little problem out of the way," Elizabeth said, "I'd like to see the pathology reports on the two dead ambassadors, and I'd also like to see complete medical reports on the remaining ambassadors. Who did the autopsy?"

"I—I—I did," Dr. Rigel stammered. "Dr. McCoy felt—that is, Dr. M'Benga's field is much more with humanoids, and I have a little more ability—well, Ambassador Neko *was* a cat, and . . ." Ruth's babbling drifted off into silence as she stood looking at her boot tips, waiting for the axe to fall.

"What exactly is your rank, Doctor?" Elizabeth asked calmly. "And would you mind telling me what your real field of specialization is?"

"I'm the ship's veterinarian," Ruth mumbled at her boots. "I specialize in biology, alien biology—alien animals?" She looked up at the SSD officer, her face quietly humble and with a bit of pleading in her eyes.

"Oh! I see. That explains a great deal," Elizabeth said. "It was really rather clever of you, Dr. McCoy, to put your veterinarian to work on this. I've seen the manifest of the ambassadors you've got on board, and if I were in your shoes I'd be terrified to deal with them. They're as alien a bunch of aliens as I've seen in one place in a long time. I congratulate you on your astuteness. Now, Dr. Rigel, since we've got that out of the way, would you please show me your records?"

With a sigh of relief, and a slightly tremulous smile, Dr. Rigel beckoned Col. Schaeffer in the direction of the pathology lab. "I'll be glad to show you what we've got," she said, "but it's not very much. From all indications, Agnatha and Neko died from perfectly natural causes—that is, if you can call simply being dead for no reason whatever 'natural causes.' "

Using the computer, Col. Schaeffer carefully examined the medical report. She had enough background in the sciences to realize that what Dr. Rigel had stated was absolutely true: the autopsies showed no sign of any organic disease in either Agnatha or Neko, nor any toxins or other foreign substances. There was nothing to explain the deaths of the two ambassadors, save the fact that they *were* dead. Schaeffer noted the high ongrene count in Agnatha's case, but dismissed it for the moment as being unimportant. Neko had showed no such elevated hormone levels; he had died calmly, without any trace of a struggle. It was as though he had simply curled up and gone to sleep, never to waken again. Schaeffer put down the records and nodded acceptance of their contents.

"Dr. Rigel, it would take someone with a great deal more skill than I have to find anything wrong with your autopsy reports, and I note that the computer concurs in all your findings. But there's something here that stinks, it stinks to high heaven." She tapped the file slabs with one slender forefinger. "They're not telling us the truth. Oh, I admit all the medical figures are there, but they're not telling us the truth about how these two ambassadors died. I can smell murder, the way other people can smell spring in the air, the scent of the ocean close at hand—and believe me, I *do* smell murder."

Dr. Rigel gathered together the information slabs and filed them. "There is Ambassador Naja's report of seeing the Angel of Death," she said. "That is, if you care to put any faith in that sort of thing. Personally

I've never believed in a death angel, and I've seen a lot of animals die."

"Yes, but how many humans have you seen die?" Elizabeth looked beyond the veterinarian as though seeing something in the far distance. "I've seen more deaths than you will ever know in your lifetime, Doctor; a number of them I've been responsible for. I accept that responsibility, but there have been times . . . I've watched someone die in my arms, and there's been an expression on their face as if they're greeting someone—it's a look of almost transcendental joy. And there've been times when I've felt the brush of wings against my own back. . . . I assure you, Dr. Rigel, I *do* believe in the Angel of Death. I've seen him, and I know when the time comes and he has slowed his journey to greet me, I too will mirror that great joy. I don't know who sends the Angel of Death, or where he'll take me, if anywhere—but I *do* believe in him. If one of the ambassadors on board this ship has seen such a being, I'm inclined to believe it. I want to meet him—now."

Dr. Rigel stared, bewildered, at the SSD colonel. Most of what the woman had said seemed sheer nonsense, but there was something in those large azure eyes, an expression of absolute belief, that made Rigel wonder—and also feel a little frightened.

"You'll find Ambassador Naja in his quarters; he says he hasn't been feeling well. I checked him out this morning, and he's fine for his age. But then," Ruth glanced back at her record banks, "Agnatha and Neko were healthy, too. I wish you luck in your hunt for Death's Angel, Colonel. And you know, I think I'm glad I *don't* believe in him."

Elizabeth nodded and moved toward the door of the office. As the door opened, she said over her shoulder, "You may not believe now, Dr. Rigel; but someday you will. Of course, when that someday comes and the Angel of Death comes for you, you won't be alive any more—so it won't really matter, will it?"

With that, the SSD agent was gone, leaving behind in the pathology lab a shadowy presence that made Dr. Rigel shiver.

14

Elizabeth Schaeffer found Naja of Dalzell's quarters without any difficulty. She was just about to knock when she noticed a creature hurrying down the corridor toward her. From his appearance, she assumed he was one of the ambassadors. She checked her mental file system and realized it was Rovar of Hemiptera. He was an enormous plump creature, his body striped vividly in black and yellow; his arms were waving, signaling her to wait for his approach, and his three eyes were revolving in their sockets like windmills. He came to an abrupt halt in front of her, clasping his six arms together in a convoluted formation which she recognized as a greeting. She repeated the gesture as best she could; lacking six arms, it was rather difficult.

"Finally you're here! What are you going to do about these killings? When are you going to catch the murderer? I won't have it! This is the first time I have ever traveled on a Federation vessel and had problems of this sort. It's too upsetting! You can't understand how important it is to an ambassador to have quiet and peace and tranquillity! Why didn't they send an SSD person along from the very beginning of this? It's so slipshod! I'm going to complain to the Central Council!" Rovar's stream of complaints poured out of him with barely a pause for breath.

Elizabeth tried to soothe the large creature. "Well,

sir, whatever has happened in the past is past, but I am here now, and I intend to make sure there will be no more deaths. I'm sure you are aware of the reputation of the SSD, so you know there'll be little to worry about."

"But you don't understand! With Agnatha and Neko dead, I am now the head of the anti-Romulan delegation. As such I am a target—I am likely to be the next victim! They're going to kill me! I can't understand why they only sent one SSD agent. There should be several, we should have protection! I don't care what Naja is saying; I want protection; and I don't believe in his Angel of Death—and don't you believe anything Naja says about it! It's only a ploy to get attention. *He* wants to be the head of the anti-Romulan delegation. It's *mine* by right of seniority. I won't allow that shifty snake to take over *my* position. I warn you, he's untrustworthy, he's crafty, and he's *lying*! There is no Angel of Death. In fact"—the creature's eyes swiveled as if contemplating a new thought, something which obviously did not occur very often—"Colonel, I would not be in the slightest surprised to find that Naja was the murderer. He's always been envious of Agnatha's position—and as for Neko, well, Neko probably knew too much. So why don't you march in there and arrest Naja, and we can all sleep a great deal more soundly in our beds."

Elizabeth tried hard not to laugh. This puffed-up, self-important creature obviously felt he had solved the entire problem—and it seemed plain that there was some sort of dispute between Rovar and Naja. She would not speculate on what that might be until she had more information. She was now more convinced that a long discussion with Naja would be very helpful. She took a deep breath, smiled at the Hemipteran ambassador and tried to reassure him, but her tongue was planted so firmly in her cheek that there was a danger of the tip showing out one ear. "Sir, I swear that I will do all in my power to bring this dastardly culprit to justice; and if it is indeed Naja I'll make sure you receive the credit for spotting the murderer so swiftly. Now if you'll excuse me. . . ."

She pressed the door button and heard it chime faintly. The door slid open, and before Rovar could start another stream of conversation, Elizabeth Schaeffer slipped into Naja's room and listened with satisfaction to the hiss of the door closing behind her.

The room was dim with a reddish twilight glow. It was difficult to spot the ambassador, but then she noticed, in one corner, a coiled, lopsided shape topped with a brush of feathers.

"Ambassador Naja?" she inquired. "I'm Col. Elizabeth Schaeffer of the Special Services Division; I'm here to speak to you about this vision you reported to Captain Kirk, the vision of the Angel of Death."

There was a dry rustle in the corner as the ambassador lifted his head. It was hard to see him clearly, but the light struck one eye, making it glitter like a large ruby. "Do you believe in the Angel of Death?" Naja's voice was soft and silken. "The Captain did not, and yet it is so very important. You see, my child, I am waiting for him to come again; and he will come—he promised me that." The great serpent's head sank down again onto his coils.

Elizabeth glanced around in the gloom for some chair or stool; the only thing available for her to sit on was the large smooth-topped bed that had been provided for the ambassador. She moved toward it slowly, perched on one corner. "While you wait, would you mind telling me about the visit? I do believe in the Angel of Death, and I am very interested in him. He and I are old friends."

"Ahh, then you know his beauty." The feathered head lifted a little higher, and the flat wedge of Naja's face turned toward her. "How majestic he is, how his body flames; and his coils are thicker than any of the beings of Dalzell. The pattern of his body is like fine jewels. It was an honor for him to come to me simply to speak. He brought me warning. It is very unusual for the Angel of Death to give warning, is it not? But I was pleased that he condescended to do so. Of course I cannot comply with his wishes, and so I must await his return; but I do not grieve. My life has been a long one; I have seen a hundred and fifty-seven of your years, my child, and it is not often given to see the Shining One's glory more than once. I have been very blessed."

"What warning did he give you, sir?" Elizabeth asked. Her pulse had speeded slightly; she knew she was at the crux of the problem, and she wanted to reach out and wrest from the serpent the answers about the ambassadors' deaths. But she knew she'd have to move slowly and carefully, and accept whatever this creature told her, in whatever form he chose to tell it. His people were very old and given to belief in courtesy, tradition, and the telling of a tale in its proper order. She would have to still her racing mind and wait patiently.

"The Angel of Death wishes the détente with the Romulans." Naja was uncoiling and moving slowly toward her, his body forming large curving S formations across the floor. "I do not understand why he should be in favor of such a thing, except that the Romulans have provided him over the centuries with many of his victims. Oh, yes, the Angel of Death often walks with the Romulans; perhaps he's fond of them. But you see, even though the Shining One said he was in favor of the détente, I cannot agree. He is only a messenger from beings far above himself, as far above himself as he is from me—and as yet I have had no word from *them* to change my opinions of the détente. Perhaps if the great Lord of All, He-Whose-Name-May-Not-Be-Mentioned, were to appear to me and say, 'Yes, the Romulan détente is a good thing,' I would bow my head and accept. But not to the Angel of Death, not merely to a messenger."

Naja had reached the side of the bed and had again coiled himself. He raised his head and slowly began lifting his body until his face was level with Elizabeth's. His great feathered crest spread like a wreath around his head. He swayed back and forth, slowly, with almost hypnotic grace. When he opened his mouth, she could see curved poisonous fangs, poised only inches from her own skin.

"You see, my child," the ambassador continued softly, "I am Naja of the Naja, greatest of the Elapidae, chief of the families of the Dalzell peoples; I do not take orders from messengers. He cannot bid me think any way other than what I would wish. There is only one order the Shining One can give me, the one order I will obey—to accompany him. But until that day comes I will remain firmly opposed to the détente. Do you understand that, my child?"

"Very well. You have a duty to your people; I have a duty to my office, and I too will accept only one order from that messenger. But I find myself wondering if he is a true messenger. Is he what he says he is? Could it be a fake? Could there be someone on board this ship impersonating the Shining One?"

Naja drew himself up three-quarters of his body length and loomed over the woman. He was swaying in wide circles, hissing menacingly. The light glimmered off his fangs.

"Never say that. Never. Never! Never deny me what I have seen! Do you think I am a fool, child, do you think I could be tricked by holograms or some human in a plastic suit? Do you take me for an idiot? I know the Shining One, I cannot be mistaken."

He swooped downward, his head resting atop her own, his feathers brushing her cheeks on each side. "Do you doubt," he said in a soft, meditative tone, "that I could kill you in an instant? It would be so simple. My fangs—you do know my fangs, child. They could pierce your scalp so tenderly that you wouldn't feel the pain, but you would be dead in seconds. It would be a painless death; your heart would simply cease to beat. Do you believe this, my child?"

Elizabeth held herself rigidly still, afraid to move. She knew the ambassador was not mad, not precisely insane—but he was making a point and, considering his fangs, a very sharp one. "Yes." Her voice was as even as she could make it. "I know how close I am to death. But the Angel of Death is not in this room—therefore I am not going to die."

"Aaahhhh." The feathers stroked her cheeks lightly. There was a scent of sandalwood, and the odor of something very old and musty. She felt the plates of his chin move slowly across her head, back and forth, as he stroked her. "You are brave. You are worthy of the black tunic. Not many beings would be so calm as you are. Oh, I sense the blood rush through your veins, I sense your fear; but it is controlled, so controlled. I honor that. Yes, I too wondered if I could have been tricked, but it is not possible. No one can mistake the Shining One for anything other than what it is. No one can mistake the wounding of a scale for the final blow; the scraping of the skin differs from the coup de grâce. We know that, you and I. And so you shall not die this time, my child; you are right, the Angel of Death is not in this room."

He gave a dry chuckle as he lifted his head and brought it down until his eyes were even with her own. "Do you know you ran very little risk? I am so old that the poison in my sacs is all but gone. That is why I do not fear the coming of the Shining One. I do not wish you to avenge my death, because my time has come."

He slowly brought his head forward until his nose rested just brushing the bridge of her own. His breath was warm, strongly scented of sandalwood. "I will be dead before morning, I know that. And I ask something of you, my brave child: stay here with me tonight, watch with me. And when the Shining One comes, perhaps you will see the glory of him and be able to tell your children's children. Perhaps you will be one of the double-blessed who have seen the Angel of Death twice. Who can tell?"

He lifted his head away and slowly devolved downward into a coiled heap, his head resting lightly on the topmost coil. "Will you stay with me?" he asked softly with a note of pleading in his voice. "Which do you fear most, Elizabeth: the great serpent of Dalzell or the Shining One? Stay with me and see."

Elizabeth reached down and gently stroked Naja's feathered crest. "I fear neither of you; the Angel of Death will come for me when he is ready, and if you were his emissary there is very little I could do about it. But I will wait with you; I'm very interested in the Shining One."

"Good. Then we wait."

The hours of the night watch slipped by slowly. Elizabeth sat on the edge of Naja's bed and relaxed herself by going over the mental exercises she'd been taught as a child to help pass time. In the life of a Special Security agent, there was a great deal of waiting. She listened to the even breathing of the ambassador, and she watched the room for any sign of the Angel of Death.

There was nothing.

The hours slipped by one by one. Elizabeth grew cramped, her feet tingling slightly until she slid off the edge of the bed and rested herself comfortably against the back of the ambassador. He sighed slightly in his sleep and made room for her, his head slipping off his coils until it rested upon her knees. She sat waiting for the dawn watch, stroking his feathered crest.

His death came between one breath and another. There was no lifting of his head, there was no greeting to anyone in the room; the Shining One, if he had come for Naja, had not made himself visible to Elizabeth. She waited, feeling a slight tremor go through the creature's body, indicating the passing of life. In the dim red light she saw his eyes fade. There was nothing left of the magnificent intellect, nothing but a large, unwieldy body. Even the feathers of his crest felt dry and lifeless under her fingers. Naja, of the great house of the Elapidae of Dalzell, was dead.

Elizabeth shifted her weight, wincing slightly at the pain in her stiffened joints. She made her way to the wall recorder and called Sick Bay.

"Dr. McCoy? Dr. Rigel? I think you'd best come to Ambassador Naja's quarters. He's dead, and I spent the entire night with him. Nothing came into this room, and nothing—unless you count the spirit of Naja himself—left this room. Schaeffer out."

She pushed the button, cutting off the transmission before McCoy and Rigel could answer. She knew the efficiency of a starship Sick Bay; there would be attendants in the room within minutes. She stretched, catlike, easing the strain on her muscles. She would sit in on the autopsy, but she doubted anything would be found, other than indications of old age.

Elizabeth Schaeffer knew without a shadow of a

doubt that Naja had slipped off with the Shining One without any evil connected to the deed. There had been no murder committed here; there was no stink of evil in the air. But a third ambassador was dead, and that was going to be unpleasant, both for the *Enterprise* and for the SSD.

"My friend," she said to the lifeless hulk of the ambassador, "they had better find a reason for your death—as I'm sure they will—or I am in serious trouble. Because I don't think you died the same way as Agnatha and Neko; and if I'm wrong—if I'm wrong . . ."

She looked down at the lifeless body, contemplating it. "No, I'm not wrong. I know death too well. Whatever angel came for you last night, it was not the one I'm seeking."

She could hear, out in the hallway, the sound of the approaching medical team. She lifted her head, glancing around at the four corners of the room. "Do you hear me, whoever you are, killer of ambassadors, fake bearer of tidings? You're no more an angel than I am, and I will prove it. I'm issuing you a challenge here and now, and we shall see in the final battle who wins. Because when the Angel of Death comes for me, it had better be the right angel!"

15

"Thank God this is a death where I can sign the certificate with a clear conscience. I can definitely attribute this one to natural causes."

Dr. Rigel turned away from the autopsy table and peeled off the thin plastifilm gloves. "A clear case of stroke; if you look at the brain you can see the blocked artery big as life. It looks like something out of a textbook, Col. Schaeffer. Come and have a look."

Elizabeth bent over the body of the dead ambassador. His feathered crest had been separated from his skull, to reveal a pale pinkish brain. She looked at the area that Dr. Rigel indicated. Even though her knowledge of medicine was mostly theoretical, she could see quite clearly what the veterinarian was pointing out; stroke was probably a very good definition of what had killed the ambassador. She was glad it had been quiet, that he had gone in his sleep; she wondered if his dreams had been troubled for one brief moment with the flash of beauty and the golden shimmer of his real Angel of Death. She wished him well, wherever he had believed he now was. She moved away from the table and nodded her acceptance of the results.

"We're going to have one problem, Dr. Rigel," she said. "I saw this one, I was there when he died. The other ambassadors—they're not going to be as easy to convince. They're going to yell 'coverup,' they're going to yell 'conspiracy,' and they're going to accuse us both of every crime imaginable, including arson, assault, barratry, and treason. Don't take it too hard or very seriously. I've gotten used to it in my profession, but I'm sure as a vet you've never had any of your patients taking verbal liberties with you. Just keep up the good work, keep the mask firmly in place, and remember, you are a *physician*!"

Before Dr. Rigel could answer, there was a soft chime from the communications panel on the wall, and Lt. Uhura said, "Col. Schaeffer, there's a message coming in for you from Détente One. Would you like to take it on the viewscreen in Dr. McCoy's office?"

Elizabeth walked over to the panel and opened the channel. "Schaeffer here. Yes, I'll take it on the viewscreen. I should be in McCoy's office in about two minutes. Schaeffer out." She slapped the panel harder than necessary. She knew only too well who was calling her from Détente One.

When the screen shimmered into life on McCoy's desk, it revealed the face of Col. Alexis Schaeffer. He was a dramatically handsome man, with large intense brown eyes, almost black in their depth. His face was lean and hawklike, and his dark olive skin was complemented by the mop of blue-black hair he wore almost a shade too long for SSD requirements. He was, Elizabeth noted, as breathtakingly handsome as he'd been eleven years ago when she had first seen him at the Special Security Central office. But she found, rather to her surprise, that her heart did not leap quite the way it had eleven years before.

"Well, my loving wife," Alexis drawled in an exaggeratedly gentle tone, "do you realize that I arrived here on Détente One and found that, much to my surprise, you were not here? I thought we had an agreement, Elizabeth, that this was going to be a chance for us to be together. Do you know how long this ridiculous blather might go on, that there's a possibility for us to really work out our problems? And what happens? At the first chance, you run off to some stinking starship. I hope you have some explanation."

Elizabeth took a deep breath and realized that

Alexis was appearing at his absolute worst. When he was angry, he was inclined to be very petulant. She would have to deal with him carefully; any attempt to sound parental or superior to him would be dangerous. She had to be calm, reasonable, and soothing. She found herself wishing there wasn't a screen separating them. Talking to him directly was always a great deal easier; she had weapons at her disposal that he couldn't counteract. But then again, the screen might be a safety factor; when Alexis continued with his petulant child routine a little too long, she always had to fight down the urge to slap him silly.

"Alexis, I'm sorry. But unfortunately I had the best reason in the Universe for being on this ship: it's my job. I was the senior officer on Détente One when the report of the *Enterprise* incident came in. The Department felt that it had to be a senior officer, and protocol demanded it; and I knew Derek was perfectly capable of controlling the situation on Détente One—after all, the Romulans aren't there yet. I knew you'd take over the proper position as a Special Security officer when you arrived and handle the job at your end. I know how much this meeting meant to you, and I really am sorry—but I didn't have any choice. I was following the Department's orders." She realized the comment about following orders was a little lame, but it happened to be the truth; even Alexis would know that.

"You could have sent Derek. He's a lieutenant colonel, that's high enough for the likes of James Kirk—or do you think the little band of turquoise around your neck is *that* important? Just once, doesn't what happens between you and me mean more than any job?"

"Alexis, that's unfair. You know as well as I do that *whatever* the Department wants comes first. Life, death, and the destruction of the Universe cannot come before obeying a Department order—and compared to life, death, and the destruction of the Universe, our problems pale a little."

"It's *always* been the Department first," he said in a sulky voice. "Ever since we were first married, it's always been the SSD first. When, Elizabeth, just *when* am I going to be first in your mind?"

"When I stop being Elizabeth Schaeffer, and you stop being Alexis Schaeffer, and the SSD vanishes in a cloud of dust. Don't play games with me; if you tried something like that, I'll remind you of all the occasions when you had to dash off somewhere because *you* were on orders. Don't waste precious communication time on trying to make me feel guilty—it won't work. I have never in my life felt guilty for anything I've had to do for the SSD, and that includes what I'm doing right now. I have two murdered ambassadors on my hands, and a third who died from natural causes. This ship is in a state of chaos. It could damage the entire détente—and if I prove the Romulans are behind it, it could mean a war. So don't play games with me, Alexis, and don't point out that my rank is a shred higher than yours. Because if you do"—her tone was measured and cold, and thoroughly that of an SSD officer—"if you dare throw that up in my face again, I'll use it. I'll remind you that I am your superior by nine months. There's one thing I want you to think about, Alexis. I don't want you to answer it honestly right now, you're too mad—but if it had been you down there on Détente One when the call came in from the *Enterprise* with a case like this, and you had been told by Central that you were to go out and handle it, would *you* have told Central no?"

"All that's beside the point," Alexis said, seemingly brushing away as incidental everything he'd been taught since a cadet. "You promised me we'd have this time together, that you'd give me a chance to convince you to renew the marriage—and now you've gone back on that promise. I need you here, I need you as my wife, not as a Security agent. Doesn't that mean anything to you?" There was an edge and a very real anguish to his voice. He had obviously been really hurt by arriving at Détente One and finding her gone.

"I can only give you the answer I gave you before. I'm following the orders I was given. There's nothing more I can say except I'm sorry." Her voice was very weary; she didn't want to continue the conversation. If he pushed just a little more, she knew she would lose control and yell at him, and that would be the worst thing possible. She promised herself she would try at least to be as open-minded as possible about continuing the marriage, and she knew there was still a very large part of her that was in love with this highstrung, sometimes impossible, sometimes very lovable man.

"Alexis, please, don't put more on me than I can handle. Please let me do my job, and I promise I'll get it done as fast as I can and get back to Détente One and to you. It's the best I can offer." There was an edge of pleading to her voice that she disliked; she quickly quashed her irritation.

"That's not enough," Alexis answered. "It's not good enough, Elizabeth. If you loved me at all, if you cared about me, you'd have been here—but you weren't, and all the 'I'm sorry's' in the world won't change that fact, that you weren't here when I needed you. And it's obvious that no matter how much I need you right now, you're not going to be here. So all right. Take your own damn sweet time on this case, and get around to me whenever you can work me into your schedule." The screen went blank.

Elizabeth stared at it dispassionately, realizing that the chances of anything successful coming out of future discussions on their marriage had been lessened by Alexis's temper tantrum. "He's a child," she murmured. "A spoiled, egotistical child. And unfortunately he's *my* child, and perhaps the fact that he is a child is what I love. May the gods help me! I wish I didn't love him at all."

She rested her head on the top of the viewscreen and tried to remember all the good things Alexis had brought to her life. She swiftly realized that in her present state of mind it was impossible to be objective about her husband.

"I'm told you'll get wrinkles doing that," Captain Kirk said from in back of her. "But I'd assume you know more about feminine vanity than I do."

"Do I?" Elizabeth lifted her head to watch the Captain circle the desk until he was facing her. "I've been told you know quite a bit about the ladies, Kirk—including their little vanities. Personally, I don't give a damn if I age a hundred years on this case. It might solve some of my problems."

"What, and destroy all that beauty? For shame, Colonel. Destruction of a natural wonder is against Federation law, you should know that." His tone was light and bantering, just the sort of thing she needed after dealing with Alexis.

"Beauty isn't all it's cracked up to be; in fact, it's sometimes a definite drawback. I wish I only had the murders and the *Enterprise* to worry about—it wouldn't be any problem; I'm trained to handle this kind of thing. But I'm afraid I've got a great deal more on my mind. It's personal, but it's important to me." She felt an incredible urge to explain Alexis to this man, a feeling that if she could once get out how she felt about her marriage—lay the burden on someone else—it might be good for her.

"Well, Captain," she said, "shall I tell you my sob story? It's got to be the oldest in the Universe. Boy meets girl, boy falls in love with girl, boy marries girl, and boy and girl have a lousy marriage. I need to talk to someone about it, and you happen to be handy. But I have no right to burden you with my personal problems."

Kirk slid into the other seat at the desk. "Go ahead and talk. Part of being a starship captain is that you get used as a sounding board. Of course, you could always go cry on McCoy's shoulder, and he'd prescribe a couple of shots of Saurian brandy and an aspirin. . . . But he's had a rotten morning too. I think it would wind up with you two getting flat-out drunk and having a great game of 'Ain't It Awful.' I don't think that's what you need, Elizabeth Schaeffer. I'm a veteran of the war of the sexes, and I understand most of the things that can happen to a human being. I might be able to offer something in the way of consolation. So tell the old captain what your problem is. I've got broad shoulders."

Elizabeth got up from the recliner and began pacing the length of the room. Captain Kirk had touched her in a surprising way. Consideration of her as a person rather than as an SSD agent was the last thing she had expected of him. It would be a relief to tell this man about Alexis.

"I married Alexis because we were in the same profession and because he could understand what it means to be a Special Security agent. We knew there'd be long gaps in the marriage when we wouldn't see each other; the only alternative was to take desk jobs, but neither of us was ready for that. We're both ambitious people, Captain. We both have duties. This—" She pointed to the collar stripe of her uniform, brilliant turquoise under the light. "—This is part of the problem. I became a colonel ten months ago. Alex just received the blue collar of a full colonel last month, and mentally he's still wearing the red stripe of a lieutenant colonel. He's got the turquoise stripe on his uniform and around his neck, but it's the fact that I got there first that sticks in his craw. There's always the danger that if I pull off this Angel-of-Death caper with enough splash and style, they may make me a general, and Alexis could never cope with that. Ambition in a marriage is as deadly as absence. Do you know that we've seen each other less than nine months, on and off, over a ten-year period? What kind of a marriage is that?"

"It can be a very good one if you do it right," Kirk said. "There's such a thing as too much togetherness. If you and your husband were together all the time, you might find out more than you wanted to know about each other and your marriage wouldn't have lasted even ten years. I suspect those reunions of yours are pretty intense, very special."

"Oh, they're special, all right. We leap on each other like a couple of rutting Rigellian bloodworms and never get out of bed for the entire duration of our leave. There's more to a marriage than sex, Captain, and that's the part that's missing with Alexis and me. There's never been a feeling of shared problems, of having to look after each other in sickness and in health. I don't even know what Alexis is like when he's sick. Heaven knows he's never had to bail me out of any troubles. What we've got is really a series of romantic encounters. I suspect that if I don't sign the marriage agreement when it comes through, Alexis and I will go on seeing one another at intervals, and it'll continue to be exciting. But the quarrels, Captain, are what's become most of the problem. Alexis and I do manage to communicate between our little weekends, and our letters back and forth used to be a way of being together even if we were halfway across the Universe from each other. But lately those letters have been nothing more than an extended quarrel, and I'm getting sick of it. I think"—she laughed bitterly—"I'm even getting a little sick of Alexis. And yet he's demanding that I renew the contract. For some peculiar reason known only to him, he's still in love with me, and he wants this farce to go on.

"It's really his only flaw. Alexis is a fantastic SSD agent, but I'm his Achilles heel. This love for me will destroy him; there's just too much of it to let him survive. Some day he'll do something stupid because of me, and it will cost him his life or his career. I'm not sure which would be worse."

"And do you love him?"

"Jim"—she switched to his first name without even warning him—"if I had the answer to that, I wouldn't be here talking to you. I wouldn't have any problem! Yes, I love him—no, I don't love him. He's Alexis, what can I say? This meeting on Détente One was important to us—we were going to try to see whether there was anything left of our marriage, whether there was any future in it. Alexis set the meeting up, and it meant the world to him. But I have to admit I wasn't that happy about it. I would have preferred to let the thing quietly die. I suppose that statement indicates clearly enough how I feel about the marriage—it needs to be put to death mercifully."

"At least the fact that you're interested in mercy shows there's some feeling left. I've known a lot of friends who've gotten divorces and been anything but merciful. A lot of blood and guts got scattered all over the place; you seem at least to be avoiding a bloodbath."

"Oh, I'm not going into court for a formal divorce; that'd be silly, there're no children and no community property. It's simply a matter of letting the contract lapse. I'm really glad the Federation allows for that sort of thing. It's tidy. I wish my thoughts on the subject were as tidy.

"It's not as if we're bound to each other. I know that in the last ten years Alexis has not remained absolutely faithful to me; I wouldn't have expected it of him. There was even, three or four years ago, an affair during which he thought *he* might let the contract lapse. It's one of those things that just happens along the way, and there's nothing you can do about it."

Kirk laughed and said, "And do you mean to tell me, sweet little Bess, in all of ten years you've never strayed from the sacred path of matrimony?"

"That would be as ridiculous as expecting Alexis to be faithful. I tried to avoid emotional entanglements, though; I didn't feel that sort of thing was healthy. My primary consideration was Alexis, and whatever activities there have been on my part were purely recreational, not because I'd fallen in love." She looked up at Kirk almost as if she were seeing him for the first time. "Do you know," she said, "if I was in love with anyone else, it would make this so much simpler. I'm not afraid of being alone, I'm not afraid of being unmarried—but I would like something to help tip the balance one way or another. I wonder if you can fall in love out of desperation, because it's a solution of some kind. What do you think, Captain?"

Kirk was silent; several possibilities were looming in his mind. She was an attractive woman; it would be very easy to make her fall in love with him in the state she was in, and he realized that having Elizabeth Schaeffer in love with him could be a very marvelous thing. It might put an end to the feelings of loneliness he'd been experiencing, the empty hollow feeling he sometimes felt in the night watch. He realized, too, that it would be very easy for him to fall in love with *her,* out of perhaps a different form of desperation.

"I want to tell you something about myself," he said slowly. "It may help, it may not. There comes a time in everyone's life when they look around and wonder if this is all their life is going to be. I find myself going through that, but the marvelous thing about being a starship captain is that I've never wanted to be anything else in my life, and I don't think there's anything else that would give me the satisfaction this job does. Yet more and more I find myself wondering, what if I'd taken another path? What if I'd been a farmer like my father or a doctor like McCoy? I start looking at all the what-if's along the way, and one of the major what-if's is, did I miss out on something? Did I miss out on some*one*? I'm going to go on—I'm going to remain a starship captain, I know I wouldn't be happy anywhere else; but those doubts, that feeling of having missed something, are still going to be there. And they manifest themselves as a feeling of incredible loneliness. I find myself wanting to reach out and touch something—some*one;* I need *someone* important in my life. And I find myself looking at every woman I meet and asking, 'Are you the woman, are you the one I should spend the rest of my life with, the one who's going to make me a complete person?' And I warn you, Elizabeth, I'm looking at you that way. I want to know if I'm possibly letting the chance of happiness slip through my fingers. So if I tell you to be a good girl and go back to your husband, am I giving up the second most wonderful thing to ever happen to me? I cannot and will not give up the *Enterprise*—but what about you? Are you that second marvel that I can't give up?"

"I don't know. Do you realize you've just added another complication? I came to you for some sort of—oh, emptying out the garbage, I guess, and I find that it's just been a mutual trade. I understand what you feel, I've felt it too—but I don't know the answer to your question. It's entirely possible I am that person; but it's too early to know. There's one thing that has to be settled first: I am Alexis's wife. For two months. That is a fact that can't be escaped, and whatever happens between you and me will depend very much on what happens in the next two months with Alexis and me. When I first came aboard the *Enterprise,* I wasn't sure how I felt about you—the great James T. Kirk, captain of the *Enterprise,* a living legend—a god. Well, the living legend is a rather handsome man with a rather nice smile and as many problems as I have."

She smiled gently at him, her hand going out to touch the side of his face, one finger touching the diagonally cut sideburn. "There's only one thing I can tell you. I don't know how much of an answer it is, for either of us, but I will say it anyway. I like you, James Kirk. I like you a great deal."

"And I like you, Elizabeth Schaeffer," he answered. "I like you a great deal more than is probably good for either of us."

16

Medical Log, Stardate 6981.5, Dr. Leonard McCoy reporting:

I find the autopsy results on Ambassador Naja extremely satisfactory; Dr. Rigel is to be commended for her work. There is no possibility whatsoever of an error; Dr. Rigel has made it clear to both myself and Col. Schaeffer that Naja of Dalzell died of natural causes. I only wish we could convince the ambassadors of that fact. They did not receive the report with any show of satisfaction—there were even accusations of a coverup, which Col. Schaeffer swiftly nipped in the bud. The ambassadors are suffering from an assortment of emotional disorders, and there are indications of hypertension and psychosomatic illness. I have given orders for Dr. Rigel to medicate as she sees fit, and I have done my best to keep the ambassadors calm. Col. Shaeffer's presence has been of help; she seems to have some sort of soothing effect on the people around her. I find this puzzling but the ambassadors, no matter how angry they are, seem to respect her a great deal. But I am not sure that one SSD agent, no matter how remarkable she is, can possibly handle all the difficulties we're having with the ambassadors. The situation is explosive. One more death on this ship and I cannot be held responsible for the resulting damage to the detente.

I do, however, wish to commend the actions of Dr. M'Benga, who has been of enormous aid and assistance, especially in his work with the ambassadors. We are very fortunate to have on board a physician who has been trained in Vulcan mind-control techniques. M'Benga has been tireless in his attempts to teach these calming and controlling exercises to some of the more excitable ambassadors. He has been assisted to a certain extent by Mr. Spock; but Ambassador Sarek is showing signs of fatigue and what in any other being but a Vulcan might be described as despair.

Ambassador Sarek was indeed distressed by the events occurring on board the *Enterprise*. He had pledged Captain Kirk on his honor that there would be no problems for the *Enterprise* on this particular mission, and even though he knew he was not personally responsible for the ambassadors' deaths, the situation still weighed heavily on him. He felt increasingly weary, and the requirements of dealing on a day-to-day basis with his fellow ambassadors were becoming more and more difficult. It was entirely possible, he reflected, that this might be his last mission; if the détente with the Romulans was accomplished and the treaty found to be binding, it could be an excellent capstone to his career in the service of the Federation. He knew that the situation aboard the ship was in competent hands. Sarek knew Elizabeth Schaeffer personally and was well aware of her record with the SSD; he felt a quiet confidence in her abilities, and knew that if anyone could solve the murders, it would be her. But could she solve them in time? Could she, by herself, save the détente?

Col. Schaeffer had decided that the most logical plan of attack was to interview the remaining ambassadors one by one and find out precisely what they knew about the deaths of Neko and Agnatha. Her conversation with Naja haunted her. He had believed in the Angel of Death; he *had* seen that angel. So there was the possibility that other ambassadors might be visited by the apparition. She had to gain their confidence, make them realize that she was their best bastion of defense. She decided to start her inquiry with Ambassador Rovar of Hemiptera—not because she felt he would know that much, but simply because he was likely to be the next victim. Rovar was the last remaining ambassador violently opposed to the Romulan détente. She easily found his quarters on Deck Four, but was surprised to discover he was not alone.

There was an apparition in Rovar's quarters—fortunately not the Angel of Death.

Elizabeth stood by the door, trying to assimilate the details of what she was seeing. The tall blue crocodile was obviously a Gavialian, but his costume was so outlandish that she was both stunned and appalled. He was clad in a long Inverness cloak of a particularly gaudy heather-blue tweed, a matching deerstalker cap, and held in one clawed hand a magnificent calabash pipe.

"What in the name of the seven sacred stars are *you*?" she asked.

"I am Si-s-s-s(click), the world's greatest detective, my dear young woman. I should think that would be obviousss." Si-s-s-s(click) folded back the cape of his coat and produced from an inside pocket a large magnifying glass, which he held up to one eye like a monocle, to peer back at Elizabeth.

She resisted an urge to laugh; she realized by now that this had to be one of the ambassadors, and since he was a Gavialian he was probably involved in one of the elaborate *persona* games his people were prone to. "Yes, I can see that, but which world?"

"Why, Earth, what else? I'm being Sherlock Holmes. Would you care to be Watson?"

"Would I care to *what*?" Elizabeth realized he was making some reference to Terran literature, but wasn't quite sure which literary character he had in mind. Ancient detective stories hadn't been part of her curriculum as an SSD officer.

"Watson—Dr. Watson! He was Sherlock Holmes's assistant on all his cases, and I assure you it's an excellent part. Holmes did manage to solve almost all his cases. Can you say the same, Col. Schaeffer?"

"No, I can't claim a one hundred percent success record," Elizabeth said, "but unfortunately since I'm not that familiar with the role, I'm going to have to continue being Col. Elizabeth Schaeffer. I'm very sorry."

"Oh! And I spent all night researching the role! I was so sure it would be perfect. Are you quite positive you don't want to be Watson? Well, in any case you *will* let me help you with the investigation, won't you, my dear Col. Schaeffer?" Si-s-s-s(click) advanced on her, his mouth open in a wide toothy smile. "You see," he said when within a jaw's length of her, "I find the whole concept of solving crimes absolutely fascinating. And I did want you to agree that I could assist. I'll take the part of Watson, if you'd rather be Holmes."

Elizabeth tried not to laugh and controlled her facial muscles to produce nothing more than a quiet smile. "I assure you, my dear Ambassador Si-s-s-s(click), I have not the slightest intention of keeping you from assisting me with this case, but I don't think it's necessary to go through all . . . this." She spread her hands to take in the Inverness, the deerstalker, and the calabash pipe.

"Well, I did think it was so much in character—but of coursse there is a problem." He held out the pipe, turning it from side to side in his hands. "I couldn't quite manage to deal with this. Every time I tried a s-s-smoke it, I either became very ill or the s-s-stem kept breaking between my teeth. I'm not at all sure this is precisely the way it ought to go, and my romanticism was such fun. I just had a new cape made, black velvet lined with red satin. Of course, it didn't become me, it clashed with my hide. So I gave it to Ambassador Damu. I musst say, it did look better on him. He is a far more romantic character than I am." Si-s-s-s(click) gave a great sigh and clutched the Inverness cloak around his large reptilian body. "But you see, if I can't play the great romantic, I have to have *some* role; so I thought this one might at least be enjoyable."

"When are you going to stop all that nonsense and start protecting me?" Rovar pushed his way into the middle of the discussion, all of his elbows akimbo. "Do you realize, Col. Schaeffer, that you are totally ignoring me? I assume you're here to talk over this terrible tragedy, and perhaps I can make you understand how much I need protection. I had a great deal of faith in the SSD, but *you,* Colonel, are not a fit representative of the Special Security Division. Here I am in danger of losing my life at any moment, and you spend your time blathering with this great blue idiot! I want protection, I want it now! I want a whole squad of security officers in here, and what I don't want"—his voice was rising into a howling bellow—"what I don't want is this silly blue booby posing and prancing in my quarters! He burst his way in here and began asking me silly questions about dogs that didn't bark at night and blue carbuncles and who was Irene Adler! It's moronic, and I want nothing to do with it. If you're to conduct an investigation, Colonel, conduct it properly." The Hemipteran paused for breath, contemplating his next tirade.

"You're quite right, Ambassador Rovar," Elizabeth said placatingly. "I did come here because of you, and I am very concerned for your safety. I'm well aware that you are the last ambassador left on the ship opposed to the Romulan détente, and I'll do what I can to protect you. There will be a squad of security guards outside your door, I'm going to have a twenty-four-hour surveillance unit set up in your quarters—with your permission, of course—and I will do everything in my power to keep you alive." Her voice was soothing, gentle, and she utilized every ounce of charm that she could muster on the large striped alien.

Her comments had the desired effect; Rovar calmed down immediately and seated himself with much huffing and puffing on the edge of his wide bed. "And what do you intend to do with this blue clown? Must I submit to his questions as well?"

"Ambassador Si-s-s-s(click) is a fellow member of the diplomatic corps, and I should think he has a certain right to concern himself in this case. But if you object . . ." She glanced at Si-s-s-s(click) and watched his face fall as he realized he was being gently eased out of the investigation.

"However," Elizabeth continued, "I understand your objection to his being here; he is, after all, in favor of the détente, and as such may be your greatest danger. So what I will have to do is put the ambassador to work in another area—that is, if you don't mind, sir."

She turned to Si-s-s-s(click) and smiled. "I would like your assistance in this investigation, but I think I might better use you in dealing with your fellow ambassadors who are either neutral or in favor of the détente. You see, it's very difficult to question a hostile witness, and as long as you're here I'm afraid Rovar is going to be hostile. So if you don't mind, would you please contact Cdr. Collier and tell him I'd like to see him in my quarters in half an hour?"

Si-s-s-s(click) bowed in acknowledgement and turned, swirling his Inverness around him like Hamlet's cape. "Very well. I know when I'm not wanted. If Rovar is going to take that kind of attitude, I shall go elsewhere. But I will be only too glad to do your bidding, Col. Schaeffer. Cdr. Collier will be in your quarters within one half hour if I have to carry him there myself!" On that line, Si-s-s-s(click) exited, and Elizabeth restrained an urge to applaud.

"Thank goodness he's gone," Rovar grumbled. "It's bad enough he's involved in the conspiracy with Sarek and Sirenia to make us all slaves of the Romulans. But that silly playacting of his is more than any intelligent being should be expected to tolerate. I can't understand how a mature individual could get any pleasure out of running around making a fool of himself. Well, there's no accounting for tastes. But I assure you, Col. Schaeffer, no Hemipteran in his right mind would consider such activities." Rovar harrumphed himself into silence, and looked up at Elizabeth, waiting to be questioned.

"I can repeat what I've already said," she began. "Naja's death was due to natural causes. I witnessed the autopsy and I've read the reports; I've also read the autopsy reports on Neko and Agnatha, and I don't like them. I have a strong suspicion that there is a murderer aboard the *Enterprise,* and I need your assistance in catching him because I'm afraid you may be the next intended victim. Would you mind giving me your impressions of your fellow ambassadors—particularly Sarek, Si-s-s-s(click), Telson, Karhu, and Sirenia? According to my notes, they are the most vocally in favor of the détente."

Rovar inflated his chest, obviously preparing for a longwinded speech. "Ambassador Sarek is entirely too slick for his own good, and the fact of having his son as an officer on this ship is entirely too suspicious. I'd suggest that you investigate those two. We all know Vulcans have some very strange habits; they do mind-touching and other mental perversions. I wouldn't put it past them to have the capacity to kill. As for Si-s-s-s-(click) . . ."

Rovar appeared to consider what he might say that would be the most damning, and then shrugged. "Well, I think his performance here explains everything you need to know about him. Telson is a nobody, Sarek's shadow—and as for that great hairy marsupial Karhu, why, he has threatened me with death more times than I could possibly count. He takes a positive delight in it. He's a vicious creature, Colonel. Don't let all that soft flaccidness fool you for a moment. He's a trickster and a vicious villain. I can say little about Sirenia; I don't know her well. But there is something cold and clammy there. I avoid her. Now is there anything else you wish to know?" He interlocked all his hands in an ornate pattern and sat there, a fat, striped, complacent Buddha, sure of every word he had said.

"What about the neutral ambassadors?" Elizabeth consulted the manifest sheet she had tucked into her belt. "I believe they include Edentata, Damu, Spiracles, and Hotep. Would you care to comment?"

"Fence-sitters, all of them. Blind, mindless fence-sitters. You won't get any help from them. Damu is a popinjay, Edentata never has anything to say for himself, Spiracles is a pompous ass, and Hotep . . . Hotep . . ."

Rovar leaned forward and lowered his voice as if about to impart some special information. Elizabeth leaned forward, fascinated by the look of puritanical annoyance on the Hemipteran's face. "Hotep is the worst of the lot. He is—a sensualist! He has no interest in politics whatever. I don't understand how he ever became an ambassador."

Disappointed, Elizabeth leaned back in her seat. She was obviously going to get little useful information out of this addleheaded being. But protecting his life was crucial. If anything happened to Rovar while she was on board the *Enterprise,* it would reflect badly not only on herself, but on the Department. She must do everything possible to maintain his security; her personal feelings toward him meant nothing.

"Well," Elizabeth said, getting to her feet, "I think I had better make arrangements with the Chief Engineer for security surveillance of your quarters—and I have an appointment with the Chief Security Officer. I assure you, Ambassador Rovar, your security is my major concern. I'd advise you to be very careful where you go aboard the *Enterprise,* try not to travel in corridors alone, don't be alone at any time with any ambassador who has been too much in favor of the détente; and perhaps it would be wisest if you spent most of your time here in your quarters."

"Oh, I can't do that!" The Hemipteran swelled impressively. "I have a job to do. I am the only representative of the opposition party; it's my duty to convert those wooden-headed neutrals to my way of thinking. I cannot sit here sulking. I must go out and do my duty—and you, Colonel, must do yours by protecting me."

Elizabeth sighed, realizing that her job was going to be more difficult than she'd expected. But then, expecting reason and logic from Rovar was asking a little too much of the Universe. She thanked the ambassador profusely and was preparing to leave his quarters when the communication panel lit up and Captain Kirk's voice was heard asking for Elizabeth Schaeffer.

Before Rovar could demand to know why the Captain would be wanting to speak to the Colonel rather than to himself, Elizabeth dashed to the wall panel and slapped the communication button open. "Schaeffer here. What is it, Kirk?"

"I'm afraid we've had a little visitation." Kirk's voice

was hesitant; he was obviously unsure how much to say in front of the Hemipteran. "I'd suggest you drop in on Ambassador Spiracles; it might prove helpful. Kirk out."

Elizabeth snapped the button back to off. "Well, it appears that I have another ambassador to interview. So if you will excuse me, Ambassador Rovar. . . ."

"He's seen it, hasn't he? Spiracles has seen that thing. Well, let me know how it comes out. And remember, I want surveillance, and I want protection, and I want it now."

"I'll not forget, sir. I'll make sure that everything is done to your satisfaction. Now if you will excuse me. . . ." Elizabeth palmed the door open and escaped into the hallway, feeling relieved to be out of the Hemipteran's presence.

A second sighting of the Angel of Death by one of the other ambassadors was something she'd been hoping for. Naja's description of the angel had been entirely too mystical to provide any concrete evidence. Perhaps Spiracles might be able to help.

His quarters were only a few doors down from Rovar's. His door was already open, and the large shiny black creature stood in the center of a ring of security officers, talking to Captain Kirk. His massive wings drooped and his mandibles clattered. His large bellowed chest rose and fell rapidly as he breathed through his nose plugs. It was quite clear that Spiracles was terrified. When Elizabeth entered he ran forward to grasp her arm with one extraordinarily long-fingered hand.

"I've seen him! I've seen him!" the Gyomorian announced. "I saw the Angel of Death, right here in this room! I was taking a nap, heard something stirring in the room, sat up, and there he was! Tall and terrible! He told me . . . he told me I had to vote in favor of the Romulan détente or he would return to me and I'd die. Help me, Col. Schaeffer. He was so tall and terrible!"

Spiracles wrapped his wings around his body, forming a great dark chrysalis; his voice came echoing out of the center of it as if he were at the bottom of a well.

"He's going to come for me again, I'm going to die like all the others, and I'm not ready for death."

"Could you be a little more specific as to what he looked like?" Elizabeth encircled the chrysalis with her arms, rubbing it gently. "If I'm going to prevent your death, Spiracles, I must know everything about the Angel of Death."

She continued slow, rhythmic stroking of his wings until he gradually unfurled. At a nod of her head, the security guards left the room. Captain Kirk paused a moment, waiting to see if she wished his presence. She shook her head slightly, and he too departed.

Spiracles was trembling in absolute terror. Elizabeth led him slowly to his bed, seated him, and then signaled the kitchen unit to supply a large mug of strong herb tea from his native planet. When the tea arrived she placed the mug gently in his long-fingered hands and helped him bring the cup to his large mandibled jaw. He sipped at the tea as if to draw security from its warmth and strange lavender-gardenia odor. Elizabeth waited until he drained the mug. She sat down next to him, close enough for actual physical contact should he again revert to a chrysalis.

"Are you feeling better? Just relax and calm yourself. I know you've been through something very traumatic and you're very frightened. I'll try to make this as easy as I can, but I will have to ask you some questions."

"It was the Angel of Death," Spiracles said, holding out the mug in a mute appeal for a refill. Elizabeth got to her feet and signaled for more tea.

"What was the oxygen level like in your room this afternoon?" she asked in a conversational tone as she brought him the second mug and again helped him drink it. The question was not an idle one; Spiracles was from a planet with a very thin atmosphere, and oxygen in excess quantities had a detrimental effect. It was inclined to cause intoxication.

"Oh, I know what you're thinking," he said between sips of tea, "but I've been very careful to regulate the oxygen levels in my room ever since I boarded the *Enterprise*. The level is high now, but that was set by the Captain so I could be questioned without the crew fainting from oxygen deprivation. And of course when I leave my room, I wear nostril plugs to filter the air for me. I assure you, Col. Schaeffer, I was not drunk—I did see the Angel of Death." He began to shiver again and almost dropped the white porcelain mug. She cupped her hands around his own to help him finish the tea, and then asked if he wanted more. He shook his head, then took a deep breath to steady his nerves.

"You're being very kind, far kinder than I expected. One hears such stories about the SSD—I didn't expect—that is, you must understand, Colonel. I'm not accustomed to working with Special Security. I wish there was no need for it now. But as to my seeing the Angel of Death, oh yes, he was here. And I intend to vote in favor of the Romulan détente." He looked up at her pleadingly. "You may consider me a coward—and you would be right, I am. I am very young yet, and there's a great deal of my life I want to live. I saw Agnatha's body and that shattered environment tank. He was terrified too, and I understand his terror. I'd do anything—*anything*—the Angel asked of me if it will prevent my seeing him again for a long, long time."

"I quite understand, sir. I too fear death, and I wouldn't willingly place my head under his blade. If you feel that voting in favor of détente is the best answer for you, who am I to criticize? But I would like to put a stop to the situation. I don't approve of ambassadors being terrified. So if you could give me a description—a minute, detailed description—of what he was like, it would help."

Spiracles was rather startled, as though the idea of describing the Angel of Death was a very odd request. "He looked like what he was. That tall, dark winged being called Death. He was black, so black—of a darkness that stretched back to eternity. He is the stuff of which black holes are made, and he wraps you in his wings and takes you away into whatever place it is that he dwells." Spiracles had the same mystical expression in his eyes that Elizabeth had noted with Naja. She had to get something a little more pertinent than mere mysticism.

"How tall was he?" It was a simple question, and simple questions were sometimes very calming. It was a technique she found useful in tense situations.

"His head brushed the top of this room. In fact, he had to stoop to fit in here. That would make him, what—three meters. Perhaps a little taller. I was not inclined to ask his height; he was giving me orders at the time."

"And width? How wide were his wings?"

"Wide enough to stretch from wall to wall. Wide enough to encompass this room. And he filled every centimeter of the room and encircled my bed. I could see nothing else but him, towering over me, and his voice was like the sound of deep space itself. Empty, and echoing with nothing."

It was not a pleasant description, but it provided Elizabeth with several clues. The Angel of Death was obviously not one being masquerading in a series of costumes. While it might be entirely possible for someone to do themselves up the way Spiracles described, the difficulty of that same being presenting himself as Naja's great glowing serpent provided too many technical problems. There was always the possibility of a projection, but she'd been told that every inch of the ambassadors' cabins had been gone over, looking for projection equipment. The manifestation was not a hologram.

"Was there anything else you noticed about him? Any odor, any strange lights?"

Spiracles nodded and said, "He smelled like death—the stinking, sour-sweet smell of death. His breath was the scent of an open grave. I have no wish to meet him again. I will vote as he demands." Spiracles lifted his head and raised his voice so he could be heard in every corner. "Do you hear me, Death Angel? I will do your will, vote as *you* wish."

Elizabeth realized the ambassador had reached the end of his strength; he was visibly panting, even in the—to him—high oxygen environment. The experience had been a terrifying one, and he was probably not finding it easy to deal with his own self-admitted cowardice.

"I'll get Dr. Rigel to come up and administer a sedative; and if you'd like I'll have several security officers monitor your room around the clock."

Spiracles turned to stare at her for a long moment. "Do you think all the security agents in the Universe could stop him if he wished to take me? No, Colonel, there's no need for surveillance. I have done as he has asked, and I am safe. What happens either here or on Détente One is of very little importance to me, as long as I preserve my life and live to see my grandchildren."

Elizabeth stood up and walked toward the wall panel to contact Dr. Rigel. She turned on her way to the wall and said, "I would like to see my grandchildren too, Spiracles. I understand—I really do understand."

17

"Well, she's managed to pull this one off," Dr. Rigel commented to McCoy after returning from Spiracles's cabin. "That poor ambassador is scared out of his skin, and I can't say I blame him. But I think Col. Schaeffer managed to make him feel a little better about the whole thing. He didn't even need a tranquilizer. All I did was fix his oxygen, tuck him in and tell him to contact me if there was anything he needed. He said he'd prefer to contact Col. Schaeffer; and I don't blame him for that, either. She can probably help him more than I can."

McCoy looked up from his desk at the young veterinarian. There were several things about Elizabeth Schaeffer he didn't fully understand, and he suspected Ruth might know something. "Look, I know your field isn't exactly alien biology, but there's something weird about Col. Schaeffer and I'd like to know what it is. She won't let me sigmund her, and yes, she had the right—regulations and all that—but the way people keep reacting to her! They keep forgetting she's a blackjak, and I don't understand it."

"Well, that's relatively simple to answer, even for me." Ruth slid onto the corner of McCoy's desk, which was one of her favorite perches. "It's part of that mixed alien ancestry she has. We know the SSD picks their cadets for very specialized reasons—and in

Schaeffer's case I think it has something to do with her body chemistry, particularly the pheromones. Everyone gives off odors—they're simply a natural function—and a lot of animals have odors that are meant to frighten anything that might want to eat them. And then of course at mating seasons, pheromones are used to attract a being of the same species and the opposite gender. It actually occurs in human beings, too, but on such a slight level that I don't think we're even consciously aware of it."

"Ruth, are you trying to tell me that Col. Schaeffer is good at her job because of the way she smells? That's too silly even for me to believe, and on this mission I've grown accustomed to believing at least six impossible things before breakfast every day."

"No, I'm serious about it. I suspect Schaeffer is part Laudarian. They give off pheromones that ensure they'll be liked; it's a defense mechanism. And knowing the SSD, I'm sure Col. Schaeffer is aware of her effect on other beings. In fact, it strikes me as an extremely useful trait for a security agent."

"But wouldn't the odor have to vary depending on the kind of alien she was talking to?"

"Oh, of course. That's part of the beauty of it. It's a semiautomatic function; it can be dealt with, oh, a little like biofeedback. Schaeffer's probably an expert at it. She can produce the right combination of chemical compounds and the right body odor that calms whoever she's talking to. I'd love a chance to get her into my lab and study the chemical balances she must have to go through. I've done some experiments with moths, and those funny little rodents they have on Miskar Two, but they just produce mating pheromones, and it isn't sex that Schaeffer's selling. It's something a lot more complex. She's not even interested in being loved—it's a likeability factor."

There was a slightly fanatical glint in Ruth's eyes as she contemplated the biochemical aspects of Col. Schaeffer. "You know, if the Angel of Death manages to get *her*," she mused, "I'd have the makings of a brilliant paper for the next Science Academy meeting. I wonder . . ."

McCoy laughed and reached over to smack the veterinarian lightly on one dark-clad thigh. "Ruth, you little ghoul, keep your mind on your animals! Don't go thinking you can dissect a sentient being just because I promoted you to physician. I'll make you a promise, though: if the Angel of Death gets Schaeffer, you get her body. But I want in on the autopsy, too; some of those SSD augmentations she's hinted at sound downright fascinating! I just hope the body doesn't blow up in our faces the first time we tinker with it."

Col. Schaeffer had barely completed her somewhat delayed discussion with Lt. Cdr. Collier when she was informed that a message was coming in for her from Détente One. She knew even before she made her way to the viewscreen precisely who the call was from and what its contents were likely to be. When she flipped on the screen, she found she was right. It was Alexis.

"Well? Are you finished playing here we go 'round the rosebush up there on the *Enterprise*?" he asked in an acid tone of voice. "Or is there some ambassador or another you haven't managed to charm yet? In case you don't realize it, you're needed down here. Derek and I are the only two SSD officers present, and if you think it's easy keeping everyone else in line, and managing the Romulans—who, by the way, I may inform you have now arrived—well, you've got another think coming. I need you down here, and I need you down here quickly."

"I have a job to do," she said. "I haven't solved the problem yet. I've got three dead ambassadors up here and the possibility of more, and I haven't the vaguest idea what's happening. I don't intend to give up until I do know what's going on aboard the *Enterprise*. You and Derek will simply have to manage as best you can—and if you don't want to take my word on that, you can contact Central. I'm sure they don't take this situation lightly."

"Dammit, Elizabeth! Do you have to invest every atom of yourself in your work? It's more than just the problems down here. I want to see you; we've a lot to talk about. Doesn't it matter to you at all that we haven't seen each other in months, and that I love you?"

Elizabeth sighed. It was going to be another one of *those* discussions. "Alexis, don't do this to me. I don't need a discussion on the nature of love right now. I've got a problem, and I'm trying to deal with it, and you're not helping me in the slightest. Now please don't call me again unless you can tell me something useful."

"And isn't the fact that I love you useful?" Alexis did not wait for an answer; the screen went blank.

Elizabeth stared at the black screen for a moment, and then murmured sadly, "Alexis you great idiot, at this particular moment it doesn't matter to me in the slightest whether you love me or loathe me. Two months . . . you've got two months."

18

Elizabeth had three more of the neutral ambassadors to interview. She was trying to decide in what order she should see Edentata, Damu, and Hotep when Si-s-s-s-(click) came bounding into her quarters.

"Ambassador Hotep is ready to see you," he announced, flourishing his absurd Inverness cape.

"Why Hotep?" Elizabeth asked. "I did intend to see him, but I'm curious why you put him at the top of the list."

"Wasn't it the right decision? My dear Colonel, do tell me if I've done something wrong. I want to learn the detecting business properly. I realize upon studying your methods that the great Holmes is sadly backward."

"Oh, there's nothing wrong with Hotep being first, I was just curious as to your reasons. But since he is ready to see me, by all means lead on."

Hotep was indeed ready to receive visitors. The pyramid had enthroned himself on the rectangular slab which was the only piece of furniture in his quarters, and placed a large sunlamp directly overhead. On the slab beside him was an enormous bowl of fruit. Hotep was manifesting ears, arms, eyes, a nose, and a good-sized mouth, into which he was busily stuffing fruit as rapidly as possible.

Elizabeth and Si-s-s-s(click) waited for Hotep to finish his snack so they could begin questioning him. But after several minutes Elizabeth realized the ambassador did not intend to stop eating for her benefit. She would have to conduct the interview while the creature was busy stuffing himself and hope that whatever answers he managed to get around his mouthfuls of food would be at least understandable.

"Your Excellency, I am very pleased that you have allowed the time for this interview. I seem to be interrupting you," Elizabeth said, hoping for some explanation of his strange behavior.

"Oh, that's quite all right," Hotep answered, manifesting a second mouth below the one he was stuffing with fruit. "You see, I don't want to stop eating, because the more energy I can put into my body, the more activity I'm capable of. A very simple equation. Go ahead and ask what questions are necessary, and don't mind me. I *am* sorry if you find the eating rude, but to me it is the most important aspect of these junkets. On my home planet I never quite get enough to eat, and this," he sighed, and began stuffing his second mouth with food, "this is . . ." He stuttered a bit, realizing his error in attempting to feed two mouths at once, and began coughing. Si-s-s-s(click) dashed to his side and began smacking the various panels that made up the pyramid-shaped alien.

"Hotep," Si-s-s-s(click) said, vigorously beating the ambassador about his slanted sides, "s-s-stop being s-s-such a fool and keep one mouth clear for the investigator. Col. Schaeffer can't waste her time watching you make a pig of yourself. Now you behave!"

The coughing fit seemed to be over. Hotep caused his second mouth to vanish and then reappear; this cleared his system, and he began to speak again in his normal tone of voice. "I'm so sorry, Colonel, you must forgive me. But I'm not sure you understand what my world of Djoser is like. My home planet is sixth out from its sun, and we're at the very edge of the inhabitable belt. Since the energy levels—and food supplies—are very low, my people travel in tribal units across the face of our planet, eating plants and whatever insects we can find. Most of the time my mouth is on what you would consider the bottom of my body. Feet and a mouth are the only essentials. It's very difficult when you're on a low-energy diet and get so little radiation from your sun to do much more. I envy you people who are able to have arms and legs and noses and eyes and ears all at once—It's so nice to be able to take all that for granted. With this lamp and all this food, I can manifest as many of those things as I need, as often as I need them. You have no idea how pleasant it is not to feel hungry. . . ."

Elizabeth was starting to feel a little sorry for the creature, and she watched as Si-s-s-s(click)'s thumpings turned to sympathetic pats. But then the nature of the equation he had described made itself plain. The more energy went into his body, the more he would be able to manifest. . . .

She found herself switching rapidly from sympathy to deep suspicion. Hotep had just placed himself neatly on her list of suspects.

"Would you mind telling me, Your Excellency, what you know about the deaths of your three fellow ambassadors, and whether or not you have been visited by the Angel of Death?"

"Oh, about that Angel of Death nonsense," Hotep answered, "we don't have one. I mean, it's a very interesting concept and all, but my people have never indulged in that sort of mythic tradition. Granted, the subject was discussed on a philosophical level several centuries ago, but we decided that since death was a simple metabolic process, there was no need to glorify it. You have to understand that on Djoser we have a great deal of time to think; we specialize in philosophy and abstract mathematics, sociology, psychology . . . and in some ways we are advanced over other races, which are quick to deal with less abstract objects. I'm afraid I find the concept of an Angel of Death, or even a God who could send such an angel, to be extraordinarily primitive. If such a being were to visit me, I would probably manifest a mouth and laugh in its face."

"Even if it had the power to kill you?" Si-s-s-s(click) was clearly amazed by the little pyramid's reaction. "I assure you, if any being that called itself the Angel of Death appeared in *my* quarters, whether I believed in it or not, I would pay very close attention to anything it had to say. I may not believe in an Angel of Death either, but I most certainly believe in dying, and I don't intend to do it.

"Of course," he added swiftly, "the Angel of Death, whoever or whatever he is, isn't likely to visit me. I've been on the right side all along. I am in favor of the Romulan détente; it's the most splendid idea to come along since the Federation was founded. We won't have to s-s-spend so much money patrolling that s-s-silly Neutral Zone—and think of the opportunity it gives me to read Romulan literature! I'm sure to find some fascinating concepts there."

"Well, Hotep," Elizabeth said, "you must agree that Ambassador Si-s-s-s(click) has made a valid point—*two* ambassadors have been killed by whatever this being is, and even if you don't believe in him, you must have some belief in death itself."

"Oh yes, I believe I'm going to die, but death for my people is simply the result of a natural wearing-down of the tissues, nothing more. Of course it can be caused by a loss of energy, but I would find it odd that any being would attempt to frighten me into voting one way or another on this issue. It would have to force me to manifest ears to hear it or eyes to see it, and that's simply not possible; if I don't want to see the Angel of Death, I simply don't. As for the Romulan détente itself, I'm in the neutral camp simply because I don't care one way or the other. As I said earlier, my primary interest in this trip is energy."

He glanced lovingly up at the heatlamp, his eyes waving about on their long stalks. For a moment he pulled them back into the surface of his body, as if to protect them from the light; it seemed to be his equivalent of closing his eyelids. "Oh, it feels so good. So warm. That's why I'm here. Warmth and food. I don't really care about the détente. If there are enough people in favor of it, when it comes time to vote I'll vote with the majority. It's that simple. The Angel of Death has no interest in me."

"What about the deaths of your fellow ambassadors?" Elizabeth persisted. "Don't they mean anything to you?"

"Oh, I suppose it matters, to a certain extent. It's difficult for me to concern myself very much with the demise of creatures I have no particular interest in. Agnatha was decent enough but inclined to proselytize; I found him boring, and we had nothing whatsoever in common. As for Neko—Neko attempted to use me as a scratching post at our last ambassadorial conference. I had no fondness for Neko. The most I can say is that his death, in the abstract, gave me some slight satisfaction.

"No," he added after a moment, "I've been considering it. I don't think I would want Neko alive again, and should I find out who did kill him, I would recommend a medal or an award of some kind. Do you know that great hairy cat actually threatened to have me reshaped as a litterbox?"

"Oh, that was simply one of his jokes," Si-s-s-s-(click) said, snapping his jaws together two or three times in appreciation of a good jest. "He was always threatening to turn one or the other of us into something esoteric. His suggestion concerning myself was a matched set of luggage. I'll admit that my hide is a beautiful shade of blue and would make marvelous luggage—not that I was inclined to let him do it. But I thought it was an attractive way to end my days. Of course," he added swiftly, "when he threatened to remove Sarek's ears, that was going a little far. Sarek is a gentleman and does place a certain amount of pride in those elegant Vulcan appendages of his."

"That's something else I don't quite understand," Elizabeth said. "I noticed from listening to recordings of the détente meetings on Deck 4 that Neko referred to pointed ears a bit too often. He had pointed ears himself, and I don't understand the insult."

Hotep laughed with both mouths, spitting bits of

half-chewed fruit around him; Si-s-s-s(click) snapped his jaws together vigorously several times, a sort of booming sound coming from the general vicinity of his midriff. When the merriment had subsided, Si-s-s-s(click) tried between jaw snaps and diaphragmatic throbbing to explain what the joke had been.

"You s-s-see, it was because Neko had pointed ears that he so objected to them on humanoids. He felt that only cats and such beasts were entitled to pointed ears, and the fact that Vulcans took pride in such a silly matter infuriated him. He wasn't really insulting Sarek much at all. You know how these Vulcans are, nothing insults them. It was just one more thing for Neko to be mad about. All of us found it terribly amusing."

Hotep, to show his feelings on the matter, produced first a perfect pair of Vulcan ears and then, just below them, cat's ears, which looked almost exactly like Neko's. The comparison was ludicrous, and Elizabeth found herself giggling.

"But aren't you at all concerned that two ambassadors have died," she said. "I assure you I'm very concerned; it's my job."

"You keep mentioning *two* ambassadors," Hotep said. "Aren't you leaving out Naja, or are you, along with Captain Kirk and the doctors, insisting that was a natural death?"

"It was," Elizabeth answered. "I have no doubt of that. You have my word as an SSD agent that his death was not due to the being who calls himself the Angel of Death. Well, if you have nothing more to add, I think I had best continue my investigations elsewhere and leave you to your eating. I'm sorry to have disturbed you."

"Oh, it was no disturbance—but as you can see, I'm not involved in this. I was more than willing to give you the time, and especially since Si-s-s-s(click) told me how charming you were. He was quite right—you are. So good luck with the investigation—and if on your way out you should see one of those excellent crew people wandering about, ask him or her to please order more fruit for me. It's very difficult for me to get down from here and across the room to signal the food dispenser myself—the energy requirement is rather high."

"Well, I can solve that problem," Si-s-s-s(click) said. "I'll simply move your slab over across the room to the food dispenser, and that way you won't have any difficulty." Si-s-s-s(click) demonstrated by shoving the great flat structure with all his might, moving it a few centimeters. He grunted and pushed again, and was rewarded by seeing the slab move closer to the wall.

Elizabeth decided that Si-s-s-s(click) would be busy rearranging Hotep's room for at least an hour or two, and decided she wanted to go on to the next stage of the investigation without the ambassador's assistance. As rapidly as possible, but without avoiding any of the necessary protocol, she left Hotep's room and hurried down to the medical labs in search of Dr. Rigel.

Dr. Rigel was in the pathology lab, studying a series of slides. Elizabeth recognized the slides as being tissue samples from Agnatha and Neko.

"Nothing," Dr. Rigel said, looking up from the microscope. "Absolutely nothing. It's getting very frustrating."

"I've got something that might give you a new train of thought," Elizabeth said. "I've been talking to Hotep, and he was telling me about the equation his people live by: energy converted into activity. I was beginning to wonder how much energy it would take for Hotep to manifest himself as the Angel of Death."

Dr. Rigel looked at a blank wall beyond her lab counter for a moment. "If I were Mr. Spock, I could work that out in my head—but since I'm not Spock, let's let the computer handle it." She climbed down from her lab stool over to the pathology computer bank. Muttering to herself, she punched in the figures relating to the biology of polymorphites like Hotep. The computer began chattering back at her, spitting out a series of numbers. Rigel nodded, again addressed the computer with another column of figures, and waited. In a few minutes the computer signaled with a single figure. Ruth nodded, turned the computer off, and returned to face Col. Schaeffer.

"It isn't possible. The energy necessary to change Hotep into the creature Spiracles described would take the entire energy output of the *Enterprise*'s main drive system, and a little more. It would have been such a massive power drain on this ship that every life-support system would have gone out and we would have been blacked out while the Angel was talking to Spiracles. Sorry, Colonel, it's a good theory, but it won't wash."

Elizabeth sighed, realizing that this was another blind alley. This was becoming the most frustrating case she'd ever had to deal with, and she knew she was getting exactly nowhere. "Well, so much for that; back to square one. You know, Ruth, if this continues and I keep running into blind alleys, I'm going to look up the Angel of Death myself. It's either that or cutting my wrists."

"Now you know how I feel," Ruth laughed. "Frustration seems to be the name of the game around here. Go talk to Captain Kirk; I'm sure he'll think of something. He generally manages to solve every problem in one way or another."

"You mean he's already got a solution for this case?" Elizabeth asked eagerly. "I wish someone would have told me, I could have saved myself a lot of time."

"Oh, not a solution for the case, mind you, but he might suggest some diversion or another—something to take your mind off the subject for a while."

Ruth studied the black-clad investigator for a moment, her large eyes pensive. "There are a great number of women who consider a tête-à-tête with the captain to be the answer to a lot of things. Go talk to him—have dinner, relax. You'll find it rather comforting to be reminded that you're an attractive, desirable woman—and if nothing else, the flirtation is fun."

She laughed at the absurdity of her own suggestion. "Don't mind me—as I said, the frustration around here is hitting hard. But consider the suggestion, for whatever it's worth."

"Thank you. I may. And—I'll do what I can about the frustration level on this case as quickly as possible. Let's make a race of it, Ruth—see who has the lower frustration level, the *Enterprise*'s veterinary officer or the SSD colonel."

Elizabeth found after some consideration that the idea of dinner with Captain Kirk was probably a good one, whatever Dr. Rigel's motives might have been. She found the Captain in his quarters, finishing up some fuel allotment records. "Thank goodness," he said, looking up and smiling. "An angel of mercy to rescue me from the bureaucratic red tape. Am I glad to see you!"

"Jim, I'd really prefer you didn't use the term 'angel' in any connection whatsoever around me. I'm fed up to the gills with the whole subject."

"Well, my poor downtrodden colonel, sit over here and tell Daddy all about it."

"A father figure was not exactly what I had in mind. It was suggested to me that dinner with you and a refined flirtation might help me a bit. I was just checking to see whether you were interested in the suggestion."

"Dinner? Refined flirtation? I like the suggestion of the dinner and the flirtation, but the refinement aspect bothers me a bit. Well, if it's your wish, I'll do my best to be as refined as possible. I'll even start dragging out my S's like Si-s-s-s(click) does, if that'll amuse you. By the way, who made the suggestion? Dr. McCoy?"

"No, oddly enough it was Dr. Rigel. I'm not sure why she did it, but I've found that woman to be extraordinarily intelligent. Since she made the suggestion, there must have been a reason, and I thought it would be a good idea to follow through. I don't know what the Department would make of my taking psychiatric advice from a vet, but since at the moment my competence in this case makes me feel I have less intelligence than a billberry bush, I might as well listen to a vet, since the *Enterprise* is lacking a horticulturist."

Kirk laughed and began putting away his papers. "Well, whatever you need, a good stiff drink and dinner can't hurt."

The dinner did indeed prove to be a help; Captain Kirk was at his most charming, making silly little flirtatious remarks all through the meal, making sure she was comfortable, soothing and relaxing Elizabeth. The more she saw of this man, the more she liked him. She couldn't help comparing him with Alexis. There had been very little satisfaction from the two conversations she'd had with her husband. Now, here was James Kirk—handsome, charming, considerate, intelligent, and a great number of other things she liked in a man. She knew she was well on the way to falling in love with him; all it would take was one more nasty conversation with Alexis, and her marriage would to all intents and purposes be over.

She found herself eyeing the Captain speculatively over her after-dinner glass of cream sherry. He was a very attractive man. She had never, in the ten years of her marriage, allowed another emotional involvement to come between Alexis and herself—but this was one man who might make an emotional involvement worthwhile. Her only concern was, would it be fair to Alexis?

"Well, Captain," she said, looking down at the sherry glass, "this has been an excellent dinner, I've enjoyed every minute of it—and Dr. Rigel's prescription was right on the mark. I'll have to congratulate her on her perspicacity. And now I suspect I really ought to leave."

She glanced at his bed and then looked away. She would find no answers to her problems there, only one more difficulty to add to her life. Regretfully, she knew she would not be joining the Captain between-the-sheets for dessert. She could not do that much damage to her marriage vows. The tension in the room was such that if she stayed, it would be Kirk's bed for sure.

19

The next day, Elizabeth, with Si-s-s-s(click) in tow, continued her interrogation of the neutral ambassadors. Edentata, the giant armadillo, proved to be of little assistance. He had quickly realized it was best to vote on the side of the Romulan détente; he wanted nothing to do with the Angel of Death.

Edentata was calm about the situation and even a little unconcerned. He pointed out that in the long run such a détente was probably only a temporary situation, and whichever way his vote went was unimportant. His life had a great deal more value. Elizabeth found herself forced to agree with the armor-plated creature.

Her next interview, with Ambassador Damu, proved to be a bit more helpful. Damu greeted her in his quarters wearing a magnificent black cape lined in red satin.

"I had that one made for *me*," Si-s-s-s(click) announced in a loud stage whisper. "That was when I was in my romantic period. But I do think it's more becoming on Damu than it ever was on my back. Red and black are simply not my colors."

Ambassador Damu grinned at the comment and remarked, "I quite agree with you, Si-s-s-s(click), but I do not think Captain Kirk finds the cape reassuring. He has been infected in his childhood with certain Terran fairy tales concerning bloodsucking creatures called 'vampires.' Because the people of my planet do drink blood, and because of my appearance, he is more than slightly convinced that I am such a vampire. It's an excellent example of what a bad upbringing can do to a child. I make him nervous, and I'm quite sorry about it, since I admire and respect him."

"I can understand his problem," Elizabeth said. "While I am of mixed blood, I was raised on a lot of those same legends, and I must admit that, were I to meet you on a moonless night, I would have a qualm or two."

Damu smiled, showing his perfect, even white teeth. "Yes, but you and I alone on a moonless night would find more pleasant things to do than biting one another's necks. Now, I assume you are here for more than a social visit or a discussion of my people's customs—you want to know about the murders. I'm afraid I can be of little help. I have not yet decided what I will do as regards my vote. The Angel of Death is a terrifying possibility; I don't relish finding such a creature in my quarters. It's entirely possible that he would resemble Captain Kirk's vampire—and I, too, would fear such a creature."

"But then, wouldn't you consider it s-s-safer to vote with the rest of usss?" Si-s-s-s(click) asked. "You realize that by stubbornly remaining neutral, you do invite his presence."

"I don't agree, my friend," Damu said. "You see, from all indications the neutral ambassadors have been given warning; this Angel of Death has at least had the courtesy to state his intentions. It is only those who have been violently opposed who have been killed outright. My position is still that of a neutral. Were I to receive a visit from the Angel of Death, I could not guarantee that I would remain neutral; but for the moment, such is my position."

Elizabeth studied the tall, elegant humanoid and then said, "But aren't you worried about even a visitation? You're taking a considerable risk."

"Oh yes, I am aware of the risk. My people are prone to take risks, and I dislike someone attempting to change my opinion by force. It annoys me. Until I am required to take another position, I shall remain as I am."

"And will you inform me if you receive a visit from the Angel of Death? I need to know that—please don't keep it a secret."

Damu bowed gravely. "You will be the very first person I will tell. From all indications, the Angel of Death gives but one warning."

Elizabeth had decided to let the interviews with those ambassadors in favor of the détente wait until after lunch. She would spend the intervening time in her cabin studying the profiles on the pro-Romulan ambassadors. She was looking for some clue in their backgrounds to point to one or more of them being behind this mystery, since they had the most to gain from the assassinations. She sent Si-s-s-s(click) off to arrange the interviews and settled down to a long, arduous study of the material in the computer banks. She was attempting to correlate what material she had on the "pro" ambassadors with the *modus operandi* of the Angel of Death, when she heard her door chime.

"Enter," she said, not looking up from the data bank she was studying.

"Do you know you're going to get a permanent curve in your back, and dowager's hump, if you keep bending over a computer like that," Captain Kirk said, coming up behind her to place one hand gently on her shoulder. "I came to see if you wanted some company for lunch. That is, company other than a stack of computer slabs."

"I'd be delighted. I haven't managed to get very far with the computer data anyway. This whole case has not been particularly satisfying to me. Jim—I've never seen so many blind alleys in my life. I almost feel like ripping my black tunic to shreds and jumping up and down on it."

"Certainly it can't be *that* bad. The great Elizabeth Schaeffer admitting failure?" Kirk laughed and went over to the food selector panel. "How does a tuna salad sandwich sound, with a cup of very strong hot tea?"

"It sounds excellent, as long as you stay and share it with me."

Kirk carried the tray back to the table, and for a few moments there was only the sound of munching and tea sipping. There was something quietly relaxing about so homey an action. It made Elizabeth realize how few meals she had shared with Alexis. In fact, it made her realize how little of anything she had shared with Alexis, other than his bed. She noted that there had been no calls from Détente One, which probably meant her husband was still sulking. She looked across the table at Captain Kirk and found herself comparing him to Alexis. They were both equally handsome, adventuresome, daring, brave men, but she was beginning to realize that James Kirk was a man, and Alexis Schaeffer was, and always would be, a boy. It was not something she found easy to consider.

She had barely finished her sandwich and tea when the door chimed. It was Si-s-s-s(click), coming to announce he'd lined up the interviews she'd requested with Sarek, Telson, Karhu, and Sirenia.

"Well, Captain, duty calls. The lunch was excellent, and I thank you for it. I might add the company was excellent, too."

Kirk rose to his feet and smiled at her. "I enjoyed it as much as you did. Whenever you have two consecutive minutes to rub together, there's something I want to talk to you about. I think there are some important things we need to discuss—you know what I mean."

Elizabeth nodded. "I'll make time for that discussion, Jim—but not now. Let it be for just a little while. I have work to do."

"I would never consider keeping you from your job, Elizabeth. I realize how important the SSD is to you, and I would never ask you to put my needs ahead of theirs."

Elizabeth left her cabin with Si-s-s-s(click), knowing Captain Kirk had said something, without even realizing it, that had damned all chances of continuing her relationship with Alexis. She knew James Kirk was telling the truth when he said he would not force her to place his needs ahead of Special Security's.

Si-s-s-s(click) had decided Elizabeth should see Sarek first. The large Gavialian was very disturbed by his Vulcan colleague's behavior; he realized there was something wrong that he did not fully understand.

They found Sarek alone in his cabin, lying on his bed, staring at the ceiling. His body looked shrunken, smaller; his face had a pinched quality. At first Elizabeth thought he was ill, and then realized he was suffering from something far deeper than a mere physical disturbance.

"Sir, do you wish to speak to me alone, or do you want Si-s-s-s(click) here with me?"

Sarek turned his head on the pillow to stare at the two of them. "I mean no disrespect, Si-s-s-s(click); you know, my friend, how long we've worked together. But with your kind permission I would speak to Col. Schaeffer alone. I profoundly regret any embarrassment I may cause you, but I do this out of my need as a Vulcan."

Si-s-s-s(click) bowed deeply, a gesture of profound respect to the senior ambassador. "I would never question your wishes, S-s-sarek. I'll go and take tea with Telson and Karhu. Col. Schaeffer may join me whenever she's ready." He bowed deeply again, turned and left the room.

Elizabeth waited until the Gavialian had left and then pulled a seat up beside the Vulcan's bed. "This has disturbed you, sir, far more than is required," she said, utilizing a formal tone of voice that she knew the Vulcan preferred. "If you have no bodily ill, you are behaving in a manner I find inexplicable. Would you care to give me some explanation? The one that occurs to me is not pleasant."

"Do you suspect me of being Death's Angel? I am not, but I hold myself responsible for his activity. I gave Captain Kirk my word that nothing would go wrong on this venture, and I have proved myself incapable of controlling the situation. I am deeply shamed; my vow as a Vulcan is broken. My word is valueless."

Elizabeth leaned forward, gathering her energies to

deal with this man. "Sarek of Vulcan, son of an ancient line, you are a fool."

Sarek stared at her, shocked, then rose on his elbow, saying, "How dare you address me in such a manner? How dare you make such an accusation? By what right do you call me 'fool'?"

"Because your knowledge of logic and your belief in that logic is going to waste. You are like a mewling child cooped up here in your room, covering yourself with a guilt that is not yours. Guilt is an emotion, Vulcan, and you are displaying guilt. Your vow to Captain Kirk was worthless when you gave it. You have no control over the destinies of your fellow beings; you had no right to make such a vow, and you are a fool to have done it. I could forgive you the folly of making the vow. What I cannot forgive is your wallowing in self-pity and guilt, two things despicable in a Vulcan."

Sarek lay back on the bed and closed his eyes. "You do not understand, Colonel. I journeyed to a diplomatic meeting on board this ship once before, and there was death and destruction and damage, and I caused Captain Kirk a great deal of embarrassment. I did not wish anything of that nature to occur again. Yet my best efforts have been insufficient to prevent it. There has been death and destruction again on board this ship, and again a good man, my son's commander, is placed in a position that is difficult for him."

"Unless you admit to being the Angel of Death, sir, your presence aboard this vessel has little or nothing to do with the occurrences we're discussing. I will only accept your guilt if you tell me you *are* that angel. And since you've said you're not, I shall expect you to get out of bed and get back to work as the leader of this delegation. Or are you too old and feeble to continue the job you've been given?"

"Perhaps you're right. Perhaps I am too feeble. I should have retired years ago. But this détente was so important to me—it was a major coup. I felt the Romulan détente was the best possible diplomatic action to end my career. I could go into my retirement content with what I have done with my life. And now I see that work in a shambles. The legend of the Angel of Death is already spreading to the other ships; votes are being altered because of it. There will be little or no honesty at the détente meeting, only fear and terror and suspicion. There are many of my fellow ambassadors who believe that the Romulans are behind this. I am inclined to take that attitude myself, though I cannot understand how they have managed it. Have you any answers for that, Colonel?"

"No, I can't prove the Romulans are doing it, but at the same time I can't prove that they aren't. I believe it's someone on this ship who cares a great deal about the outcome of this meeting. And I don't think he, she, or it is a Romulan. I've dealt with them before; they are an honorable race. Now if it were a Klingon—a Klingon is capable of anything. But this, this smacks of dishonor, and I have never known a dishonorable Romulan."

Sarek nodded quietly. "I agree, Col. Schaeffer. This is not the act of an honorable man. And the Romulans are honorable. Therefore we must look for our murderer here among us. I would almost prefer for it to be a Romulan; if it turns out to be one of my fellow ambassadors, it will damage the Federation a great deal; it will damage this meeting, and I am not sure any of us will recover easily from it."

Elizabeth rose to her feet. "I quite agree with you, sir, this isn't something we will recover from easily—particularly Agnatha and Neko. They won't recover at all."

20

When Elizabeth joined Si-s-s-s(click), Telson, and Karhu, the tea party was progressing as if Lewis Carroll had written the script. Telson, the lobsterlike ambassador, was lying full length on the floor because he could not remain upright. Si-s-s-s(click) and Karhu were both seated at the table, and Karhu was casually resting his feet on the back of the large yellow Manteigan ambassador. Telson was not objecting to being used as a footstool, but the sight was ludicrous.

Elizabeth accepted a cup of tea and a plate of cookies from Si-s-s-s(click). She had a choice of sitting on the bed, somewhat removed from the center of conversation, or taking her place on the floor with Telson. Neither Si-s-s-s(click) nor Karhu seemed to have heard of the custom of rising to give a seat to a lady.

Elizabeth found a section of floor close enough to the table to carry on a conversation, yet reasonably out of range of Telson's enormous claws. She did not wish to be impolite to the ambassador, but she knew that he was capable of snapping off an arm or leg with a single stroke of those sharp-bladed limbs.

The tea was excellent, and Karhu took credit for brewing it. It had a faint spicy scent, very similar to eucalyptus. The cakes were small and quite sweet. They were obviously alien, and not from the *Enterprise*'s standard food processing equipment. Elizabeth ate them with relish and refrained from asking their exact composition. She had learned through long experience that it was often unwise to ask precisely what an alien meal was composed of.

"I'm sure Si-s-s-s(click) has kept you informed of my investigation," Elizabeth said, "and I have to admit I'm not having much luck. At the moment the ambassadors in favor of détente are the best suspects, which includes all of you. So if any of you have slipped arsenic into the tea, I'm in serious trouble."

Si-s-s-s(click) snapped his jaws two or three times, and Karhu giggled. Telson wiggled his antennae, his equivalent of a chuckle.

"Don't worry," Telson said in his high-pitched, somewhat tinny voice. "Even if any or all of us were guilty, we would have to do ourselves up as the Angel of Death first, remember? And I don't think the Angel of Death comes to tea parties."

"Speaking of tea," Karhu rumbled, "would you care for a refill?"

Elizabeth held out her empty cup, and the marsupial filled it carefully. It gave her a chance to study him. She realized that his aura of sweet, cuddly lovableness was about as real as her own ability to project likeability. She took a deep breath, checking the air for pheromones. She could smell the sea-scent of Telson, the faintly leathery odor of Si-s-s-s(click), but Karhu gave out only a sharp odor of eucalyptus leaves.

She listened with half an ear to the conversation, most of it consisting of commentary on their fellow ambassadors; while some of it bordered on the slanderous, none of it was truly helpful. She was at the Mad Hatter's tea party, and it was going to be just about as useful to her.

"I notice the absence of Ambassador Sirenia," she said. "Doesn't she drink tea? Or didn't you include her in this rather exclusive gathering?"

Si-s-s-s(click) looked across the table at Karhu; the furry ambassador ducked his head slightly, looking into his teacup as if to find the answer there. "Well, it appears I will have to explain it," Telson said. "Sirenia is in mourning for Agnatha; she loved him, you see. We try not to talk about it. It was an embarrassing subject; although both of them were amphibians, still there was a problem of miscegenation. Her people would not have approved of the relationship. She was planning—that is, how can I explain it?—spawning?"

Elizabeth nodded. "I think I understand what you're saying. I understand your reluctance to discuss it. Don't worry, it won't go in my official report; it's not applicable. It's unlikely she would have killed him, and whoever killed Agnatha probably killed Neko as well."

"But Neko deserved to die," Telson said. "I could in the space of five minutes think of at least a hundred good reasons for him to die. I don't think you'll find anyone in the Federation grieving for Neko."

"Not even his own people?" Elizabeth was surprised; this was an aspect of the situation that was entirely new to her.

Karhu giggled deep in his round fat belly. "Why do you think they made him an ambassador? They wanted to get him off the planet! Even on Gyuunyuu Neko was known as a troublemaker. The ambassadorship is a very polite way of making someone into a remittance man. Essentially what his people were saying was, 'Go away, bother someone else, and *stay* away!' "

"I'm told that all three of you have had your share of run-ins with Neko. What about the possibility of any of you killing him?"

"Oh, I had to discipline Neko more than once," Karhu answered. "In fact we had a quarrel at the ambassador's reception before we even came on board the *Enterprise*. But fear was an adequate weapon to use on Neko, and he was afraid of all three of us. Telson almost severed his tail last year, and Si-s-s-s(click) bit him on the ear at our last major ambassadorial get-together. As for myself, I was fond of picking him up and giving him a good shaking, but that was as far as it went." Karhu smiled, revealing rather sharp teeth for a vegetarian. "Mind you, had it gotten too far out of hand and Neko done a little more than the minor claw-sharpening he had been involved in, I might have found it necessary to inflict a certain amount of damage on him—but he knew better than to go beyond a certain point. Besides, you must take into account that whoever killed Neko also killed Agnatha, and we three are all in agreement that Agnatha was a perfectly acceptable sort. We didn't like his politics, but we were fond enough of him personally. Your case falls apart, my dear Colonel, if as you insist both ambassadors were killed by the same person. We three are innocent."

"So you're all innocent because you say you're innocent? I have Sarek's word as a Vulcan that he is not responsible, and I put a great deal of trust in the word of a Vulcan. But I'm not inclined to put a great deal of trust in the silly go-round you three have been giving me. I don't like it; you're trying to keep me from suspecting any of you, and I don't know whether it's because you're all guilty or because you're all so totally ludicrous."

She paused for a moment, studying each ambassador carefully. "It's an excellent act. Si-s-s-s(click) running around acting like a buffoon in one costume or another, Telson lying there so close to the ground and difficult to notice, and you, you great shaggy beast," she said to Karhu, "playing at sweetness and light, pretending you're swacked out of your mind on Hunaja-grown leaves. Oh, it's a marvelous act, and I've appreciated every minute of it, but I recognize it for what it is. Shall I applaud now or later?"

The three ambassadors looked as sheepish as each one was capable of appearing, given their varied countenances. "Gentlemen, I think we've been found out," Karhu said. "I don't suppose it would do me any good to go all sleepy and languid? I'm very good at it, you know."

"No, it wouldn't do you the slightest bit of good. You have everyone on this ship convinced how sweet and cuddly you are. In fact, I'm told you gave orders that no one was to refer to you as cute. It was an interesting bit of psychology; naturally when told not to think of you as cute, everyone would."

Karhu laughed. "They do make these SSD agents intelligent! But if you'd like, my dear," he beamed at her, "you can call me cute; I hereby give you permission."

Elizabeth studied the furry behemoth without the slightest trace of a smile on her face. "No, sir, I would not call you cute. You are entirely too shrewd and too dangerous to ever be considered cute."

Karhu nodded and reached for the teapot and teacup. "But you see, that's why I made the offer." He poured himself another cup of tea. "I knew you wouldn't take me up on it. My reputation for cuteness remains intact."

Elizabeth left the tea party when it was still in full swing. She felt that it had been a total waste of her time; no one was going to tell her anything, and there was the possibility that all three were as guilty as sin. She'd have to wait for one of them to slip up and tell her what he knew of Death's Angel. Until then, all of them were suspects and to be viewed as such. Si-s-s-s(click), for all his posturing, was obviously their leader, and therefore the one to watch most closely.

She now had Ambassador Sirenia to interview, and Elizabeth knew that would be less than pleasant. She found the woman alone in her quarters, singing sadly of the glories of Agnatha, daring Elizabeth to comment. Sirenia was in no mood for any kind of discussion, but she did acknowledge Elizabeth's right to question her. She sat on her bed, waiting as if for martyrdom, while Elizabeth sat down across from her.

"I am not here to discuss your relationship with Agnatha," Elizabeth began. "It is not my concern, so put yourself at ease. I have no intention of prying into your private life. The only thing I want to know is, did you sense anything suspicious about his death? I'm told you were the one who demanded an investigation long before it was established that Agnatha was murdered."

"I knew it was no accident," Sirenia said. There was the sound of unshed tears in her voice. "He had no reason to die, and he was a courageous male. I know they tried to say it was suicide, but I don't believe it. Someone killed him, and I want that someone. I have songs of mourning that I have sung, but there are songs of vengeance yet to sing."

"What were Agnatha's beliefs about an Angel of Death? Did his people believe in such a being?"

Sirenia nodded. "Oh yes. The Angel of Death is a persistent legend; most races believe in that being. My people view it as the great devourer, Leviathan—that which eats its own young. Agnatha saw it as the Depths, the depths of the sea so dark that only the flickering lamps of luminescent fish marked its path. Death was sinking further and further down into the depths, and the Angel of Death was darkness—all-encompassing darkness and pressure. Whatever was in that room with him caused the pressure in his tank to increase. Agnatha's struggles were an attempt to somehow relieve that pressure."

"But did he believe in a being, a *creature* that was the Angel of Death?"

"Can you consider darkness and pressure a creature? If you can, then yes, Agnatha believed in the Angel of Death. If that is what killed him, I could understand his thrashing about in the tank. But he did not break the walls—it was the pressure, something pushing down on that tank so hard that Agnatha knew death was the only result. The only conclusions I can come to, if what Cdr. Scott said was true and the tank was broken from the inside—then yes, the Angel of Death did come for Agnatha."

"And do you seriously expect me to catch this Angel of Death? I feel like I'm fighting the fog, and on my home world that's almost as unpleasant as pressure or darkness. I was hoping you could help me, but it appears you have no more information for me than anyone else."

"No, I can't help you with any information as to what killed Agnatha. But I can report on something that was rather odd. Captain Kirk—who really is a very nice man—propositioned me. I refused him, and that night when I went to Agnatha's room, I noticed the Captain following me. But when he saw where I was going, he turned and walked away. I don't think that's very much help. Captain Kirk is not the sort of man who would kill over a woman. There have been too many women in his life for one more to matter."

Elizabeth stored the small fragment of information away and found herself feeling somewhat uneasy with Sirenia's description of the Captain as a man who would not find any one woman that important.

Elizabeth returned to her cabin intending to study the case further. But as she approached her quarters, she sensed that they were not empty. The door was slightly ajar. She moved slowly toward the room, wondering just who might pay an unannounced call. She drew her phaser from the back of her belt and slipped swiftly through the narrow opening in the door.

Si-s-s-s(click) was sitting at the table, calmly reading her reports on the Angel of Death.

"Do you generally enter an officer's room without knocking?" She held the phaser on him for a few seconds and then put it back in her belt clip.

"I did knock, but there was no one here, so I decided to come in." He stacked the information slabs back in place. "I hope you don't mind, but you did agree I could help with this case, and I must admit it's quite a tangle. I doubt even the great Sherlock Holmes could do anything with it. I believe, Colonel, that we are at a standstill."

"You, my friend, might be at a standstill, but I'm not. I have a motto to live up to—I must solve my case. The SSD expects nothing less of me. Now if you don't mind, I'm going to get some dinner and go through those reports."

"Oh, I don't mind at all, and you go ahead and have dinner and deal with these reports if you wish. I'd have dinner with you, but my eating habits are such that I'm told most humanoids find them unpleasant. What I would suggest is that after you finish these reports, come over to my quarters and we'll sit around and talk about them, and see what the two of us can discover. Perhaps an analysis in depth would do some good—and perhaps while we are analyzing we might indulge in assorted alcoholic libations. It's amazing what alcohol can do for the mind."

"Generally the only thing alcohol does for me is

make me sodden drunk, and I don't think that's very helpful."

Si-s-s-s(click) smiled, displaying all his teeth. "I use the word 'alcohol' in a generic sense. There are many fascinating fluids that beings around the Galaxy pour into themselves to produce interesting effects. Most of them are mind-altering in one way or another. What I suggest is that you and I sample a great number of them and go over these reports and see if something falls into place. If nothing helps, at least we will have enjoyed an interesting evening in each other's company. You s-s-see," he said as he stood up and moved toward her, "I find you very attractive, Elizabeth. Easily the most attractive humanoid woman I've ever met, and that's very unusual. While I do playact rather well, I think my romantic mode was one of my best. I find most humanoid women to be a bit on the repulsive side—all pink and squishy and soft, and no jaws to speak of. Yet I do like you, as a person, and so all I'm suggesting is that we get ripsnorting drunk together, baby. We can't do anything else; anatomically it would be very difficult."

Elizabeth grinned and nodded acceptance. It might give her the opportunity to discover whether Si-s-s-s(click) was involved in a conspiracy with his fellow pro-Romulan ambassadors. Liquor was known to make the tongue quicker. "Would you mind telling me what mode you're about to go into? You've shed the Sherlock Holmes, and this isn't the Three Musketeers. What have you been reading, Si-s-s-s(click)?"

He tilted his head to one side and said, "Dashiell Hammett, sweetheart. Wanna help me look for the Maltese Falcon? When we meet later this evening, I'll have myself a gray fedora, and you can call me Sam Spade."

Si-s-s-s(click) was true to his promise. When he let her into his room he was wearing a battered blue trenchcoat and a sweatstained gray fedora. There was a large array of bottles of various shapes and styles littering the top of the table in his room, and he had managed to acquire from somewhere a couple of shot glasses.

"Well, sweetheart," he said, trying with difficulty to talk out of the corner of his mouth, "are you ready to tie one on?"

Elizabeth was no more familiar with the works of Dashiell Hammett than she was with A. Conan Doyle. She gathered that it was some sort of detective fiction, and definitely not Victorian. The outfit Si-s-s-s(click) had adopted appeared to be Twentieth Century Earth, and she was not sure what was expected of her in the game. Deciding to avoid role-playing altogether, she took her place at the table and held up one of the shot glasses.

"My training in the SSD has made me acutely aware of details, and one detail I am aware of at the moment is that this glass is empty. Are you going to do something about it?"

Si-s-s-s(click) hurried to pour out a rich amber fluid that Elizabeth recognized as Saurian brandy. The shot glasses were inappropriate for the beverage but served to assist the two of them in emptying the bottle. Si-s-s-s(click) shook the oddly shaped jug hopefully, realized it was empty, and tossed it over one shoulder into the corner, where it shattered on the floor. He reached for another bottle labeled in a script that neither he nor Elizabeth could read, and the fluid inside proved to be a deep purple and tasted strongly of blackberries. It was rather pleasant. The bottle was swiftly emptied, and Si-s-s-s(click) repeated his over-the-shoulder-and-onto-the-floor gesture.

Four bottles later, Elizabeth was beginning to realize that she would have trouble matching the ambassador drink for drink. "I think . . . I've about . . . reached my limit," she said very slowly, being careful of the pronunciation of each word. "One more drink . . . and I'm going to fall over, and that would be very embarrassing . . . both for me and my uniform. . . ."

"Oh, but there's one thing you've got to try." Si-s-s-s(click) was in as poor a shape as Elizabeth. "It's s-s-something s-s-s-s-special. I was s-s-saving it for lassst. It comes from my home planet, and we drink it only with clossse friends. And you're a clossse friend, Lizzie. I'm going to drink it with you."

He moved an unsteady hand through the conglomeration of bottles until his claws closed around a small brass flagon about the size of a perfume bottle. He pulled it toward him, stared at it, lifting it first to one eye and then to the other. "Thisss is the s-s-stuff. It's good s-s-stuff, and I want to share it with you, because I like you."

He took her shot glass and very carefully poured into it a fluid that was colorless, yet had all colors; it shimmered in the light of the ceiling panels and gave back a light of its own. One moment it appeared to be mercury floating in the glass, the next a clear transparent fluid in which a rainbow floated. Si-s-s-s(click) gravely handed her the glass and then filled his own. He signaled for her to wait before tasting it, and then lifted his own glass in a toast.

"I give you illusion," he intoned. "I give you dreams. I give you the s-s-stuff of which magic is made. To all our illusions." He ended the toast by tossing back the contents of the shot glass, and Elizabeth copied the gesture.

The fluid felt as strange as it looked. It was cold, then hot; it was thick, then thin; it flowed down her throat as if it were alive and crawling toward her belly with a tickling sensation. It was easily the oddest substance Elizabeth had ever voluntarily ingested.

She knew she was very drunk; she had consumed more alcohol in this one evening than she had previously consumed in months. But then she began to realize just how drunk she really was. Si-s-s-s(click) appeared to waver and shimmer in the air. He too began to take on strange colors and consistencies, and then with mounting horror she realized she was sitting across from a large pink hairy worm that towered over her, a being that bore no physical resemblance to Si-s-s-s(click).

There was absolute quiet in the room, and she could feel a slow chill traveling up her spine. The Angel of Death—could it be this creature?

As she watched the pink hairy worm coalesced into

a multicolored crystalline structure, its facets gleaming like ice.

"That's very pretty, Si-s-s-s(click)," she said slowly, wondering when he was going to turn into the black-robed woman who was her herald of death. "I didn't know you could do anything like that. It's really very interesting."

Her voice was slow, but not from the effects of the alcohol. She realized that she had never been so sober in her life—and that her life might be about to end very swiftly. Si-s-s-s(click)—dear, sweet Si-s-s-s(click) was a shapechanger.

21

Elizabeth reached slowly down into one boot to remove her SSD special-action phaser. An attempt to kill the Angel of Death might not be easy, but she was fairly sure she could kill Si-s-s-s(click). There he was, corporeal, visible and, though looking a bit peculiar as he changed shape again, still obviously Si-s-s-s(click).

"What is this odd little substance?" she asked him. "It's having a peculiar effect on my mind."

"Yesss, isn't it marvelousss?" the large blue bat remarked. "It's not entirely legal at home, which is why you share it only with friends, but it makes the imagination come to life. It produces magnificent imagery. My world is so dull; something like the illusion fluid is a necesssssity."

The great blue bat reshaped itself into something vaguely humanoid, but still bright blue. "Of course, what I'm waiting for," the blue humanoid said with a leer, "is for you to start looking like a Gavialian. I think that would be very interesting. Much as I like you, Elizabeth, I couldn't quite cope with all that pink softness."

She had eased the phaser onto her lap, and had set it on kill. She looked up at the blue humanoid and realized that Si-s-s-s(click) was attempting to look as much like Captain Kirk as possible. "Do you mean you did this simply for purposes of *seduction*? This is a visual illusion, I assume—I mean, you're still Si-s-s-s(click) and I'm still Elizabeth, and no matter which shape you took it would still leave us with the anatomical problems you mentioned earlier."

A thought was filtering through her chemical-sodden brain. He *was* Si-s-s-s(click) and she *was* Elizabeth, and never once during the experience had she lost track of that. That fact was important, it meant something; she had to hold onto it somehow. She realized that the being across from her was losing his blue tinge, and his eyes were turning to a very familiar hazel.

"Yesss," Si-s-s-s(click) admitted, "it is only a visual illusion. But I would try to be very careful, and it might be fun, you know. Don't look at it with a closed mind. Who knows? We might discover something new in the annals of biology."

Elizabeth slowly lifted the phaser up onto the tabletop, its blue-black shell glimmering coldly in the overhead light. "Do you know what this is, Si-s-s-s(click)? It's a weapon with twice the speed of the average phaser. It's a weapon capable of splattering you to atoms, and I've been thinking about that for the past few minutes. You've come very close to meeting death here in this room. I almost was, and still might be, *your* Angel of Death. Anyone capable of appearing in so many varied guises might be the murderer I'm looking for.

"There's only one thing saving your life, and that's the fact that I *know* you're Si-s-s-s(click)—but I don't know whether Agnatha and Neko knew you were Si-s-s-s(click). It makes for an interesting problem. This scale of justice on my uniform gives me the right to be judge, jury, and executioner. I could kill you right now and no one would question my judgment—no one but myself. But because I know you are Si-s-s-s(click), I'm not inclined to believe you were what Neko and Agnatha saw, and I'm positive you're not what Naja saw. Naja would have recognized you. He wouldn't have been fooled."

An expression of dismay crossed the face of the pseudo-Kirk. There was a rapid shimmer, and he again formed himself into Si-s-s-s(click). The transformation was not complete—he was still quite pinkish in spots, and his eyes were very much those of the captain of the *Enterprise*. "You know, I really should be very angry with you for suspecting me. I was only trying to share a marvelous experience with a friend—or someone I felt was a friend—and you sat there with a weapon on me! You were going to kill me, Elizabeth! I'm hurt, I really am cut to the quick! I gave you something precious to me, and in return you've given me suspicion and fear. It hurts, it really hurts. . . ." Si-s-s-s(click)'s head fell forward on the table, and a soft snore escaped from his jaws. He had retreated from the situation in the best possible way, by going to sleep.

Elizabeth looked at him and felt a mixture of pity and self-hatred. If what Si-s-s-s(click) had said was true, and he was merely trying to share a pleasurable experience with her, she had wronged him and he had every right to be angry. But at the same time, she must continue to think as an agent of the SSD. She would deal with his anger later. Neither of them was in any shape for a fight.

She pulled herself slowly to her feet; it was not easy. The hallucinogen was wearing off, but the full effect of the alcohol she had consumed was hitting her hard. She moved carefully around the table, clutching the rim of it, and when she stood beside the now loudly snoring body of the Gavialian, she reached out to gently stroke his eye ridges.

"I'm sorry, my friend. I am sorry. There are so many things required of me in my job, and most of them do not allow friendship. Caring, affection, even love, are all suspect, and I can't help it." She patted him gently on the top of his head, not at all sure how much of what she'd said had penetrated.

She tried to lift his inert body out of the seat, but found it impossible. He would have to spend the night with his head on the table, snoring. She turned to study the room, looking for something to wrap around him to keep off the chill he would feel as his body temperature dropped. His Inverness cape lay crumpled in one corner of the room. She made her way toward it, and then staggered back to him, wrapping its heavy folds around his body. She studied herself, wondering what she should do next. An attempt to reach her own quarters in her condition would be unwise; she was too drunk to navigate the halls. She glanced over at the large sleeping platform, shrugged, and muttered, "The hell with it." She managed to reach the bed in two wobbly steps and collapsed across it into oblivion.

Elizabeth woke with the positive conviction that a squad of Vulcans had been celebrating a sand ritual in her mouth. Her head ached intolerably; there was a horrible thunderous noise in the room. She covered her ears and found she could not block it out. Turning her head, she realized that it was Si-s-s-s(click), still asleep at the table, snoring loudly. She found herself fascinated by the pattern of his snores; there was a strange sort of teakettlelike whistle, accompanied by a snort as his nostrils fluctuated. It was an unpleasant sound.

She tried to sit up on the sleeping platform, and her stomach told her this was unwise. She realized she had a choice of staying on the sleeping platform and vomiting, or attempting to cross the room to the basin and vomiting. The latter course was tidier, and she felt it much more in keeping with her role as an SSD agent.

She got to her feet and wobbled to the bathroom, where with a great sense of relief she upchucked several times. When there was nothing more than dry retching, she reached for a glass and rinsed out her mouth. Her head still complained bitterly, and she realized she would need a good detoxicant for all the alcohol in her system. Dr. McCoy could probably provide that. She supposed she would have to do something about Si-s-s-s(click), who when he woke up would probably be just as sick as she had been. The prospect of dealing with a Gavialian with a massive hangover wasn't pleasant; also, she remembered vaguely that he did have some cause for complaint concerning her behavior. She wasn't entirely sure what she had done, but she knew it hadn't been polite. She glanced around the room to see if there was a clue to her actions and noticed, with surprise, a phaser lying on the tabletop. It wasn't her belt phaser, but her SSD special. She picked up the weapon and found that it had been set on kill.

"Whatever happened here last night must have been a dilly," she said to herself. "I wonder what happened. I must have threatened to kill him, I don't bring this toy out unless I mean it. . . ." She glanced at the sleeping monster and shook her head; she wasn't about to wake him up to find out what it was she had done.

She was saved the effort of deciding what to do next by the shrill beeping of the wall communicator. Si-s-s-s(click) came instantly awake, or as instantly awake as a badly hung-over Gavialian could. He lifted one eyelid, closed it again, snapped his jaws once or twice experimentally, and then said in a calmly conversational tone of voice, "I think I'm going to be s-s-sick."

Elizabeth pointed him gently in the direction of the bathroom, and then decided if her head was going to survive at all she had better answer the signal from the communicator panel. There was a moment or two of bumbling while she tried to remember how the on-switch worked, and then managed to weakly mumble, "Col. Schaeffer here."

The person on the other end was Captain Kirk. "Schaeffer? I think you'd better get your butt down to Rovar's room. He was murdered last night when you were supposed to be watching him."

Elizabeth leaned her head against the cool metal. She wanted to scream but knew the agony of her voice would be more than her head could take. "I'll be right there, Captain. Will you please ask Dr. McCoy to be present with an alcohol detoxicant?"

"Do you mean to tell me you spent last night drinking? It's bad enough imagining you playing bounce-and-tickle with that big blue lizard, but the idea of an SSD agent getting drunk on duty is more than I can stomach! I want an explanation from you, Schaeffer, as I'm sure your superiors will. Kirk out!"

"I am in trouble," Elizabeth said to no one in particular. "I am in real trouble. I have been a prize idiot." She looked down at her rumpled uniform and debated changing. But Rovar had obviously been dead for some time, and a change of uniform wouldn't make any difference. Ambassador Rovar's quarters were only two corridors away from Si-s-s-s(click)'s, and she would have to pass them on the way to her room to change. There was no point to the gesture. She would go to the dead ambassador's room precisely as she was and face the consequences.

Ambassador Rovar of Hemiptera was badly mutilated. His quarters resembled a butcher shop; the walls were liberally splattered with blood, and the ambassador's body had been torn apart with a ferocity that was utterly appalling. To Elizabeth's experienced eye, it was quite clear that someone or something had attacked him with both teeth and claws. His legs, tongue, and most of his arms had been torn off, his eyes yanked from their stalks; his larynx was smashed and his body gaped open, revealing his tattered internal organs. His heart was still in place, bloody but intact, and his brain was undamaged—two facts that had to mean something. Elizabeth made a mental note not to overlook either one.

Lamps were overturned, the bed had been torn up, the table tipped on its side; everything was splashed with blood, bristles and bits of flesh.

"Not very pretty, is it?" Dr. McCoy said, coming up behind Elizabeth. "I believe you requested a detoxicant." He pressed the hypospray against her arm, more sharply than necessary.

Within seconds Elizabeth felt the medication acting in her brain, changing the wet, soggy sponge into something capable of functioning normally. "I thought I spent last evening with the Angel of Death," she said. "Obviously I had the wrong angel. Do you want to tell me about this, Doctor? I assume you and Dr. Rigel have done a thorough examination of the room."

"What you see is what we've got. Someone or something literally tore Rovar to shreds. Look at this mess. It's positively savage. What hatred the murderer must have felt for him. I'd hate to meet whatever did this."

"Obviously what did it was his Angel of Death."

Spock came into the room from the bathroom. "No sign of anything damaged in there, Doctor. All of the killing was done out here." He looked over at Elizabeth and took in the rumpled state of her uniform without comment. "Colonel, I took the liberty of checking the computer for an explanation of the Hemipteran concept of the Angel of Death. It is viewed as the great Devourer, a beast so fearsome that it is customary to place money in the hand of the dying to buy off the Angel, to avoid a fate such as this. Of course, given the Hemipteran burial customs—placing the bodies of the dead on platforms and exposing them to the air—and the fact that Hemiptera has a great number of scavenger beasts, it is logical to assume that Rovar's people had seen bodies in various states of dismemberment, and evolved that particular legend."

"You might find it logical, Spock," McCoy said, "but every test I've made indicated that Rovar was alive when this was done to him. He wasn't a dead carcass out on some platform in the wilderness. He was alive, and whoever did this let him live for a long time." He glanced over at Elizabeth as he repeated, "A *long* time. Rovar suffered a great deal before he died."

"I set up a complete defense perimeter around this room," Elizabeth said. "You were there, Doctor, when I put in all the visual equipment necessary for a 24-hour surveillance. I also had given orders for a rotation of security guards. Would you mind telling me what happened to the equipment and the guards?"

"I can answer that," Spock said. "At about 2200 hours last night the visual equipment showed signs of breakdown. There was static obscuring the image of Rovar's room and no signs of what was going on—or whether the Angel of Death was even present with Rovar. Mr. Scott attempted repairs at his end, and when he could not clear up the distortions in the visual equipment he came to the ambassador's quarters and requested entrance. Ambassador Rovar, or someone speaking in Rovar's voice, told him to go away and not bother him. Mr. Scott, stating that he had a right to examine that visual equiment, demanded entrance and was refused it. He contacted the Captain and they attempted to force the unlocked door, which had mysteriously jammed. They were not successful, and all the while they worked, they could hear Rovar inside the room demanding that they go away."

"Then there was no screaming, no cries for help?" Elizabeth asked.

"None whatsoever," Spock said. "But Dr. McCoy did find it interesting that the first areas of Rovar's body destroyed were his larynx and vocal cords. By the time Lt. Cdr. Scott had requested permission to enter Rovar's room, the ambassador was most probably incapable of uttering a sound."

"And when did you discover all this?" Elizabeth gestured at the bloodstained room.

"Not until this morning," McCoy answered. The security force spent the night outside the room, ripping into the bulkhead to get the door open, but nothing short of tearing the whole ship apart was going to work. Scotty tried everything, even shorting out the security system to start a fire; all doors on this floor, locked or otherwise, open for a fire signal. But even that didn't work. He couldn't get Rovar's security system to do anything but mess up the viewscreens even more. They finally blacked out entirely. Then, at 0600 this morning when Scotty was still working on the door, it opened easily as if there had never been a problem in the first place. Then he saw all of this."

"Where is Captain Kirk right now?" Elizabeth asked. "I need to explain to him what happened. I spent last evening with someone I suspected of being a part of a plot. I had a theory that there was not one Angel of Death, but several, and I suspected a conspiracy among Si-s-s-s(click), Telson, and Karhu. Yesterday afternoon they gave me such a runaround that my suspicions were, to my mind, confirmed enough to warrant further investigation. I considered Si-s-s-s(click) to be the one ambassador I would be able to get to admit the truth, because he trusted me. I spent last night in his room and came very close to killing him, because he did manifest an ability to shapechange."

She looked at the doctor to see what effect her words were having. He was listening with a little more respect than he had shown earlier. "I *was* drunk and disorderly, Doctor. There are a great number of things that an SSD agent has to do in the line of duty, and sometimes getting stinking drunk is one of them. I don't apologize for what happened; I was following a legitimate lead. I feel *sick* and disgusted with myself that it seems to have been a wrong lead, but I will not apologize for more than that. If my job calls for me to prostitute myself, to kill, to steal or lie, or even do something like this"—she glanced at the vomit staining her boots—"I'll do it. I will do everything necessary to solve this case. I set up what would have been adequate perimeters under the circumstances, and from what you're telling me the screens did not go black at once, nor were they ripped out of the wall or anything similar; they malfunctioned. I want to know why. I suspect Mr. Scott is the best person to give me some sort of explanation, so I'd best talk to him. Whenever Captain Kirk is finished sulking, I'll talk to him, too."

"It won't do you any good to talk to Scotty." McCoy's voice was calmer, even a little sympathetic. "He went over every centimeter of the security setup in the room. It was as innocent as a May-born mongcat. There was absolutely nothing wrong with it, except for the fact that it didn't work. Whatever we're dealing with, Elizabeth—" She noted with pleasure his use of her first name. "—This isn't anything any of us has ever coped with before. It's a being who can walk through walls, seal doors that aren't locked, and make surveillance equipment malfunction. This is a being so diabolical I don't think any of us could cope with it. If it's any consolation—and you will need consolation in the small hours of the night—I don't think drunk or sober you could have made any difference here. None of us could stop it, and why we should expect you to have supernatural abilities just because you wear a black uniform is more than I can understand. When I saw this room this morning, I would have cheerfully strangled you with my bare hands. Not because I loved Rovar—I thought he was a pest—but because you had failed and the Angel had managed to make fools of all of us again. But that's the point, Elizabeth, he made fools of *all* of us."

Elizabeth reached out to gently touch the doctor's shoulder. "Thank you, Leonard, for believing me. I do feel like six kinds of fool, and it's going to take me a long time to get over that; and you're right, some of those small hours of the morning are going to be very hard to take. This room won't be easy to forget. I've seen a lot of bloodshed in my life, but this one . . . this one is definitely a twelve on a carnage scale of ten. I do promise you this, though: I am going to get the Angel of Death no matter what it takes. I'm going to get him."

"But how many more lives will it cost?" Spock asked. "We still have several ambassadors left, Col. Schaeffer. How many of their lives will you risk to catch this elusive being?"

Elizabeth turned on the Vulcan, an expression of cold determination on her face. "All of them if need be. There are only nine ambassadors left here, and on Détente One, counting the Romulans, there are nearly two hundred and fifty. I am willing to let every ambassador on the *Enterprise*, the crew, and myself die by the Angel's hand before I'll let this ship move another meter toward Détente One. Does that answer your question, Commander Spock?"

22

Captain's Log, Stardate 6982.3:

Col. Schaeffer has explained to me her activities during the time Ambassador Rovar of Hemiptera was killed. I am inclined to believe that she was acting in a responsible manner; she was performing her duty and following a legitimate trail. What happened to the ambassador was not her fault, and I agree with Dr. McCoy that even had Col. Schaeffer been present at the time of the ambassador's death it would have made little or no difference. We are dealing with a being of supernatural abilities.

I use this term guardedly, and only with the meaning that there is nothing truly supernatural, only what we do not understand. I have, as captain of this vessel, encountered phenomena on other missions that lack adequate explanation. If Col. Schaeffer fails to capture the Angel of Death, I will request that this not reflect poorly on her record. If an agent of the SSD cannot capture this murderer, no one is capable of solving this crime.

I am faced with the continuation of the quarantine of my ship and the ambassadors therein. We have all come to realize that such a quarantine is necessary. There has been no indication of the Angel of Death on Detente One; his or her activities are confined to the Enterprise, and as such my ship must remain where it is, and my crew and the ambassadors on it targets for a being whose existence I cannot explain. . . .

Elizabeth Schaeffer sat in her quarters alone, shifting data slabs from one corner of her desk to the other. She had read them all, and she had checked the computer for every possible piece of evidence. There was nothing; she was no further along with the case than when she first boarded the *Enterprise*. It was a temptation to say, "I can't solve it," and give up. She could send for additional SSD personnel—but the mere presence of more agents would not guarantee a solution. There had to have been some clue, some crucial factor which had escaped her notice. She would find that clue. She reached again for the stack of data slabs; then the communications panel on her desk lit up and Lt. Uhura's face came into focus.

"Col. Schaeffer, you have a call from Détente One. Will you accept it?"

Elizabeth knew it was Alexis, on schedule with an apology; that would fit the pattern of their previous quarrels. But accepting the apology might give her a little more satisfaction than sifting the evidence one more time. "Put Col. Schaeffer on, Lieutenant."

The screen blanked, and then Alexis shimmered into view. He was wearing his contrite, little-boy-who-stood-in-the-corner expression. "Elizabeth, I've been an idiot. I realize that. I've been reading the reports sent down here from the *Enterprise*, and I can see what you've been going through. I am sorry to have made things more difficult for you. But you've got to understand how much I love you and need you. I wanted you here, I wanted time to convince you of how much I love you. I knew this détente thing would go on for months, and you and I would be together—and I was looking forward to that because of how I feel about you. I assumed our duties would be nominal and give us time for each other—and when I found that had been spoiled, well, I guess I lost my temper. I know I shouldn't have." He smiled sweetly at her, a boyish smile that had always worked in the past. "Please, dear, try to hurry up with the case, and come down here to the station, to me. And try to forgive me. I've been an idiot."

Elizabeth found herself watching almost as if it were

a film or a play. The manipulation her husband was attempting had no meaning for her anymore. The play had become stale, the lines dulled from too much use. She realized with a distant sadness how often in the past that particular method of boyish contrition had worked. It wasn't working now. She found that she had very little to say to him, and nothing whatsoever that would comfort him. She knew she had to accept the apology, it was the least she could do. She steeled herself and tried to smile.

"It's all right, Alexis; it's happened before and I know you are sorry, and I accept your apology. I'll finish up here as soon as I can, and I promise you that you will have time before our contract runs out to convince me of the advantages of renewing it. If this case takes longer than I suspect, I'll ask for an extension on the renewal until we do have some time together. I promise you two months from the end of this case. I think that's the fairest thing I can do." She watched Alexis and knew that the expression on his face meant he thought he had won. What he didn't realize was though he might have won this battle, he hadn't won the war.

"I love you, Elizabeth. I will always love you." Alexis blew her a kiss and then the screen darkened before he let her answer. It had probably been wise on his part, because she could not have said "I love you, Alexis" in return.

Elizabeth had made her formal report to Captain Kirk via communications panel rather than in person. She didn't feel quite ready to cope with Captain James Kirk of the *Enterprise*, and she knew that was the position Jim was taking. Eventually, when he read the reports, she knew he would revert to being dear, sweet Jim Kirk, but in the meantime she had a job to do, and it was time she did it. She stood up and stretched, catlike, and mentally compartmentalized the problem of Alexis. He was not something she was going to worry about at the moment. She might never worry about him again. He was no longer important to her.

Her goal was Sick Bay, and she found Dr. McCoy

and Dr. Rigel in conference, studying the autopsy reports on Rovar. Both Rigel and McCoy had thawed somewhat from their earlier attitude, and McCoy was even going out of his way to be friendly and apologetic for his blowup that morning.

"Oh, Elizabeth. There's a few things here in the official report I think you'll find interesting," he said in a voice that sounded a little too cheerful. "Whatever it was that tore Rovar apart didn't use any weapon that I can recognize. No knife wounds, no evidence of surgical instrumentation, nothing but the use of teeth, claws, and brute force. To the best of our knowledge, Rovar was simply torn apart. It was as if some gigantic animal in that room was killing for the sake of killing. Nothing was eaten or taken away. I've got no explanation for it whatever. We have no animals on board the *Enterprise* capable of this kind of violence."

"After Neko and Agnatha, this case was a little more complex," Dr. Rigel commented. "The other two were simple; they were dead, that's all. But Rovar—I've never seen anything like that. There was a wild tigrex loose from the zoo on Diana Four once, and after I killed the critter I saw some of the bodies being brought out. I should say pieces of the bodies—they were all chewed and clawed to death. Rovar was like that. But a tigrex is as big as a Tyrannosaurus Rex and twice as mean. I'd have noticed one if I saw it galumphing down our corridors, and so would anyone else. They're kind of hard to miss. I think a carnivore got him—a not very hungry carnivore."

Dr. Rigel shrugged. "That's about as scientific as I can get. But after all, I'm only a poor veterinarian, and not a real xenologist. If you and Dr. McCoy can come up with something better, I'll appreciate it."

"My knowledge of physiology was just enough to get me through the pathology courses I had to take," Elizabeth said. "I can tell with some accuracy whether someone's dead or not, and I can make an educated guess as to what he died of. But I agree with you two, this is definitely one for the books. I like the tigrex theory, but if we can't make it play, we can't. I think we've gotten everything we can out of the autopsy reports, and it's time to consider other factors. Do either of you know what Rovar was doing before going to his quarters?"

McCoy nodded, and glanced at Rigel. "Do you want to talk about it, Ruth, or should I?"

"You have a more dramatic speaking style, Doctor, I think you ought to explain it. Besides, if I try to describe last night, I don't think I have the right expletives in my vocabulary."

Dr. McCoy carefully stacked the autopsy report files, one on top of the other. "There was a meeting on Deck 4 in the ambassadors' lounge. It started out pretty much like the meetings we've been having—I noticed that you weren't there, and that Si-s-s-s(click), Telson, and Karhu were all missing, but other than that it was the usual crowd: Sarek, Sirenia, Edentata, Damu, and that funny little pyramid fellow—Hotep. And some of the crew people were there: myself, Dr. Rigel, Spock, Dr. Carter, Scotty, M'Benga, Uhura, two or three of the guys from engineering—oh yes, Grace Temple from my medical lab. Then Bobby Robinson from Security came in with three of his friends to maintain order. Bobby's been on duty since the beginning of this mess. We needed him. It was the loudest shouting match I've heard yet. Rovar was accusing anyone and everyone of murder, arson, treason, buggery, and barratry on the high seas. He was in one of his usual paranoid blathers—you know, everyone was guilty of everything but him. He went a little too far with an accusation about Sarek, and Spock got more heated than I'd ever seen him. Sarek hasn't been too well, you know, I've been very worried about him."

"So am I," Elizabeth said. "I don't think he ought to involve himself in too many more of these get-togethers; it's about time he went home to Vulcan and took up cactus gardening, or whatever it is that Vulcans do. But tell me about the upset with Spock. I'm curious about that."

"Well," McCoy said, "Rovar came out and accused Sarek of treason, claiming that Sarek was actually a Romulan agent. Spock couldn't take that—he knows how sick his father is—and he jumped to his feet and really harangued the Hemipteran. You know how Spock is, his voice is usually so quiet and calm—well, it wasn't this time. If a Vulcan could be said to be angry, Spock was angry. M'Benga was backing him up, asking what right Rovar had to attack Sarek—it was well known throughout the Federation that Vulcans were the most peaceful of races, which is more than can be said for the Hemipterans. Rovar took exception to that and called M'Benga six kinds of names—including one rather involved insult which I didn't entirely understand, even though it was in Federationese; it had something to do with an obscene biological function involving at least three Vulcans. It was the first time I'd ever seen Spock's ear tips turn bright green; whatever Rovar said, it was pretty vulgar."

"Then there were a great number of witnesses to Rovar's burst of stupidity," Elizabeth said flatly. "It doesn't help very much—it only adds a roomful of new suspects. But I'll look into the whereabouts of each of them and see if I can get anywhere. Anyone who thinks Special Security is a glamour job ought to try it. There's a lot of slogging, dead ends, and more red herrings than you would ever want to cope with in your life—and this case is loaded to the gills with those stinking fish."

Elizabeth, her errand completed, was about to leave Sick Bay when the door slid open, revealing Captain Kirk. Elizabeth paused for a moment, unsure what her reception from the Captain would be. He smiled at her sheepishly and said, "I read your report, Elizabeth. I think I know how you feel. Why don't I take you to lunch in my cabin and you can cry on my shoulder about it. The fabric they make these uniforms out of is waterproof, and I don't mind getting a little soggy. Frankly, I think you've earned it."

Elizabeth smiled warmly. She had Jim Kirk back again rather than James Kirk, Captain of the *Enterprise*. She reached out one hand, placed it on his arm, and like an empress with her favorite consort, swept out of Sick Bay.

23

The lunch did help. Jim commiserated, consoled, and did what he could to pull Elizabeth out of her mood of borderline despair. He reassured her that no, she hadn't been an idiot, the case was extraordinarily difficult, and she was doing the best thing possible. He admitted he'd been angry over her drinking spree while Rovar was being killed, but after reading her report he realized why she'd done it.

"It's just this feeling of being in the wrong place at the wrong time, Jim," she said, clearing away the luncheon dishes. "I keep thinking that this whole case is some kind of dream. You know, the sort where you're knee-deep in molasses and something horrible is chasing you and you can't move at all? That's the way I feel, knee-deep in molasses—and if it keeps up I think I'm going to turn in my uniform and take a desk job. Maybe I'm losing my edge and my brains have been scrambled by one too many high-powered assignments, but I wish it were a dream. I wish I'd wake up and find this whole mission didn't exist."

"I know how you feel. I had a problem with that a month or two ago. We were exploring a planet called Delta Gamma Four, and there was some sort of plant life there—well, Spock said it was more an animal than a plant—but whatever it was, we got a lot of spores in our heads, and the entire landing party went into coma.

Several of my people died of it. I spent ten days having nightmares, things I can't really explain—and when I woke up I wasn't even sure I was awake. It was the oddest sensation, not being able to tell a dream from reality."

"Did the dreams stop happening?" Elizabeth leaned forward on her elbows, resting her chin on her interlaced fingers. "Because that's the way this case feels sometimes—as if I don't know a dream from reality."

"I'm still having trouble with it. Dr. McCoy sigmunds me about once a week, and he says it's perfectly normal, but I still have the dreams. I had one the night the ambassadors first came on board—I dreamt that I was standing outside Sirenia's room and I followed her down the hall. It was so real. . . ."

Elizabeth's nostrils quivered, recalling the scent of murder. She remembered that Sirenia had mentioned Kirk following her to Agnatha's room—but Kirk now said it had been in his dream. Another piece had appeared that might be extraordinarily important, a clue that might solve the whole case. Elizabeth mentally looked at the puzzle piece and realized that its name was James Kirk—a fact she didn't like in the slightest.

In as calm a voice as possible, without betraying any excitement over what he'd said, she asked, "Are you sure you were dreaming? Or could you have been walking in your sleep?"

"Oh, I was dreaming, all right—I saw Sirenia go into Agnatha's bedroom. It was so painful, realizing she cared for him more than she could ever care for me, that I just sort of stumbled away. I wasn't even too sure of what was happening in the dream, it was very vague . . . there was this piece of funny-looking statuary I tripped over, and then I woke up in bed, feeling incredibly lonely, and there were tears on my face. I don't understand it exactly."

Kirk ducked his head as if he didn't want to face Elizabeth as he added, "I propositioned her, you see, and she turned me down—and it hurt. I think that's why I dreamed about it. I was jealous of Agnatha, but the dream was terribly, terribly real."

"You seem to get very involved with the ladies on

board your ship, Jim," Elizabeth said coolly. "First Sirenia, and now me. You're too charming for your own good or mine."

Her mind was busy sorting the information she'd gotten from Kirk concerning the dream, and the matter of the strange little sculpture, something new she would have to investigate. Yet on another level she was considering her relationship with Jim. If he turned out to be the Angel of Death, she realized it would be extremely painful for her to kill him. She wasn't even sure she could pull the trigger and end his life, angel or not. That sort of thinking was dangerous for an SSD agent. It could cost her life or his—not a pleasant choice.

It was startling, but not totally unexpected, for her to discover she was more than a little in love with this man. But she was very aware of her duty; no matter how much she loved him, if he turned out to be the Angel of Death, he would meet his destruction at her hands or she would have to take her own life as an admission of her failure.

"Elizabeth, you're not the same as Sirenia, or a lot of other women I've met," Kirk said softly. "You're a person first. Oh, I admit when I first met you I was definitely interested in your body, but all I knew about you was how beautiful you were. But it's different now. Can't you see that? You mean more to me than anyone I've ever met—in fact, you mean enough for me to ask you something that's very important."

He reached out and took her hand, placing it gently against his cheek. "Elizabeth, Elizabeth my darling, in two months when that ridiculous marriage of yours is over, I want you to come back to the *Enterprise* as my wife. I want you to be Mrs. James Kirk. Because I think you're the answer to the loneliness, the empty feeling I've been having since my illness on Delta Gamma Four, and with you and my ship I think I will finally recover and be as complete as a human being can possibly be. Dearest, will you marry me?"

Elizabeth felt a slight burst of irritation. Why did the men in her life always manage to do the wrong thing at the wrong time? At any other point in the investigation she'd have been elated by Jim's proposal—but now that strange dream he'd described was foremost in her mind. She was all SSD agent and very little an emotional woman. The proposal was interesting, but something to file away and consider at a later time.

She could tell by looking at Jim's face how much he wanted a favorable answer, and also how much he really loved her—for now, at least. "Jim," she slid her other hand up to cup his face gently, "I care about you a great deal more than I ever should. For the first time in my marriage I've allowed myself an emotional relationship with another man, and I'd love to be able to say yes to your proposal—but Alexis contacted me this morning, being his usual contrite self after one of our quarrels, and I made him a promise: I promised him two months. I keep my promises, Jim. He'll have his two months, and I won't under any circumstances say yes to a proposal from another man while at the same time I'm allowing Alexis to try proving that there is something worthwhile in my marriage. I'd consider something like that dishonorable; I'd be a cheat and a liar. I'm perfectly willing to lie, cheat, or steal in the course of my work, but when it comes to my private life I can't do it. I have to retain some integrity somewhere, and I cannot and will not give you an answer until those two months are over."

She bent forward and kissed him gently, trying not to let her fears show on her face. She might well, she knew, be in love with the Angel of Death himself.

24

Elizabeth left Captain Kirk's quarters determined to get to the bottom of the situation involving the dreams of Delta Gamma Four and James Kirk's nocturnal visit to Sirenia. She had to know if the man she was in love with could possibly be the Angel of Death—a possibility she wanted to deny. She knew only too well that the denial was coming from her emotions and not from her mind.

She found Sirenia on Deck 4, in the ambassadors' lounge, talking to Sarek and Hotep. Elizabeth waited politely until the conversation was over, and then asked Sirenia for a private discussion. They moved to one side of the room, out of earshot, and Elizabeth again asked Sirenia for the details of Kirk's nocturnal prowling of the hallway. Sirenia could only repeat what she'd said before, that she had noticed Captain Kirk following her, and that he had seen her enter Agnatha's room.

"But I don't think he killed Agnatha," Sirenia added.

"But can you think of anything unusual at all that was in the hallway? Anything different, or that shouldn't have been there? Captain Kirk spoke of stumbling over a piece of statuary. I checked out that hallway. There is no such sculpture."

Elizabeth felt a tugging at the hem of her tunic. She

looked down and noticed Ambassador Hotep. At the moment he had feet, one arm, eyes, ears, and a mouth. He obviously had not felt the need of a nose or another arm.

"I overheard your conversation from across the room," the ambassador said. "I'm afraid I enjoy listening in on secret confabs. I know I shouldn't do it, but you pick up the most fascinating pieces of information that way. However, I can solve your problem with the statuary in the hallway. I'm afraid it was me. I was in search of a crewperson to bring me another supply of fruit, when I noticed Sirenia coming down the hall. I wasn't that interested in speaking to her—she'd been haranguing me earlier in the day over the détente, and I was tired of the subject—so I simply reverted to natural form and stayed as close to the wall as possible. It's surprising how many people don't notice a one-meter high gray pyramid if they're not looking for one."

"And was James Kirk in the hallway outside Agnatha's quarters?" Elizabeth said.

"Oh, definitely. But it was very odd; it was Captain Kirk, yet it wasn't Captain Kirk." The pyramid pulled all his appendages into his body for a moment, presenting a totally blank visage; and then, his period of contemplation over, the ears, eyes, mouth, and other accouterments popped out suddenly. "I know this is going to sound very silly, but after Captain Kirk watched Sirenia go into Agnatha's room he turned around and there were . . . I think you call them tears on his face. He moved down the hall in a very random fashion, stumbled over me, and then—now this is the odd part—he vanished into thin air. I have to admit it's a very good trick, and one of these days I'll have to ask him how he did it."

"Are you sure of that?" Elizabeth leaned down until she was face to face with the ambassador. "He didn't just turn a corner or go into a room? Or did you stop using your eyes? Are you sure he really did disappear?"

"Without a doubt, Colonel. I was watching him all the time, because he did stumble over me rather rudely and I was waiting for an apology. I didn't get one. I admit, it must be difficult for people to apologize to a pyramid, but still. . . ."

"He disappeared into thin air," Elizabeth mused. "Do you know," she said, addressing both ambassadors, "I feel for the first time that I'm approaching some sort of solution in this case. I'm not sure if I like it, but it is a possible solution."

"May I remind you, Col. Schaeffer," Sirenia said, "you have had several theories in the past as to who the Angel of Death was, and you've been proved wrong. What makes you sure that this one is correct?"

"Oh, it's not entirely that I suspect Captain Kirk. It is the disappearance that fascinates me. Captain Kirk swears that he never left his quarters; he was sound asleep and dreaming, and he woke up in his own bed after tripping over a piece of sculpture—and as far as he knows he was never physically out of his room."

"Astral projection?" Sirenia said. "I have heard of such techniques, and there's a great deal of Terran literature on such phenomena. Do you think our Death Angel is such a projection?"

"Not quite." Elizabeth was growing excited. "True astral projection doesn't work that way. It's usually much more tenuous, and I doubt that any being, particularly a Terran, would be capable of killing anyone astrally. There seem to be certain rules governing the process. But Captain Kirk made reference to an incident that occurred on a planet called Delta Gamma Four. There's a chance that our murderer may have something to do with that incident. Now if you two will excuse me, I have some heavy research to do."

She bowed to both ambassadors and turned, striding purposefully in the direction of the nearest turbolift. She and McCoy needed to have a long talk, quickly.

Several hours later, Elizabeth had covered all the reports concerning Delta Gamma Four and its strange spores. The dream aspect was utterly fascinating. Only Captain Kirk had spoken of having dreams. When she questioned McCoy, he said that the Sigmunds of all the other members of the Delta Gamma Four party had indicated very strong REM patterns, but none of them spoke of dreams, either when they regained consciousness or since. In fact, most of them said they'd had no dreams at all, which was odd for such deep REM sleep.

"That is," McCoy admitted, "I can speak for all but Spock—it's almost impossible to get a decent EEG on a Vulcan. I frankly can't tell whether he's dreaming or not. You'd have to ask Spock about it, but if you want to talk to a couple of the victims of Delta Gamma Four, Dr. Carter and Dr. M'Benga are both on duty in the medical lab."

"Yes, I think I'd find that very interesting. Would you ask them to come to your office, Doctor?"

Drs. Carter and M'Benga were very little help. Both of them stated they'd had no dreams, nor any memory of dreaming. In fact, Dr. Carter pointed out that the one odd phenomenon he'd noticed since returning from Delta Gamma Four was that he could remember no dreams at all.

"Yes, I was aware of that problem," M'Benga said. "I did some REM tests on the landing party and myself. They all show deep REM, so we *are* dreaming, whether we can remember it or not. There's been something out of the ordinary there. But I'm not sure it's important."

"And what about you personally, Dr. M'Benga?" Elizabeth asked. "How has not being able to remember your dreams affected you?"

"Not enough to worry me very much," the doctor said. "I miss dreaming a bit. It's funny how in most cases dreams are just such a jumble, and you don't pay much attention to them—but I used to have some rather nice ones, all about being on Vulcan again. Those two years I spent interning there were some of the most pleasant months of my life, and I used to dream that I was back on Vulcan and it was so peaceful there. Now—nothing. I go to bed at night, I go to sleep, I wake up in the morning. According to McCoy the bodily toxic levels are well taken care of, and I am showing REM patterns—but I miss my dreams. Of course, if that's the only thing Delta Gamma Four has done to any of us, I suppose it's a small price."

"Yes, gentlemen, but there is a problem. Captain Kirk is having dreams and, worse of all, he remembers them." McCoy, Carter and M'Benga looked at each other, and then back at the SSD agent.

"Then there's a possibility," McCoy said slowly, "that Jim, *our* James Kirk, could be the Angel of Death?"

"I refuse to make any further accusations," Elizabeth said. "I've made an idiot of myself a little too often on this case. I'm not going to say it's Kirk. All I'm saying is that Kirk says he's had dreams; and I would suggest, Doctor, that you get the Captain down here at once and give him the fanciest Sigmund you can come up with, because right now his dreams are the only clue we have. I have proof that when Captain Kirk thought he was dreaming, he wasn't. He *was* physically someplace else than his bed, and I want to know everything I can about that."

McCoy, Carter and M'Benga broke into a babble of questions, comments, and defenses of their captain. Elizabeth heard them out. She was inclined to agree with them; James Kirk seemed a most unlikely suspect for the Angel of Death. But she reiterated the importance of the Sigmund, and Dr. McCoy, with some reluctance, signaled the Bridge and demanded that Captain Kirk put in an appearance in Sick Bay for a special Sigmund.

Elizabeth waited for the captain to arrive. She repeated to the three physicians the information she'd received from Hotep and Sirenia, and they were not able to explain it any more readily than she could. Carter was positive that it didn't fit the standard pattern of astral projection—in fact, it didn't fit the standard pattern of anything. But then, as M'Benga pointed out, nothing about Delta Gamma Four had been standard.

"You know," McCoy said, "I remember something strange that Scotty said while we were still circling Delta Gamma Four. I'm not sure if it's important, but there was some problem with the fuel consumption. We were all half out of our minds with worry, but

Scotty says he didn't sign the bloody thing. Could someone else—like Jim, in his sleep—have signed those forms?"

"Doctor, if you're correct you could be damning your captain as the Angel of Death." Elizabeth moved to the computer and requested a readout of fuel consumption sheets for the Delta Gamma Four time period. There, clear and bold, was James Kirk's signature on the form.

"Congratulations, Dr. McCoy," Elizabeth said without a trace of emotion. "One more bit of proof that Jim can move in his sleep."

"But a fuel consumption signature doesn't prove he's the Angel. . . ."

Captain Kirk came into the room, looking decidedly irritated. "All right, Bones, what's this about a Sigmund? You've been giving them to me once a week since Delta Gamma Four, and I'm not scheduled for another one for at least three days. I hope you've got a good explanation."

"I'm afraid I ordered it, Jim," Elizabeth said. "I've been researching the Delta Gamma Four problem, and those dreams of yours—well, they were more than just dreams. You *were* outside Agnatha's quarters that night—both Sirenia and Hotep saw you there. And you signed a fuel consumption report while you were lying here in a coma. There's something a little odd going on that's more than just dreams, and since you're the only one from the Delta Gamma Four landing party who's reported dreaming, I'm afraid we have to run some tests. I think it ties in with the 'Angel' problem."

"Are you accusing *me* of being the Angel of Death? If you are, you're way off base. My position on the Romulan détente has always been neutral; the whole crew knows that, and so do all the ambassadors. I've made it quite clear that if there is a détente, I will honor it; if there's not, I will continue opposing the Romulans. I take my orders from Star Fleet, and I don't get involved in politics. As for my being the only one from the landing party who dreams, that's not so; Mr. Spock had dreams. He told me so when we were recovering from that coma; we were both rather upset about the dreaming, which was the only reason he mentioned it. I think before you start running all these fancy tests on me, you should do the same with Spock."

"Col. Schaeffer, the Captain is right," McCoy said. "If I have to do a Sigmund on him, and Spock has been dreaming too, Spock should have the same type of Sigmund. In fact, as Chief Medical Officer I would demand that he have the same test."

"And you'd be within your rights," Elizabeth said. "I quite agree that Spock should be sigmunded. It'll take you a while to sigmund Jim, and while you're doing that I'll have a talk with your First Officer. Is he on the Bridge?"

"No, I think he's in his quarters," Kirk said. "It's his rest period. I'm not sure how he'd like having that interfered with."

Elizabeth nodded and turned toward the door. As it opened she moved out into the corridor, and Kirk and McCoy could hear her cheerfully whistling a chorus of *What Do You Do With A Grumpy Vulcan?*

25

Elizabeth had to lean quite heavily on the door signal several times before she got an answer from Mr. Spock. The door finally opened, and the First Officer looked decidedly displeased at being interrupted. For the first time since she boarded the *Enterprise*, Elizabeth saw the Vulcan looking rumpled. His normally smooth bangs were awry, and his tunic had been yanked on so hastily that he had not fastened the neck opening.

"Col. Schaeffer, I'm sure you are aware this is my rest period. I was indulging in meditation and had no wish to be disturbed. I hope whatever reason you have for being here is of sufficient importance."

He was not pleased to see her, but he at least showed enough courtesy to pull out a seat and make sure she was comfortable. He sat down across from her and reached up to smooth his hair into place. "Now, Colonel, may I ask what this is about?"

"Yes, Mr. Spock. I have come to talk to you about dreams. Delta Gamma Four dreams, to be precise." She watched the Vulcan's face and saw a faint flicker of light in the depths of his flat black eyes. She had touched a nerve of some sort.

The Vulcan arranged his face in rigidly formal lines. "I do not dream, Col. Schaeffer. I do not find dreaming a necessity, and as for Delta Gamma Four, I did not dream before or after the experience. Now that I've answered your question, may I return to my meditations?"

Elizabeth leaned forward slightly, a catlike smile on her face. "Then tell me, oh wise and honest Vulcan, why did you tell your captain you dreamed after Delta Gamma Four?"

The question obviously took Spock by surprise. He half-rose from his seat and then slumped back into it. "I did not dream," he repeated almost mechanically. "As a Vulcan I am not capable of dreaming. That is my last word on the subject."

Elizabeth reached to the back of her belt and removed her standard phaser; she placed it on the table in front of her. "And this is my last word on the subject. I want to know what happened after Delta Gamma Four, and I want to know quickly—or you will be a very dead Vulcan. You keep insisting you did not dream. Your captain says you did. At this particular moment I am inclined to believe him. But we'll try another tack."

She picked up her phaser and set it on kill. She sighted down it, positioning it in such a way that the bolt of energy would go right through the Vulcan's heart. "Now, we will begin again, Cdr. Spock. After Delta Gamma Four, did you at any time experience out-of-body activity that might be misconstrued by another person as a dream?" Her words were as evenly paced as a sentence of execution.

Spock ran one hand down the side of his face and glanced at it as if surprised that he was sweating. "That is unfortunately a question I will have to answer. As a Vulcan I cannot lie, and when you asked whether I dreamed I could say no and not be lying. I did not dream. But when you asked about an out-of-body experience—that is a direct statement of what occurred, and I must answer it. I ask you, Colonel—no, I beg you—do not force me to reveal what that experience was. I assure you on my oath as a Vulcan that it had nothing to do with the Angel of Death; I am not that being, I am incapable of killing in the fashion that the Angel kills. But what happened is so personally distasteful to me that I cannot readily discuss it." He looked up at her with naked pleading in his eyes.

Elizabeth felt a certain pity for the First Officer. He was obviously laboring under the effects of a very traumatic event, but she *had* to know what the experience had been. She lowered the phaser carefully to the table and turned it back to neutral. "Spock, Sarek's son, whatever you say to an SSD agent is sacrosanct. I am under no compulsion to repeat anything told me in confidence. It would not even be possible to torture the information out of me. Whatever you relate will go with me to my grave, as secret as if you had kept it in your own mind alone. But I must ask you again: what did you experience? Remember, while you might feel shame or embarrassment, the lives of a number of people are at stake. If I can't get the information out of you voluntarily, there are ways of forcing it out of you. None of them are pleasant, and I do not speak of torture. Your father Sarek would be willing to assist me by mindmelding with you and finding out exactly what you know. Do you want to tell me about it, or do you want to tell Sarek?"

Elizabeth had pushed precisely the right button. At the mention of Sarek's knowing anything about the incident, Spock's face registered absolute dismay for a fraction of a second. "No! I can't let my father know about this. You have won, Col. Schaeffer, and I hope you find it as bitter a victory as I find it a bitter defeat. You will learn nothing from it."

Spock leaned back in his chair and closed his eyes. "The plant beings of Delta Gamma Four are intensely telepathic. Their spores enable the mind of whatever host creature they inhabit to travel at will to any place on the planet's surface and to carry the spores with it. Then the spores can be deposited on fertile ground and grow. It is not necessary for the host's body to travel, only his spirit. It is an interesting biological mechanism—but also, as you have noticed, deadly. Because what travels with the spore is not what people might call the soul, but a subconscious—the deep dark part of oneself that is hidden from the light. The part of every being that is capable of dishonorable acts, capable of cruelty, of pain, or even—of murder. I can understand the Angel of Death now, and I am beginning to suspect that Delta Gamma Four is a clue to the ambassadors' deaths. That was the subject of the meditation you so rudely interrupted. Whoever the Angel is, it was one of the people on Delta Gamma Four. I know this from my own experiences of such mind travel. McCoy was able to kill the spores but not the urge to leave the body that the spores engendered. I do not understand the process, only that it does exist.

"The coma state I was in allowed me to travel at will throughout the *Enterprise*. It is the same for the Captain. Both of us have rather high psychic readings for our respective races. I am, of course, a great deal more capable than the Captain; I can control to a certain extent what I do, and I know that I am doing it. I would suggest you do a rundown on the psi patterns of everyone who was on Delta Gamma Four, and those readouts will more than likely give you your murderer."

"What you're saying is rather interesting, Mr. Spock, and I intend to do just that, but you're avoiding the question. What was your experience?"

The Vulcan sighed deeply. "Must I tell you? I've given you all you need to know to find the murderer. The knowledge of my darkside is not necessary to you."

"I remind you, Mr. Spock, of your choice. You will tell me, or you will tell Sarek." Elizabeth realized she was being cruel, but not, she felt, needlessly. She had to have an accurate description of what the out-of-body experience was like; a description from someone who knew that he was indeed out of his body. Though she would probably hate herself for what she was doing to the Vulcan, that hate could be turned aside with one word of justification: duty. She was doing her job, and the question of who might get hurt along the way was unimportant.

"The experience, Mr. Spock. I'm waiting."

Spock shifted uncomfortably in the chair. He seemed ill at ease and, for a Vulcan, intensely nervous. "I committed an act that was immoral," he said. "I feel shame at my actions, but if it will assist you I have no other choice. While in the so-called coma state I left my body and traveled to the quarters of a young engineering lieutenant on board the ship. She is a woman of exceptional promise and is extraordinarily intelligent. Also"—his face contorted—"by Terran standards she is very beautiful. I do not allow myself as a Vulcan to notice beauty, but under the influence of the spores I found myself desiring this woman. Such desire is a part of the dark side of my personality. It is something I can normally hold at bay, but under the influence of the spores I had no such control. I am ashamed of my actions and I deeply regret them."

"What did you *do*?" Elizabeth prodded. "I must know what capabilities the spores can produce in breaking down resistance to an immoral act."

"I went to the woman's quarters late at night while she slept, and I indulged in certain biological activities with her." The Vulcan's ears and face were suffused with a deep green. His hands twisted and untwisted as they revealed his shame.

Elizabeth wanted to make some consoling comment, pointing out that what he had done was not so bad; a shipboard seduction was not necessarily a terrible crime. But then she remembered how it would seem to a Vulcan, going outside the normal channels for such activity. "Did the woman know you were with her?"

"No-o-o-o. I made very sure that she remained in a half-dreaming state—but it was not rape. Not even the spores could force me to such an act. The lieutenant was more than willing."

He held up his hands and looked at them. "With my ability to mindmeld it was not difficult to clear her mind of the incident. If you were to question her, she would admit to having had a highly erotic dream, nothing more. I would prefer not to tell you her name; it is of little importance. But it is something I found thoroughly reprehensible in myself, that I could use another person in such a way. It was shocking, totally and completely shocking. . . ." The Vulcan's words drifted off; he covered his face with his hands. It was clear he had nothing more to say.

Elizabeth wanted to comfort him, to say something to make him feel a little less guilty, something to make him aware that allowing the Terran part of him to indulge in something Captain Kirk would consider as casual as breathing was not a crime. But she knew from his demeanor that it meant a great deal to Spock. She set her mind pattern and adjusted the chemical balance of her body to match that of Spock's mother, Amanda.

Taking a deep breath, she reached forward and gently stroked the Vulcan's hands. "Spock," she said softly, "what's done is done. No amount of remorse can change that; and I assume from what you have said that there have been no further dreams." She watched him shake his head swiftly. "It was an isolated incident, something you could not entirely help. You were under the influence of an alien life form; you must not blame yourself for what happened. It's entirely possible that the lieutenant in question enjoyed the dream she had. Try not to dwell on it; free your mind. You know the proper techniques. You've been beating yourself over the head with something that wasn't your fault. That is illogical, and it isn't proper Vulcan behavior. I would suggest you deal with the situation in a manner your father would approve of. It is past."

Spock lifted his head to look at the woman, holding his hands in hers. The dark green tinge was fading from his skin to reveal the normal golden-tawny shade of his complexion. He looked deeply into Elizabeth's eyes and saw forgiveness there. He took a deep, gulping sigh, almost a sob.

"I didn't want it to happen," he said. "I really didn't want it to happen. But I couldn't help it!"

Elizabeth rose from the chair to stand in front of the seated Vulcan. She slipped one arm around his shoulder, noting his unusual lack of resistance to her closeness. She pulled him to her body, one hand reaching out to stroke his dark, sleek head. "It's all right, it's all right." She pitched her voice as closely as she could remember to the voice pattern of Sarek's wife, Amanda, an old friend from a long time ago.

"You're a Vulcan who happens to be part Terran. It's something you fight every day, and you fight it well. Without meaning to, you lost a battle. But you've not lost the war, Spock. You know that. What has happened will never happen again. So be at peace with yourself."

His arms slid around her waist and he held her close. There was nothing romantic in the gesture; it was simply a request for and an appreciation of comfort. She continued to hold him, stroking his hair until he let go of her and sat up, once more the proud Vulcan first officer of the *Enterprise*. He looked up at her, nodded quietly, and then said softly, "Thank you. As you can see, I still suffer from the aftereffects of the spores. My touching you, or allowing you to touch me, is quite unusual for me. I would not normally react that way, even for my mother. But you mimic her voice and body scent quite well; you are to be commended for that. And I admit I find some comfort in it—illogical, but a fact nonetheless."

"You're quite welcome. I was afraid I'd end up hurting you very badly, and I regretted it; there are a great number of things I regret about my job, and if I've left you feeling comforted, perhaps it's one good point to counterbalance a lot of the black marks." She nodded quietly and turned to go, then realized the Vulcan had reached for her hand. He lifted it to his lips in a formal gesture.

"Colonel," he said, "the credits you have accumulated in your lifetime far outnumber the debits. May you go in peace."

26

Elizabeth sat in her quarters, attempting to correlate in her mind the material she had accumulated. The Delta Gamma Four expedition was definitely the place to start her search for the Angel of Death. It was obvious from her talks with both Kirk and Spock that the Delta Gamma spores had a variety of strange properties. She read in the coroner's reports that the dead crewmembers' brains had been packed with the spores, crushing the tissues. Something Spock had said about psychic ability itched at the back of her mind. The dead crewmembers had no psychic abilities at all, so of course they couldn't transport the spores out of their bodies. That was what killed them.

She drew from the stack of information slabs the report on Spock's latest Sigmund, the one she had ordered McCoy to give. By making comparisons with past Sigmunds, it appeared normal; she could see why McCoy had not been concerned. But she did note the high telepathic ability, the strength of Spock's mind, and his ability to influence other beings through the use of the mindmeld. She put down the computer slab, looked at it and sighed. He would make such a magnificent suspect, and also a very unlikely one. She tossed the slab aside and reached for Captain Kirk's Sigmund, done just before Spock's. It too revealed that the Captain was functioning perfectly normally. There was an indication of deep REM sleep, but little of the light delta fragments that generally occur in a human between stages of deep REM sleep. There was also some indication of disturbance in his alpha wave sleep pattern as he fell asleep. The alpha state was far too short. There was none of the subconscious rambling to be expected from that twilight period of sleep. She found that most intriguing.

But the spores had been killed in Kirk, Spock, M'Benga, Carter, Temple, and Robinson. Or were they? Elizabeth rechecked McCoy's report on the use of antibodies, and found that while he had indeed killed the spores, the organic remains had been absorbed by the crew and filtered out of their bodies. There was the possibility that, while the spores were gone, the command to do *something* remained. She carefully correlated the behavior patterns of the landing party both before and after Delta Gamma Four. There were several differences.

Grace Temple had gained fifteen kilos, almost enough to get her removed from active duty. Carter had difficulty controlling his temper and had been in several fights. Bobby Robinson had become compulsive about his job. Kirk suffered from loneliness. M'Benga wanted to go back to Vulcan. And Spock—Spock was being entirely too human for his own good. The scene in his cabin had proved that to her satisfaction and placed him firmly on her suspect list. A Vulcan who could feel sexual desire might also be able to overcome his aversion to killing. The spores did indeed bring out some very interesting characteristics in the victims, but which characteristic pointed to the Angel of Death? Wanting something very badly seemed to be the answer, but what in this conglomeration of unfulfilled needs would add up to killing ambassadors to preserve a détente? There was nothing to do but check and double-check the Sigmunds of the Delta Gamma Four party. She reached for the next slab, that of Dr. M'Benga, when the intercom signaled that there was a message for her.

Cursing intercoms and messages in general, she

turned off the computer and went to the wall panel. It was Lt. Uhura.

"Col. Schaeffer, I have been told by Star Fleet Command that the quarantine of the *Enterprise* has been lifted." There was a long pause, as though Uhura wasn't sure how the message was being taken. Then she said, "I assure you, Colonel, no request for lifting the quarantine came from the *Enterprise*. It seems to have originated on Détente One."

Elizabeth knew who had lifted the quarantine. A cold anger welled up in her, a feeling of destructiveness and hatred, a feeling of the Goddess wanting revenge. She reached up blindly for the first thing at hand, a small pottery vase, and threw it across the room as savagely as she could.

"Lieutenant, patch me in to Détente One as quickly as possible. I want to speak to Col. Alexis Schaeffer. No, better yet, ask that I speak to *Lieutenant* Alexis Schaeffer. Because by the time I get finished with him he'll be lucky to be *that*!"

"Yes ma'am!" The screen went blank quickly. Uhura, obviously startled by the cold fury that she had never heard in the Colonel's voice before, was taking care of the message as quickly as she could.

Elizabeth stood by the communications panel, drumming her fingernails against the wall. Throwing the vase had only helped somewhat, and she knew Alexis was extraordinarily lucky not to be in her physical presence. The communications panel came to life again, and Uhura's voice said, "I've contacted Col. Schaeffer for you; he wants to know if you want the message put on viewscreen or simply as sound."

"Sound will do, Lieutenant. If I have to look at him, I will probably do something I'll regret for the rest of my life."

"Elizabeth? You dragged me out of a rather important meeting. I hope this is essential. . . ."

"*Essential!* You addlebrained backside of a pig! What do you think you're doing? How dare you lift the quarantine on the *Enterprise* before I've given a clearance? I know who went to Star Fleet, because you're the only one on Détente One with enough power to do it, and I'm telling you, mister, I don't like it! How dare you interfere with an assignment of mine?"

"And you're interfering with one of mine. Unless you've forgotten, Elizabeth, I have a conference to put on here, and we're missing several crucial ambassadors. I felt it was time we got things moving, and since you can't deal with the Angel of Death yourself, you might as well bring the *Enterprise* in and let Derek and me have a hand at it."

"You, Derek, and the entire station? Do you want the Angel of Death doing wholesale slaughter among the Federation ambassadors? Alexis, I made you a promise, to give you two months—but that promise was on a basis of my finishing this case. You've violated your side of the agreement; what is there to make me keep mine?"

There was a long pause, then Alexis said, in a small, childlike voice, "Your sense of duty? You've got to admit, you're not doing very well alone, and there would be three of us. We could contain the *Enterprise* in orbit around the station, and I'm sure three SSD agents could handle the problem quickly." His voice was apologetic, and more than a little scared.

"I want that order rescinded, Alexis, and I want it rescinded now. The quarantine stays."

"It's too late for that." His voice took on a more positive note. "I've already convinced Star Fleet that it was necessary. Your captain is already getting his orders to continue to Détente One. The case is, to a certain extent, over—your part of it, at least. You're getting a little egotistical there, thinking you could handle it by yourself. It's clear you need help, and I am more than willing to give it to you."

"I don't want your help. I don't like the underhanded way you went about this. You're not concerned about the *Enterprise* or the détente mission, you're just trying to get me to Détente One a little faster. Well, let me tell you, Alexis Gregorovich Schaeffer, you've goofed, and goofed badly. You *are* going to get your two months—every minute of it—and that's all you're getting. As far as I'm concerned, this marriage is over. Col. Elizabeth Schaeffer, *out*!"

Her fist slammed the off button with such force that the button snapped in two, and the jagged edge slashed into her wrist. She watched it bleed, feeling a certain perverse pleasure in the pain. "I'll kill him," she murmured. "So help me, I'll kill him. If one ambassador on Détente One dies, so does Alexis Schaeffer."

Elizabeth systematically destroyed her room. She took a great deal of satisfaction in the act. She had to get the anger out. Tearing apart pillows and smashing bric-a-brac was a far safer way than facing a sentient being. When she had finished and the adrenalin surge was over, she looked at the debris and shrugged in quiet acceptance of her act. There was a great deal of blood splattered about; she realized her wrist had been cut more severely than she'd first thought. The communications panel did not function, and she was unable to call Sick Bay.

She went to the door and stuck her head out into the hall to see who was available. A young lieutenant that she recognized as one of the Bridge crew stopped to stare at her. She realized she must look like some kind of wild woman, her hair on end and blood dripping down her battered uniform.

"You, Lieutenant," she said, "will you please get Dr. McCoy for me? I seem to have injured myself."

The lieutenant, his Oriental face alight with curiosity, approached her door, where he could just see a fraction of the damage. "I'm Lt. Sulu, Colonel. Is there anything I can do to help? Your room—was it the Angel?"

"No." She leaned against the doorframe feeling thoroughly drained. "It wasn't the Angel of Death. But," she added, holding up her arm to reveal the blood-soaked sleeve, "I'm afraid he will be paying me a call if you don't get McCoy quickly. I don't think I hit an artery, or I'd have bled to death quicker than this. But I seem to have severed something major."

Lt. Sulu nodded, turned and trotted swiftly down the hall, where Elizabeth could hear him signaling not only Dr. McCoy, but a couple of security guards as well. *Well,* she reflected, *I probably look like I do need to be put under restraint. I can just see what this is going to do to the* Enterprise *scuttlebutt: "Did you hear that Col. Schaeffer went completely crazy today?"*

She looked down at her wrist, watching the blood flow over the triggering bracelet which had slid almost to her elbow from the force of the blow to the communicator panel. *I wonder if that's the answer. Pull this and it's all over. No more Alexis or Kirk, no more* Enterprise—*and no more Angel of Death.*

She touched the slippery plastic, wiping away the blood. *One pull and I have a clean record; case solved. I'm free of Alexis, Jim's free of me, and the SSD will probably make me a general—posthumously.* Elizabeth giggled hysterically. *No, I can't do it; I haven't any proof, no case. It's not professional. If I die now I'll never know who the Angel is, and Jim would never forgive me for destroying his ship or him. I can't do it . . . I don't even want to do it. . . .*

Dr. McCoy was able to patch up her wrist with little trouble. She had severed a couple of blood vessels and torn a tendon; her arm would be sore for a few days.

"I see, Colonel, that when you get mad, you really get mad," McCoy said, taking in the damage to her room. "I assume it was something important. You don't seem the sort to indulge in feminine outbursts for no reason whatsoever, and I know that it isn't time for your moon cycle. . . ."

Elizabeth sighed. "I don't often lose my temper, Doctor, but when I do I prefer to take it out on inanimate objects. It's safer; they're easier to repair than people. No, it wasn't a feminine snit. I was angry. My lamebrained husband, Alexis, has gotten Star Fleet to lift the quarantine on the *Enterprise.*"

"*What*?" McCoy was stunned. "On what grounds? You haven't caught the Angel of Death yet, and this ship is the mechanical equivalent of Typhoid Mary. I wouldn't take it anywhere near Détente One. Isn't your husband aware of what would happen with the Angel of Death loose among all those ambassadors?"

"He knows, Doctor. But he doesn't care. Alexis unfortunately is the victim of an old and honorable affliction: he loves me, and he wants to see me. Anything else is immaterial. He's lucky, it'll take us at least a day and a half to reach Détente One. It will give me time to contemplate all the possible ways I could kill him, none of them pleasant—and by that time I'll have calmed down enough so that I can face him without doing him great bodily harm. There are times when I agree with Vulcans—emotions are hell, and love, my dear Doctor, is the worst one of all."

McCoy shook his head. "You know," he said, "if I were a betting man, I wouldn't bet a counterfeit credit on your chances of renewing the marriage contract. Sounds like your Alexis has messed himself up pretty badly, both with you and with the SSD. But then, people do a lot of odd things in the name of love. That's something I think you find hard to understand, Elizabeth; you're not Terran enough. If you were, you might be willing to make some of his mistakes yourself. Or you might even be able to love him enough. But enough philosophy for the moment—you need to get some dinner into you, you've lost a lot of blood. I recommend high protein, and if you don't mind I'll stay here with you."

"Afraid I'll go on another rampage? Don't worry, Doctor, I've taken care of it."

"No, not that. It may surprise you to find that I'm angry myself." McCoy made his way to the food dispenser and signaled for a high protein dinner for Elizabeth and a small steak and a salad for himself. He brought the trays back to the table and motioned her to sit. "If you don't eat every bite of that, I'll force feed it to you," he said, grinning.

"You said you were angry. What have you got to be angry about? You haven't fouled up a case. You have Dr. Rigel handling the medical end; frankly, you seem to have been ship's dunsel this trip out."

McCoy picked up his fork and knife and cut himself a piece of steak. "I'll pretend I didn't hear that; I'll put it down to what you've just been through. But yes, I am angry, and I have every right to be. The loss of life angers me, killing angers me, and most of all waste angers me—and I've watched this ship be torn apart by a phantom no one can put their hands on. I'm also having to watch an extraordinarily competent woman whom I've come to admire tearing herself apart over this. I think I have a score to settle with the Angel of Death myself. But before I get my adrenalin flow going, I'd better get on with my dinner—and I advise you to do the same. There's going to be a meeting in the ambassadors' lounge in half an hour; we'll both need to be there. Captain Kirk will no doubt have informed them of the lifting of the quarantine, and it's going to be very messy. I'm getting very tired of all this messiness on *my* ship."

Elizabeth looked up at him, surprised by his use of the possessive. "Do you think Jim Kirk is the only one entitled to call it *his* ship?" McCoy asked. "It's mine as much as it is his. I have the responsibility for the crew's health, mental as well as physical; Scotty runs the engines and Kirk gives the orders. If any of us fall down, the *Enterprise* ceases to exist. Well, there are a lot of ways I've fallen down on my side of this, and I don't like it. Now eat your dinner. I want to pour a good stiff brandy down you before we go to that meeting; I think you'll need it. And I think," he said, nodding, "I think I will prescribe one for myself. I'll probably need it, too."

The meeting was already in progress when Elizabeth and McCoy arrived. McCoy's prescription of a glass of brandy had been an excellent idea; Elizabeth felt relaxed and warm, yet coldly sober.

The room seemed much more crowded than usual. All the surviving ambassadors were there, and as many of the crew as could fit themselves into a small space. The senior officers were present, and a variety of people that Elizabeth wasn't even sure she could identify. Dr. McCoy pointed out some of the Delta Gamma Four party members as they made their way around the room looking for empty seats. Grace Temple was seated with Dr. Carter. Bobby Robinson was, as usual, in charge of the room's security, directing the various security officers to their positions. Dr. M'Benga had saved a couple of seats for McCoy and Schaeffer.

He looked up and grinned when he saw the two of them. Patting the empty sections of the bench, he said, "I wasn't sure you two would make it. I heard from Sulu about the mess in Schaeffer's room, and I thought you'd be giving comfort and counsel into the wee small hours, Doctor."

McCoy leered, and assisted Elizabeth into place next to M'Benga with an artistic flourish. "Oh, I was more than willing to do comforting and counseling half the night, but Elizabeth and I felt this meeting might be more important. Not nearly as much fun, but a little more important—and as you can see, I'm even willing to share her company with you, as long as you don't take the sharing too far!"

McCoy seated himself on the other side of Elizabeth and looked around to pick up the thread of the argument that was going on. Sarek, as usual, was chairing the meeting, and Karhu stood beside him, a large looming reminder that order was necessary. So many people were speaking at once that McCoy could make no real sense of the discussion. Finally, in desperation it seemed, Karhu slammed his fist down hard on the tabletop, and at the top of his voice yelled for silence. The room was instantly still. It was the first time that many of the people in the room had ever heard the Hunajan ambassador raise his voice.

"Thank you very much," Sarek said. "I am well aware that all of you are opinionated concerning the recent lifting of the quarantine, but I do feel that if we're going to establish any sort of consensus, it is necessary for one person to speak at a time. I would recommend, therefore, that anyone with anything to say please stand and be recognized. I want no more of this vulgar hubbub."

Captain Kirk raised his hand and, when recognized, he faced around toward the crowd. "Look, the lifting of this quarantine was not my idea. The orders did not come from the *Enterprise* or from any ambassador aboard her. It was Star Fleet and Col. Alexis Schaeffer on Détente One who decided that there was no more need for the quarantine."

The battle broke out again, and once more Karhu

signaled for silence. "I don't like this any more than the rest of you," Kirk continued. "We have a very dangerous being on board. We've given him the name of the Angel of Death because that seems to be the most applicable, but he's our problem . . . and I do mean *our* problem. Col. Elizabeth Schaeffer was sent here by the SSD to handle the matter, and she is doing her job. But we're dealing with something none of us really understands. It is my concern that whatever it is, we may be taking it to Détente One. For those of you who are still neutral in this matter, you have some small idea of what the effects would be on *your* fellow ambassadors should they receive a visit from the Angel of Death. As for those ambassadors opposed. . . ." Kirk did not need to continue. Everyone in the room knew how Rovar had died.

Captain Kirk sat down, leaving a moment of hush behind as the ambassadors and crew considered the possibilities of the Angel of Death on Détente Station One. The silence was broken by the sound of Si-s-s-s(click) getting to his feet.

"Captain, I would normally tend to agree with you." He adjusted his trenchcoat around his shoulders and set his ridiculous fedora at a jaunty angle. "But you s-s-see, the Angel of Death has managed to unify the viewpoint of the various ambassadors aboard this ship. I'm sure Edentata and Damu and S-spiracles and Hotep are now fully in favor of the détente. So I see no harm in continuing on our way to Détente One."

"And you're a stupid blue idiot!" Heads turned to see where the comment had come from. Dr. McCoy was on his feet; he had not waited to be recognized. His face was suffused with red. "I don't know how you've visualized all of this, Mr. Ambassador; I know your people's fondness for illusion and games. Perhaps all of this has been a cute little holiday for you, a chance to wear fancy costumes and pretend to be all sorts of marvelous things. Well, that's all very well for you, but it's been entirely different for the rest of us.

"I had to help clean up Rovar's cabin after his death, and that's an experience I never want to repeat. I don't want the quarantine lifted, I don't want this ship taken to Détente One, and most of all I don't want the Romulans to win. Can't you see those arrogant, overbearing warmongers laughing up their sleeves at this whole mission? We haven't been able to catch the Angel of Death, and we're dumb enough to bring it right to Détente One. We're handing the Romulans the Federation, lock, stock, and barrel. I won't have it. I'm going to lodge a protest; I'm going to get every officer on this ship to protest; and I'm going to talk to every neutral ambassador within reach when we get to Détente One. I wasn't sure of the wisdom of this treaty when I first heard about it, and now I *know* I don't like it. If something like the Angel of Death is necessary to create a détente between the Federation and the Romulans, that détente is wrong.

"We've had three ambassadors die over that détente, and in my opinion they died for nothing. How long do you think the Romulans will keep a treaty with us? The first time the Klingons come sniffing around with a better deal, that treaty won't be worth the parchment it's written on. We're on a fool's errand, and I'm going to do everything I can to prevent this folly going any further. I'm sick of it, totally sick of it!"

Before Dr. McCoy could continue, Elizabeth had jumped to her feet. She reached across M'Benga and grabbed the startled Doctor by his arm. Half-pulling him across the unprotesting M'Benga's lap, she dragged McCoy out of the room.

As soon as they reached the hallway she grabbed the Doctor by both shoulders and slammed him hard against the wall, wincing at the pain in her arm.

"Si-s-s-s(click) may be a fool, but you're twice the fool he is, Doctor! Do you realize what you've done? One of those beings in there *is* the Angel of Death and you have just set yourself up as the next target. And it will be my responsibility to try saving your life. If I had my way I'd hand you over to that being, because stupidity like yours is totally uncalled for. Do you think I want another death on my hands? Your blood dripping from my fingers? So help me, McCoy, there's still some rage left in me, and you aren't an inanimate object."

She slowly let go of his shoulders, watching with interest McCoy's face go deathly white. He was terrified. She was not sure whether the fear was over the expression on her own face, or whether it had occurred to the Doctor just what he had done. She waited, watching him lean against the wall, regaining his composure.

"You don't think . . . but it was only my opinion, I do have the right to say what I feel. . . ."

"And you have the right to die, too. What does the Angel of Death look like to you, Leonard? I have a feeling you're going to get a good look at him tonight."

She pulled herself together, the rage fading slowly. She took a deep breath and stretched, pulling her muscles out to their full extension, favoring her sore arm. It was a relaxation exercise taught her by the SSD, and at the moment very necessary. "I'm going to set up a surveillance team around your quarters; we'll put in the cameras and do everything we did for Rovar," she said in a calm voice. "But there's going to be one additional factor. This time I'm going to be in the room with you. If the Angel of Death comes for you tonight, he'll not only have one rather foolish doctor to deal with, he'll also have me. I think the time has come to meet my enemy and find out who he is. Even if he kills me, those few seconds of knowledge might be worth it."

She took McCoy's arm tightly with her own good arm, leading him down the corridor toward his quarters. "We've got a lot of work to do, Doctor. Let's get started."

27

Elizabeth supervised the construction of the security network. She double-checked every security camera Scotty and Spock installed; she helped lay out the fine mesh network across the door, so sensitive it would pick up the footsteps of a flea. The door would be left unlocked and ajar. She had arranged with Scotty that the locking mechanism would be removed to make sure there was no way the door could be sealed. She had examined every corner of the room, every possible hiding place, every crevice that might have contained holographic equipment or anything that could cause a manifestation. The room was as safe as Star Fleet technology could make it. There were six security guards stationed outside McCoy's door, Lt. Cdr. Greg Collier among them.

On a table beside McCoy's she had set out her armory: a dozen grenades, poison dart guns, gas bombs, phaser rifles, and three phasers—two standard, one a double-action SSD special. She had even taken the precaution of adding to the collection a stiletto, a rapier, and a double-bladed throwing axe; there was always the chance that the interference noted in Rovar's room could also affect her weaponry. Very little could interfere with a rapier in the hand of an expert, and Elizabeth Schaeffer was an expert—and ambidexterous.

She had gone about her precautions in silence, making no answer to the comments Spock, Scotty, or McCoy directed at her. She was completely the agent, a prowling machine from which all humanity had been removed.

Finally the room was prepared to her satisfaction. She nodded to Scotty and Spock and said, "You've done the best you could. Now it's just a matter of waiting." Her voice sounded odd in the room, almost hollow.

"Would you be wanting any further assistance, mum?" Scotty asked. "I canna think of anything we've overlooked. There must be something. . . ."

"I would advise you, Colonel, to accept my presence in the room with you," Spock said. "It might be safer if there were two of us guarding Dr. McCoy."

Elizabeth looked up at the Vulcan as if she had never seen him before. "No, I'd rather you didn't," she replied in a curiously flat voice. "I know one fact—I am not the Angel of Death; I can assume that Dr. McCoy is not the Angel. Beyond that . . ." She looked up at Spock.

The Vulcan lifted one eyebrow and nodded. "Yes, it's logical. I could indeed be an excellent suspect. But my only concern was for your safety and the Doctor's. If you wish me to go, I shall, but I will not be far away. I have decided to spend tonight in the empty cabin across the hall, rather than my own quarters. Should there be a problem, I will be readily available."

"Thank you. I would suggest that you put Captain Kirk on alert, also. We might as well have as many people at the party as possible, although I have a strong suspicion that it's going to come down to just the three of us—McCoy, myself, and Death." She watched Scotty, Spock, and the technical personnel leave the room. She was now alone with McCoy. She took her place at the table and prepared to wait and watch.

"Doctor, I'd suggest you make whatever preparations are necessary for going to bed, go through whatever sleep ritual you use, and don't be too concerned about my presence. If you generally sleep in the buff, don't worry about that either. Yours won't be the first naked male body I've seen."

"Aren't you ever embarrassed about anything, Schaeffer? I am, and even if I did sleep in the nude I certainly wouldn't do it with you in the room. Not out of any sense of false modesty," he added. "It's just the idea of myself naked in the room with a beautiful woman leads to thoughts that don't involve death. If you don't mind, I think I'll just take my boots off and sleep in my uniform. I like the feeling of being ready for whatever you expect will happen here, although I'm not entirely sure I agree with you. Yes, I mouthed off down at the meeting, but I don't think what I said was that horrifying. I'm sure a lot of people in that room were thinking the same thing."

"Thinking, yes, but not saying it. That's what makes you a target." She watched as he removed his boots and climbed into bed.

"Are you going to be comfortable there?" McCoy asked her. "Sitting up all night doesn't sound very appealing to me."

"It isn't, but I've been trained to go at least seventy-six hours without sleep if I have to. The body toxins aren't fun, and I generally have to spend several days recuperating. But if necessary I can do it—and believe me, I won't sleep tonight. You can, if you wish. I might even suggest you take something to keep the tension down. Try a tranquilizer, or whatever it is you use to soothe your nerves."

"I don't generally indulge in pills, and I find my tranquillity more often than not in a bottle. But if I'm going to meet the Angel of Death tonight, I think I'd prefer to do it sober."

Elizabeth glanced at the bookcase by the bed. "You might try reading. I often find that soothing."

"What do you generally read? Your case books?" The comment was uncalled for, and McCoy realized it. "Look, I'm sorry, I'm nervous about this, too. But I don't think I could read. Why don't we just talk about anything at all. Tell me about the SSD, yourself—anything at all." He settled his head back against the pillow and looked at the ceiling. "I have never felt more awake in my life," he observed. "Can you think of anything boring to talk about that might help me sleep?"

"All right," Elizabeth settled back in her seat, deliberately letting the muscles ease so that they would be uncramped. "You want something dull to talk about? Let's talk about my relationship with James Kirk. Oh, I'm perfectly aware you've been dying of curiosity about the whole thing. I've noticed those sly looks. Is there anything in particular you want to know?"

McCoy turned his head on the pillow, grinning. "I've watched a lot of Jim's romances over the past few years; one more or less isn't that different. But if you want to talk about it, go ahead. I'm pretty sure I know the script."

"Has he ever told women he was involved with how lonely he was?" McCoy looked a little startled, and she realized that perhaps there was some strength in her relationship with James Kirk. "He's told me he's going through a sort of midlife crisis; it's the usual one that comes to a man his age. Here he is, enormously successful, top of the heap, likely to be made an admiral—but he feels there's something missing in his life, and he thinks what might be missing is me. He asked me to marry him, Dr. McCoy. How many times has he asked *that* of his lady friends—or do you think it's just the spore sickness talking?"

McCoy looked thoughtful for a moment, as if trying to remember. "Well—he's married one that I know of, and there's probably been a proposal or two. While there may be some difference in James Kirk, there's a lot more of a problem for you. For one thing, you're already married, even though it is just for two more months. What are you going to do, Elizabeth? Wait out the two months, let the contract slide, and then come racing back to the *Enterprise* to marry Jim, even if it is his reaction to the spores?"

"I thought about it. I was so mad at Alexis today I didn't even want to give him the two months together he'd asked for, but I realized I'm cursed with one sickening attribute, a sense of honor. Alexis is entitled to his two months of persuasion. It's not going to work, you and I already know that. My marriage to Alexis Schaeffer is over.

"But at the same time I'm not sure I'm going to come back to the *Enterprise*, either. You know, there are certain pleasures to be found in being a free woman. I've been 'married' for ten years; I'd like to see what it's like being single for a while. It might even improve things for Alexis and me. As for Jim, I love him and I think he loves me, but I'm not positive—and until I am, I won't be coming back to the *Enterprise*. Love is a two-edged blade, Doctor; it can harm as well as heal, it can give release from torment or pain beyond belief. I need some time to think before I inflict that blade on James Kirk. . . ."

A gentle snore from the bed told her that McCoy had drifted off to sleep somewhere in her soliloquy. She smiled to herself, wondering how much he had heard or even cared about. He was probably right, he had seen a lot of Kirk's women traipse in and out of the *Enterprise*, but Elizabeth found herself feeling a quiet pride at being one of those women. Even if there was nothing lasting between herself and the Captain, she had been his woman for a short length of time, and there was a great deal of joy to be found in that. It would give her an idea of what she wanted in the future from other men—not necessarily from Kirk, though that was a possibility. But he had provided the means of escape from Alexis, and for that alone she knew she loved him.

The hours passed slowly, leaden little cat feet moving across the room. Elizabeth checked her armory for the umpteenth time; everything was in perfect order.

She was beginning to wonder whether she'd been mistaken and the Angel of Death was not going to put in an appearance. It was entirely possible she had been fooled again. If that were so, it did not surprise her; she had more than used up her foolishness quota on this particular mission. Then she noticed a drop in the room temperature, a chill in the air.

There was a sense of foreboding, of something evil, something lurking. She had dimmed the lights when she'd realized McCoy was asleep, but there was still enough light to make out every feature of the room. She tensed slightly, like a cat. There was a prickling sensation in her fingers. Something was coming, coming to this room—and that something smelled of death.

She waited, unsure where the apparition would first appear. She was tempted to call out to the security guards, but knew that if she did the presence she sensed would vanish, and there would be nothing in the room when Collier and his squad burst into it. No, she would wait a little longer.

The room began to brighten. She knew she had not touched the light controls. There was a glow in the room, fluorescent, sparkling at the edges with a fine gold glitter. She found herself wanting to turn away from McCoy's bed, wanting to leave the room; it was an urge, extraordinarily strong, telling her she did not belong here. Her injured arm ached intolerably. Her bladder felt full. She glanced toward the bathroom, then vowed that not even the pain in her body would make her move from this spot. Whatever was happening, she would stay to observe it.

A figure was forming at the foot of McCoy's bed, a figure clad in flowing white robes and carrying a gold-bladed sickle in one hand, and in the other a golden hourglass filled with silver sand.

Elizabeth wanted to cry out, and found to her horror that she could not. She sat mute, staring at the figure. She knew who the Angel of Death was.

He did not look at her. His attention was directed at the sleeping man on the bed. Elizabeth wanted to cry out his name, to distract him, but she had no voice. She reached for her wrist trigger, but the gesture was not completed. The message had traveled from brain to muscle but had not been fulfilled. Her hand remained on the edge of the table, where it rested. She tried to stand up, and found she could not move. She was held fast in her seat by a force far stronger than anything she had ever encountered. Her struggles attracted the attention of the figure at the foot of the bed, and he turned to face her.

She looked up at his ebony face, as still as a carved

African figure. The Angel of Death was Dr. M'Benga.

"I have not come for you. It is not your turn." His voice was soft, gentle, and unlike that of the man she knew as M'Benga. "You have done nothing wrong," the Angel continued. "You are not trying to end peace. You have merely attempted to search for me, a search which was futile from the beginning. And now the *Enterprise* will go to Détente One, and I will continue my work. There will be peace between the Federation and the Romulans. I will make sure of that. Ambassador Si-s-s-s(click) was not mistaken; my powers are everything he said they were. I will convince the neutrals and destroy those who oppose the détente." As if reminded of the opposition, he turned back to face the sleeping doctor.

"Doctor Leonard McCoy, arise!"

McCoy sat up in bed suddenly, staring wildly about him. Then he saw the figure and froze.

"I am Death, and your time has come. You must go with me."

"But I'm too young," McCoy said. "I don't have any terminal illnesses, my heart is in good shape—there's no reason for me to die." It was obvious he did not recognize the man standing in front of him—he saw only the Angel of Death, not M'Benga.

Elizabeth realized that she alone knew the identity of the Angel—probably because he had not come for her, and he could not be both her concept of the Angel of Death and McCoy's at the same time. That was a point in her favor. She watched as he grew in size and stature, looming over the bed, and she knew that this was not simply Dr. M'Benga; this was something else, some dark and subconscious part of the doctor, some portion of him which had required the détente, that hungered for it.

She knew she would have to tell someone who the Angel of Death was. He had said he hadn't come for her, but he would be foolish to leave her alive if he had the slightest inkling of her knowledge. She was not sure what abilities the pseudo-M'Benga had in the way of telepathy; she hoped he had no more than he was currently using. Her own psychic rating was high enough for her to scream soundlessly into the void. Spock had said he was across the hall. Spock would hear that wordless scream. She concentrated all the effort of her mind into one loud, agonized shriek. Her mind cried out, but there was silence in the room.

The Angel ignored her as though she did not exist. He looked only at the man on the bed. "You see, Dr. McCoy, you stand between me and my goal. There must be peace in the Universe, there must be a détente between the Romulans and the Federation, and eventually between the Federation and the Klingons. We have had enough bloodshed. I am tired of bloodshed. I grieve at the bleeding bodies I must deal with day after day. I am the Angel of Death, and as long as there is no peace in the Universe I must go on plying my trade. I became what I was, thinking to play the part of the Angel of Mercy, but that ironically is not so. It is only death that I see around me, and it must be ended. You stand in the way. I have no wish to take you with me; the others I did not know, they were simply impediments. But you were his friend, that one who sleeps, and he will grieve for you, and I will grieve for him. But it must be. Come, Leonard. Come with me."

Kirk sat bolt upright in the bed. There had been a scream, Elizabeth's scream, yet she was not there with him. She was—with McCoy! Kirk bounded from the bed and raced to the communications panel. "Red alert! Red alert!" he cried into the speaker. "The Angel of Death is in Dr. McCoy's room! Red alert!"

Without bothering to pull tunic or trousers over his undershorts and T-shirt, he raced out of the room and down the corridor, running desperately to save Elizabeth. He knew from the scream still echoing in his head that she was in deadly peril.

He found the security guards, Greg Collier, and Mr. Spock clustered around the door to McCoy's quarters. They had heard the red alert sound throughout the hall and knew it could mean only one thing.

The door itself was fused to the lintel. There was no lock, no locking mechanism, but it would not move. Only a thin line of darkness showed in the space Elizabeth had left open, and that darkness was as hard as the durasteel of the doorframe.

"Send for Scotty!" Kirk demanded. "I want that door opened, and fast. The Angel of Death is in there with Bones and Elizabeth."

Spock turned to consider his captain. "You heard it, then," he said. "Her scream. She can't help McCoy, Jim. But she can link with us. The three of us together can help McCoy. I know who's in there with them. I have become a part of Col. Schaeffer's mind by tracking back her cry. My mind is more finely tuned on the psychic level than your own, but I need your help to conquer the Angel of Death."

Spock reached out, grabbing his captain by the arm. "It's M'Benga. He was on Delta Gamma Four with us, and he's dreaming. I sent a security guard to his room; it's locked. But you and I together, using Elizabeth's mind as a guide, we can get inside this room. If M'Benga can do it, so can we. Remember the dreams, Jim. The possibilities in those dreams."

Spock's face was intense, trying to will Kirk to understand what must be done. Kirk looked at the door to McCoy's room, and then back at Spock. "Get Scotty to break into M'Benga's room and *wake* him up! That's an order, Mister."

The Vulcan shook his head. "It won't stop what's happening, and it might kill Elizabeth, McCoy, and M'Benga. He doesn't know he's doing this, Jim, any more than you knew when you dreamt. But you, Elizabeth, and I, as one—melded, our minds together—let us help you." Spock led Kirk away from the door to the other side of the corridor, and pulled him downward onto the floor in a seated position. The Vulcan knelt beside his captain, his long slender fingers reaching for the nerve points on Jim's head. "Consider what the Angel of Death might fear, Jim. Consider who controls the Angel of Death—and go with me to Elizabeth!"

Inside McCoy's bedroom, Elizabeth watched in frozen terror as M'Benga beckoned to McCoy. She saw an ashen tone creep across the doctor's face; she saw him slump gently back onto the bed, and knew that the life force was beginning to drain from him. There was nothing she could do. The scream for help had not been answered.

Then there was light in the room, the light of millions of candles blazing from the walls. There was warmth and an intensity that caused Elizabeth to be flattened back into the chair. There was another being in the room, larger and even more impressive than the Angel of Death—a being she could not look at, something that shimmered and glowed with the brightness of a thousand suns. And a voice came out of the brightness—a voice that was every sound from the tiniest whisper of a bird's wing to the loudest thunder ever heard.

"WHAT DO YOU DO HERE, MY SON?" the voice asked of the Angel of Death. M'Benga turned to face the being, his control over McCoy ebbing. He stood before the light, which vaguely suggested a humanoid figure.

"I am doing my duty, bringing peace to the Universe," M'Benga answered.

"I SENT YOU ON NO SUCH MISSION OF PEACE," the light announced. "YOU HAVE DISPLEASED ME. RELEASE THE TERRAN, LEST I UNLEASH UPON YOU MY TERRIBLE AND SWIFT SWORD."

The Angel, smaller now, visibly cowed, turned back to the bed and waved aloft the scythe, only this time in a gesture of benediction. McCoy's color returned to normal; Elizabeth could see his chest rising and falling in a gentle rhythm. But to her amazement, she realized she was seeing it from two angles—her own, and that of the glowing light.

The Angel stood at the end of the bed and let fall the scythe and hourglass. He was a small and pitiful figure now, simply a man in a white robe. Elizabeth found she could move, and that it was possible to reach across the table for her phaser and put an end to the being called the Angel of Death. She lifted her hand, but the voice stopped the gesture.

"DO NOT HARM HIM, ELIZABETH. HE DOES NOT KNOW WHAT HE IS DOING. WE WILL LET

HIM RETURN TO HIS BODY, BECAUSE IF YOU DESTROY THAT WHICH IS HERE, YOU ALSO DESTROY THAT WHICH SLEEPS. WOULD YOU HAVE M'BENGA'S DEATH ON YOUR CONSCIENCE?"

She let her hand fall back on the table. "I have the right to be executioner. I have the right to be *his* Angel of Death." She was arguing with the light and with herself at the same time.

"BUT THERE IS PERHAPS A GREATER RIGHT, THAT OF KNOWLEDGE. WE MUST KNOW WHAT CAUSED THIS SO IT CAN NEVER HAPPEN AGAIN."

Elizabeth looked up at the light, shading her eyes with her hand. She thought she saw within it Jim Kirk's features, Spock's, and her own, but she could not be sure; the incandescence was too brilliant to make out details. "I want to be there when he returns to his body. I do have the right to interrogate him."

The great awesome light indicated that she had that right. "GO," it/she said. "GO TO M'BENGA'S ROOM AND BE THERE."

She stood up and walked past the now pitiful figure of what had been the Angel of Death. It was hardly more than a shimmer in the air, the features vague. She did not even glance at it. The door opened easily at her touch, the brilliant yellow light spilling out into the hallway. The security guards clustered around her, asking questions, but she could see only James Kirk across the hall, and Spock, his hands pressed to his captain's head. She knew the sources of the light and of the being in McCoy's bedroom, and that was enough. She heard the door hiss closed behind her, the brightness shut in; she blinked in the comparatively dim light of the corridor, broke mind contact with Spock and Kirk, and then made her way to M'Benga's bedroom.

Either Scotty had managed to unlock the door or the door had simply not been locked in the first place; Mr. Scott was never able to say. But he stood aside to let Elizabeth enter the room. It was dim, bathed in the light of the red alert signal.

M'Benga's quarters were still, almost monastic in their simplicity. He had added very little to the room: a small handwoven rug by his bed, an ebony carving of some African deity, and a few medical books—very slight indications of the complexities that a man could be. The only sound in the room was the gentle breathing of the doctor in his bed. Elizabeth stood beside him, looking down at her enemy, the being she had fruitlessly chased. But she felt no hatred, no sense of revenge. If M'Benga did not know what he was doing, the knowledge he would have to face would be punishment enough.

Watching the man stir in his bed, pushing the bedcovers aside, revealing a deep-copper-colored chest with a sparse scattering of hair, Elizabeth felt a sense of profound sympathy for a being who cared so much about peace that he was willing to kill for it. She bent over him to readjust his bedding, gently tucking the covers around his body.

M'Benga stirred, frowning as if at some unpleasant dream, and then his eyes opened suddenly. He looked about, startled, and saw Elizabeth standing over him, a look of maternal protectiveness on her face.

"Col. Schaeffer? What are you doing here? Is there something wrong?" His questions were so matter-of-fact, she hesitated to break in on them. She wanted to preserve for another second the calm tranquillity in this man's face before it was shattered by the knowledge of what he was.

She heard the door opening behind her, and the light was turned up. M'Benga sat up in his bed, puzzlement in his face as he stared at his captain, Spock, and the squad of security men entering his room. He looked at Kirk's face and saw there the answer to this rude awakening. Slowly he bowed his head and covered his face with his hands.

"Did I do it?" he asked, all the pain in the Universe in that question. "Was it me? Am I the being Col. Schaeffer looked for?" His words were half choked by gulping sounds, sobs. Tears sprang from between the fingers to fall on the cover of the bed. "I don't understand. I don't understand. How could it be me? I would have known! I would have felt something. . . ."

Elizabeth sat down beside him and drew a soft white silken kerchief from her sleeve, pressing it into M'Benga's fingers. She put her arms around his shoulders, rocking him gently as he wept. "Tell me, Dr. M'Benga," she said softly, "do you ever dream? Since Delta Gamma Four, do you ever dream?"

The doctor looked up at her, his tear-streaked face a mask of anguish. "No. I can't dream. But I obviously can kill."

28

The U.S.S. *Enterprise* was in orbit around Détente One. The ambassadors had left the ship and the bodies of Agnatha, Rovar, Naja, and Neko had been removed. There remained only three people in the main Transporter Room. Lt. Kyle stood at the console, trying not to notice Captain Kirk and Elizabeth Schaeffer standing at the edge of the transporter platform.

"What will the SSD do to M'Benga?" Kirk asked. "He's a brilliant doctor, and you heard what Sarek said after examining his mind—he never knew he was the Angel of Death. He's not to blame for it."

Elizabeth smiled sadly, reached out to stroke the gold braid on Jim's tunic, the gold that was so lifeless and faded in comparison to that brilliant glow she'd seen in McCoy's room. "He won't be harmed, I assure you. My report makes it quite clear that he didn't know what he was doing. It was simply a subconscious part of him, something that desired peace so badly," she sighed. "I wish I had that much mental power, to want something that much."

"But why couldn't he remember his dreams?" Kirk asked. "Spock and I were able to remember ours."

"Yes, but you weren't killing anyone. M'Benga's desire for peace was in direct conflict with his ability to kill, so his conscious mind blocked out all thought of the dreaming. I can't say I understand all of what happened. Spock and Sarek both mindmelded with M'Benga and the best they could come up with was that the spores should not have been killed. If they had been left alone, all of you who lived would have simply deposited the spores in a suitable place to grow and there would have been no problem of your desires getting mixed up with that of the spores."

"I'm not sure I'd care for that on my ship, Elizabeth. The only suitable place for spore growth would have been Hydroponics. We would have had an epidemic of spores throughout the ship as the new plants grew, taking over the minds of more crewmen who would have died for lack of psychic ability, like Raymond, Matthews, and Jamison. I would have lost a lot of my crew, and frankly, I'd rather lose a few ambassadors."

"It's all how you look at it, Jim. I'm sure Rovar and Neko wouldn't have agreed, nor will Sirenia if you repeat your opinion of the worth of ambassadors to her. She did care for Agnatha. He was a good ambassador. His only fault was in being on the wrong side of this dispute. That's not enough to merit death."

"And what about Rovar?" Kirk said. "I didn't like him, but that was a horrible way to die. Can you forgive M'Benga for that piece of mindless butchery? Can you ever forget the sight of that cabin? I know I can't."

Elizabeth turned away from Kirk, hiding her face from him. "M'Benga didn't tear Rovar apart," she said slowly. "Rovar did it to himself. It was his Angel of Death after all—his great devourer and shredder of flesh that killed him."

Kirk grabbed her shoulders, pulling her around to face him. "Explain," he snapped. "Explain how any sentient being could do that to himself."

"It was the two arms still connected to the body and the undamaged heart and brain that proved it to McCoy, Rigel, and me. A real beast would have smashed his head and torn out his heart, too. But Rovar believed in an Angel of Death that would tear him apart, and that's exactly what his subconscious mind gave him. The damage was self-inflicted . . . at the orders of the Angel. He actually died of shock and loss of blood—all at his own hands."

"But how did he live long enough to do it? How could he do so much damage to himself and not die just from the pain of smashing his own larynx? McCoy said that part was damaged first."

Elizabeth's face was rigidly under control. "When you feel you can face it, read some of your Terran history on the art of drawing and quartering as practiced in the Sixteenth Century. It's amazing how much pain a human can endure and still live. Rovar had a central nervous system that was less involved than a human's, and he suffered a great deal more damage before dying than either you or I could have withstood. He was a nasty-tempered fool, but I can still grieve for the horror of his death. Perhaps that proves I'm not just some unfeeling product of SSD brainwashing." She shrugged and tried to hide the tears in her eyes.

"Did anything good come of all this?" Kirk pulled her into his arms to comfort her yet again. "M'Benga may well have changed the direction of the détente. The Romulans may win because of his 'dreams.' I'm not sure I like that one bit."

"What M'Benga felt was not harmful in and of itself," Elizabeth answered, swiftly regaining control of herself. "He merely wanted an end to war and killing. I can't blame him for that. Neither can the SSD. But we'll need to study more about the Delta Gamma Four spores, and he will have a team of Vulcan doctors to assist him in repairing his mind. I doubt he'll ever be able to manifest the Angel of Death again—that part of him is gone for good—but he's going to have a great deal of difficulty dealing with himself. It will take him a long time to heal. As soon as the Department is sure he's safe and no longer a threat, I think they'll probably send him to Vulcan. He does love Vulcan, almost as much as Spock or Sarek do. I think I'll get in touch with Sarek's wife, Amanda. There's a great deal of compassion and understanding in that woman. Anyone who would remain married to a Vulcan for as many years as she has needs a lot of understanding. I'll ask her to look after M'Benga."

"I couldn't think of better hands for him to be in,"

Kirk said. "With one exception, and that's yourself, Elizabeth. You had the right of an SSD agent to destroy him, and yet you didn't. There's a gentleness and a compassion in you, too."

Elizabeth looked down, her hand absentmindedly brushing the gold-embroidered scale of justice on her tunic. "Don't give me credit for anything I don't deserve. Had I believed that Dr. M'Benga was doing what he did deliberately, he would not have left this ship alive. What I did was, as your First Officer so charmingly put it, logical. There is no point destroying an entire man to remove a small cancer. That's all the Angel of Death was, a cancer, and I can take no credit for its removal, or even for M'Benga's healing. There will be others who will soothe his mind and enable him to live with himself, and this will be one case where I amply display my own foolishness. In years to come, when I've handled a case extraordinarily well and am feeling very smug, I'll take out the file on the Angel of Death and read it, and it will keep me humble. Humility is a quality an SSD agent sometimes lacks."

Jim reached out to take her in his arms. "Don't blame yourself for what happened. It was something larger than any of us could have handled by ourselves. What I don't understand is how you did it. My psi rating isn't bad for a Terran, but it's not good enough to pick up the sound of a silent scream."

"Yes it is—if the screamer has my bloodlines and willpower. I admit I was screaming for Spock—that was the logical thing to do. But emotionally . . . emotionally, Jim, I wanted only you. So *you* did hear me. Spock would say it wasn't logical, and he'd be right. But then, what does a Vulcan know of emotion?"

"Not much, but he knew it would take all three of us to turn the trick. If you hadn't screamed, Spock and I could not have known what the problem was; I wouldn't have been able to go into that room, and not even Spock would have had that much energy. But the three of us together—and it was the three of us *together* who defeated Death's Angel. We were able to become something bigger and better than the Angel of Death. We all had a hand in what happened there, and

I feel the case was well handled. Congratulations, Col. Schaeffer."

Elizabeth nodded, accepting his words. "I have to go down to Détente One now. I have a job to do." She glanced at him, a slight smile in her eyes. "Alexis always did say I was very tiresome about my sense of duty. He's right; I won't leave Détente One until the entire Federation-Romulan discussion is over, and that might take several months or even several years. But as long as it goes on, I will be there, and in command. Alexis has been demoted a rank for his part in this mess; he's back to lieutenant colonel now, and I think the red collar chafes him."

"Will he get his two months?" Kirk asked, hope in his eyes.

"Alexis will have my physical company for two months; that's all. I refuse to share his bed after what he did to me. As far as I'm concerned he broke the agreement. But I can't help being around him for the next two months, and he can't help arguing with me—but when that time is up I'm not signing a new marriage agreement. My marriage with Alexis Schaeffer is over."

"And your marriage to James Kirk?" He slowly lifted one of her hands to kiss the palm and fold her fingers over it.

"I don't know the answer to that. I can't give you one. I know that's cowardly of me, but I have to think—and so do you. We have no way of knowing how long the spore effect continues. *You* must be sure of what you really want from me before marriage can be discussed again. You have your ship, that is your prime duty; I have the SSD, that is my prime duty. We will both make the best of our respective positions. And if it turns out that our paths cross or that we both want to follow the same path, time alone can answer that. I can't." She kissed him gently in farewell and then turned away and took her place on the transporter platform.

"Whatever happens between you and me, now or in the future," she continued, "I will always remember that great glowing figure in McCoy's cabin. I'll never forget that. And I'll never forget you."

She signaled Lt. Kyle that she was ready to transport down to Détente One. Kirk took a step back from the transporter platform. He looked up at her, memorizing every line of her face and body. "And remember this, Elizabeth Schaeffer—remember, spore or no spore, I love you!"

She was shimmering out of view, but her voice came back clearly. "I love you too, James Kirk. . . ."

APPENDIX

Costume Notes on the SSD Uniform:

The ranks of the Special Security Division are color-coded as follows:

Cadet: Gray tunic and slacks, with black collar and stripe.

All other ranks wear black tunic and slacks, with the differentiation in collar and stripe to denote rank.

Second lieutenant: Black stripe and collar.
First lieutenant: Black stripe, gold collar.
Captain: Gold stripe and collar.
Major: Red stripe and collar.
Lieutenant colonel: Red collar and turquoise stripe.
Colonel: Turquoise collar and stripe.
General: White collar and stripe. Gold sword insignia are fastened to the collar to indicate each of the four ranks of generals, one sword for each rank.

ALL SSD OFFICERS WEAR ON THEIR TUNICS A GOLD-EMBROIDERED SCALE OF JUSTICE OVER THE RIGHT BREAST TO REMIND OTHERS OF THEIR ULTIMATE GOAL IN THE FEDERATION.

I wish to credit Alice E. LaVelle and David Gerrold for the creation of the basic SSD uniform.

ABOUT THE AUTHOR

KATHLEEN SKY is the author of *Vulcan!* and *Death's Angel*. She lives in California with her writer husband Stephen Goldin, and is currently writing a non-Star Trek fantasy trilogy.